Forever EAGLES

JIM CROWGEY

Order this book online at www.trafford.com
or email orders@trafford.com

Most Trafford titles are also available at major online book retailers.

Printed in the United States of America.

ISBN: 978-1-4269-6805-1 (sc)
ISBN: 978-1-4269-6806-8 (e)

Trafford rev. 05/09/2011

 www.trafford.com

North America & international
toll-free: 1 888 232 4444 (USA & Canada)
phone: 250 383 6864 ♦ fax: 812 355 4082

This book is dedicated with love to my wife, Phyllis. The picture which graces the cover of this book shows her as a beautiful teenage girl dressed for a dance, capturing the essence of small-town life during the 1950's, a Golden Age for our country.

Stony Ford High School
Jefferson Davis Road
Stony Ford, Virginia

1958

	SU	M	T	W	T	F	S
JAN				1	2	3	4
	5	6	7	8	9	10	11
	12	13	14	15	16	17	18
	19	20	21	22	23	24	25
	26	27	28	29	30	31	

	SU	M	T	W	T	F	S
FEB							1
	2	3	4	5	6	7	8
	9	10	11	12	13	14	15
	16	17	18	19	20	21	22
	23	24	25	26	27	28	

	SU	M	T	W	T	F	S
MAR							1
	2	3	4	5	6	7	8
	9	10	11	12	13	14	15
	16	17	18	19	20	21	22
	23	24	25	26	27	28	29
	30	31					

	SU	M	T	W	T	F	S
APR			1	2	2	3	5
	6	7	8	9	10	11	12
	13	14	15	16	17	18	19
	20	21	22	23	24	25	26
	27	28	29	30			

	SU	M	T	W	T	F	S
MAY					1	2	3
	4	5	6	7	8	9	10
	11	12	13	14	15	16	17
	18	19	20	21	22	23	24
	25	26	27	28	29	30	31

	SU	M	T	W	T	F	S
JUNE	1	2	3	4	5	6	7
	8	9	10	11	12	13	14
	15	16	17	18	19	20	21
	22	23	24	25	26	27	28
	29	30					

	SU	M	T	W	T	F	S
JULY			1	2	3	4	5
	6	7	8	9	10	11	12
	13	14	15	16	17	18	19
	20	21	22	23	24	25	26
	27	28	29	30	31		

	SU	M	T	W	T	F	S
AUG						1	2
	3	4	5	6	7	8	9
	10	11	12	13	14	15	16
	17	18	19	20	21	22	23
	24	25	26	27	28	29	30
	31						

	SU	M	T	W	T	F	S
SEPT		1	2	3	4	5	6
	7	8	9	10	11	12	13
	14	15	16	17	18	19	20
	21	22	23	24	25	26	27
	28	29	30				

	SU	M	T	W	T	F	S
OCT				1	2	3	4
	5	6	7	8	9	10	11
	12	13	14	15	16	17	18
	19	20	21	22	23	24	25
	26	27	28	29	30	31	

	SU	M	T	W	T	F	S
NOV							1
	2	3	4	5	6	7	8
	9	10	11	12	13	14	15
	16	17	18	19	20	21	22
	23	24	25	26	27	28	29
	30						

	SU	M	T	W	T	F	S
DEC		1	2	3	4	5	6
	7	8	9	10	11	12	13
	14	15	16	17	18	19	20
	21	22	23	24	25	26	27
	28	29	30	31			

Contents

Acknowledgments

With sincere thanks to:

Mary Beth Crowgey, my daughter, for offering her literary talents as both my editor and my teacher during the writing of this third novel, reprising her roles in both of my earlier books, *The Battle of Eden Springs* and *Guardian of Eden Springs*. The many hours she spent creatively critiquing my original draft and suggesting improvements has greatly improved the final work. I would also like to acknowledge her major contribution in designing the cover for this book. For all of this I am most grateful.

Hal Cantrill, my friend for many years, for his major role in the creation of this book cover, providing excellent computer and photography skills just as he did earlier for the covers of my first two novels. I am greatly indebted to him for his capable assistance.

Prologue

"I recall something I once read," Samuel Hundley observed to his brother Elias, as he slipped off his uncomfortable high-top work shoes to rest his blistered feet. "The promised land always lies on the other side of a wilderness."

He spoke more seriously as the two surveyed the small community below them from their hilltop vantage point. "But I truly think that we've discovered the place we've been searching for. It has everything we need for a furniture manufacturing business: proximity to hardwood forests, level land, water, electric power, access to highways, laborers who will work for reasonable wages."

"I agree with you that we've spent as much time as Moses did wandering in the wilderness, but I'm not quite as certain as you that we have finally arrived at the Promised Land," Elias replied wryly to his older brother while pulling off his equally ill-fitting boots.

"Don't you think you might be jumping to that conclusion too quickly? For generations, people in this part of Tazewell County have farmed, logged, or gone off to work in the mines. I doubt that many of the men in Stony Ford have ever seen the inside of a factory, much less worked on a production line."

The men found a place to sit on the trunk of a fallen tree, contemplating the quiet countryside surrounding them. They had traveled for weeks throughout southwest Virginia and West Virginia, searching for a suitable factory site, shrewdly dressed in rummage store clothes and driving a dilapidated Ford Model T pickup truck to avoid tipping off land owners that they were prospective buyers with ready cash.

Finally, Samuel broke the silence with a conciliatory suggestion. "Let's go back to that boarding house and check in for another day's stay, if you're agreeable. I have a good feeling about this town, but any decision to proceed has got to come from both of us, and I can see that you're not yet ready to sign off on buying property."

It was starting to rain by the time the two reached Main Street and approached the unpretentious Victorian house with peeling yellow paint fronted by a sign advertising O'Brien's Room and Board. That was when the engine abruptly quit, and the truck came to a dead stop in the middle of the street.

The brothers had lifted the hood and were standing in the downpour futilely searching for the problem when two young men, wearing neither rain coats nor hats, approached them to offer help. "We saw your truck stall and thought you might need a hand," the dark-haired one said in a friendly voice.

"We can push you over to the side of the road and then take a look to see what's wrong," the second one volunteered. "If you want to head inside out of the rain, we'll try to get your truck running for you."

The front door of the house opened, and a short, stout woman with gray hair tied up in a bun called out to them in a distinctive Irish accent, "You gentlemen come on up here where it's dry before you catch your death of pneumonia.

"Let the Tucker boys take care of your vehicle. They're young and used to working out in the weather on days like this. Both of them know right smart about engines."

The Tuckers, soaked to the skin from head to foot, joined the other three on the porch a short time later. "We found the problem," the sandy-haired boy proudly informed them.

"You've got a cracked distributor cap, and it's grounding out because of water splashing up under the hood. Tim and me will go over to Coulter's garage and see if we can find a replacement. That is, if you'd like for us to."

Back in their room after a family-style dinner that evening, now wearing warm clothes that had been dried by Mrs. O'Brien beside her kitchen stove, Samuel and Elias discussed the events following their arrival in town.

"I can't get over how willingly those two young men stepped in to help us, and how they refused to take a penny more than the half-dollar cost of the distributor cap," Elias commented. "Both of them were soaking wet by the time they'd finished working."

"And Mrs. O'Brien wouldn't let us pay her for drying our clothes," Samuel added. "These people look at us and think we don't have a dime to spare. I'm sure that's why they're acting so charitably. There are clearly some good salt of the earth folks living in these parts."

"What happened here today seems like an omen that this is where we ought to build," Elias observed. "I'm agreeable now to going back to the Jamison farm tomorrow and talking with the family again. If they still want to sell off a piece of their farm, you have my blessing to start bargaining with them."

"Then that's what we'll do," Samuel replied. "We ought to offer the old man a decent price for the land. He told us the farm's been passed down through his family for generations, starting from the time of the Revolutionary War.

"We've have made it our practice to treat people well, and I believe that's why we've been blessed with good fortune. Practicing the Golden Rule is to be the right way to run a business."

He reached over to switch off the light, adding, "I like the name we agreed on for the new company. Southern Styles Furniture sounds like a good fit for a furniture manufacturing operation here in southwest Virginia. Goodnight, Elias."

"Goodnight, Samuel," his brother called back, pulling the thick patchwork quilt up snugly around his shoulders. "It's best that we get to sleep right away. We've got a big day ahead of us come sun-up."

Chapter 1

Bob Slater stared through his windshield at the dimly lit highway ahead and watched the impending wreck unfold before him, yelling, "Look out! He's heading right for you! Get out of the way!"

The driver of the station wagon ahead was unaware that a tractor trailer had veered across the median into his lane, bearing down on him and his four teenage passengers at fifty miles an hour.

Bob heard a horn blast at the last minute and watched his friend's vehicle swerve violently toward the right shoulder of the road. But it was too late to prevent the sickening head-on crash and ball of fire which lit up the night sky.

Springing upright in bed with a cold sweat soaking his pajamas, he heard the sound of his anguished "No!" echo through the dark house. He had relived the accident once again, seeing Coach Callison and four members of the Stony Ford High School wrestling team, Red Burke, Lonnie Spellman, Rick Johnson and Tolly Smith, die right before his eyes.

Bob glanced at the alarm clock, noting that it was almost 6:00 AM. He rolled out of bed and headed for the bathroom, rather than remaining under the warm covers with the risk of dropping off to sleep and being drawn back into that hellish nightmare. He was still having a hard enough time coping with memories nine months after the accident, without experiencing a traumatic early morning double feature.

Bob regained his composure as he stepped into the shower, allowing the soothing warm stream to calm him. He focused on his schedule for the upcoming day, September 1, 1958, the start of his fifth year as a math and science teacher at Stony Ford High School.

Introducing a new class of boys and girls to the abstract world of algebra and geometry might not be everyone's cup of tea, but it was one that he looked forward to on this Monday morning.

He still found teaching teenagers to be enjoyable and rewarding at twenty-eight. If classroom boredom lay ahead for him, as it had for many others, it was far enough down the road that he could not feel it yet.

He stepped from the shower and ran an electric shaver over his sun-burned face, dressing in his usual school uniform, khaki pants, white shirt and tie, tweed sport coat, and brown moccasin loafers. Running a comb through his short brown hair while standing before the mirror, he glanced down at the picture on the dresser, a silver framed photograph of his grandparents, Kyle and Emma Anderson.

Their fragile health was the reason that he had come back to the struggling town of Stony Ford to live five years earlier. Shortly after he had gone off to VMI to earn a BA in Math and Science, his father had died, and his mother had entered into a good second marriage with a wealthy widower, giving the family home to him, and moving to Florida. His mother's good fortune left him with no obligations to an ageing parent.

However, his grandparents were another matter. Both were in declining health, his grandfather suffering from arthritis, and his grandmother with a deteriorating memory, and they needed someone nearby to lend a hand to remain in their home.

After all that they had done for him during his boyhood, Bob felt an obligation to be that special person. He had experienced only a few misgivings over the years about being confined to a quiet life in a one-horse town, and these were usually triggered by contacts with college classmates like his former roommate, Stan Walton, who was already a wealthy vice-president with a bank in San Diego.

Before heading to school, Bob drove down an almost deserted Main Street, pulling his black '55 Chevy into the empty parking lot in front of Turner's Café. Inside, he slipped into the front booth where he had breakfast every morning.

Billy Turner, the balding middle-aged proprietor, who functioned as cook, waiter, and stand-up comic, greeted him with a deadpan Buster Keaton delivery. "How's Professor Slater, the academic genius of Stony Ford High this morning? What's the latest news from the world of math and science?"

"E equals MC squared, Billy, but I guess your good friend Albert Einstein has already filled you in on that. Where's Kaye?"

"I see that you regret not having the lovely Miss Davidson here to wait on you this morning. Kaye's taking a day off. Chris is starting in the first grade, and she wanted to walk over with him to meet his new teacher."

"I knew that Chris would be starting school this month, but it slipped my mind that this was his first day, and Kaye wouldn't be at work. I suppose that absent mindedness goes along with mathematical brilliance. I've heard that Albert had the same problem."

Billy poured a cup of coffee from the steaming pot behind the counter and set it on the table in front of him. "Maybe this'll help clear up your confusion. You having the usual this morning?"

"Yeah, except make the eggs scrambled instead of fried, and give me grits instead of hash browns. Will Kaye be working tomorrow?"

"She'll be back on the job in the morning. Her landlady, Helen, will start getting Chris off to school along with her own son."

Billy returned shortly with the breakfast plate, inquiring, "Have you heard whether anyone's been lined up to replace Callison as coach this year? This town is deader than a hammer since the wrestling team disbanded after the accident."

"That wasn't even discussed at the faculty meeting last week. I don't think anyone has the heart to bring it up. How do you even talk about rebuilding a team when the coach and half of the starters from last year are gone? Do you think Johnny Burke and OL Spellman would come back out for the team after each of them lost a brother in that wreck?"

"I can't answer that, Bob. But I do know that no matter how torn up everyone still feels after that accident, this town's got to find a way to put it behind and move on. Stony Ford's been going downhill for a long time.

"When Southern Styles moved their manufacturing operation down to Georgia and laid off most of their work force, things went from bad to worse. Half of the people around here are looking for a job. And all of that unemployment has killed business for the local merchants. I know it's cut into my dinner trade. Just look up and down Main Street at the vacant store fronts.

"The glue that held this community together and gave people something to cheer about was Callison's winning teams. Everyone around here turned out hooting and hollering at the wrestling matches on Saturday night, watching those feisty Stony Fork kids getting after the boys from the bigger schools."

"I hear what you're saying, Billy, but I don't see any signs that the people in this town are ready to pick up the pieces and move on. I can't imagine anyone stepping in behind Buck and trying to rebuild the school wrestling program for a long, long time. I hope I'm wrong."

"Don't just stand around hoping and moping, Bob. That's what everyone else around here's doing. Get involved and do something to help turn things around and pump some life back into this town. You've got some influence over at the high school. Why don't you try using it?"

Bob was still mulling over that challenge as he left the café and drove over to the high school. He walked past the principal's office and waved at Albert Carter, reminded again of how much his tall, raw-boned boss resembled a clean-shaven Abe Lincoln, continuing down the hall to his personal domain, Room 104.

The ear-splitting bell announcing classes would start in fifteen minutes rattled lockers and set students scrambling just as Becky Thompson, the young auburn-haired English and commercial math teacher, stepped into his doorway. "Ready to start the new school year, Bob?"

"I've never been ready for anything a day in my life," he replied, looking at Becky's ever-present, friendly smile and realizing again how attractive she was, wondering why anyone who had so much going for her would choose to live and work in Stony Ford. "How about you?"

"I'm ready, but remember that I get to teach business math and don't have to deal with all of the complex theorems that cause so much confusion for your students." Becky turned to walk away, calling back over her shoulder, "Try to have a good day. I'll catch up with you this afternoon to hear how things went."

The students filed through the door for homeroom, talking and laughing as they found seats, the usual knots of gossiping girlfriends and mischief-minded boys unchanged by the passing of another summer. Their high spirits were infectious, bringing a smile to his face as he began establishing law and order in the classroom once again.

Chapter 2

In the lounge later that day, Bob saw that several of his friends had already settled into their customary seats on the old vinyl-upholstered chairs near the front of the room, kicking off their shoes and sharing a pack of Chesterfields. Their cigarette smoke sought him out and burned his eyes as he walked by to drop a dime in the vending machine and take out a cold Coke.

Several of his friends had retreated from the smokers to the far end of the room, near an open window, and were waving to catch his attention. He joined them with a cheery, "Another day, another dollar."

Virgil Akers, industrial arts teacher now nearing retirement, and Virginia Swecker, middle-aged and matronly government and history teacher for countless years, shifted over to make room for him on the sofa. "Come on over and join us, Bob," she invited. "Virgil and I don't take up much space, and you can squeeze in."

Bob settled in beside them, noting how old and tired Virgil appeared. "Looks like both of you survived the first day of school," he commented.

"Just barely," Virgil answered in a voice two octaves too deep for his small frame. "Every year, the new kids in shop class spill that damn construction glue all over the work benches, and I have to spend an hour after class trying to chip it off. And to top it all, today one of them lost my key ring with every single key I own."

Virginia glanced sideways at Bob and rolled her eyes, signaling him to not encourage Virgil to go on. He got the message, and changed the subject. "It seems like most of the kids are in a happier frame of mind than they were when school let out for the summer. Even Johnny Burke and OL Spellman seem to be in better spirits."

"I hope you're right," Virginia replied, "When I looked at them today, I could see that both are still pretty subdued, trying to deal with the loss of their brothers."

Bob glanced toward the door and watched Principal Carter enter the lounge, striding across the room to loom directly in front of him. "Bob, I wonder if I could have a word with you in my office."

He followed the gangly gray-haired principal from the room, glancing back at his friends with raised eyebrows and shrugged shoulders as if to inquire, "What in the world have I done now?"

Albert invited Bob to take a seat as soon as the office door closed behind them, cutting right to the chase. "Tazewell School Superintendent, Sanford Williams, called earlier today to give me some bad news.

"I'm not going to get approval to replace Buck Callison due to a budget shortfall. So, I'm using my personal lottery system to pass out his former duties to the remaining faculty members, and you're the first person with a winning ticket. Congratulations, Slater. You're the new boys' varsity coach."

"You're pulling my leg, aren't you, Albert? We both know that I've never done anything here but teach math."

"Unfortunately for you, I'm dead serious. Just be thankful you aren't also getting one of Buck's civics or driver training classes. Since we don't field a football or basketball team, your only new responsibility will be to rebuild the wrestling team."

"How did you settle on me to become the wrestling coach? What about one of the other men on the faculty? Or even one of the women, maybe Grace Blevins? She helped two burly guys and me move an old upright piano out of the music room into the back of her pickup truck last week, and it must have weighed a ton."

"You can joke around as much as you want, Bob, but you know I'm not about to give the job to Grace, and that you're not going to wiggle your way out of this. You're the youngest and most athletic male member of the faculty, and I've seen that you have a lot more rapport with the boys than any other teacher in the building.

"Your personnel folder shows that you were a two year walk-on at VMI on the wrestling team. When Sanford told me that I had to handle all of Buck's former teaching duties with my staff, picking you as the coach seemed perfectly logical."

"Is there any way I can appeal this assignment?"

"You could try that, but it wouldn't do you any good. I function as head of both the executive and judicial branches in this school."

Albert peered closely at Bob with a sly smile, adding, "I hear that some members of the faculty think I bear a striking resemblance to the sixteenth president of the United States."

The principal grew serious again, continuing, "But in fairness to you, Slater, I'm going to have Becky Thompson take over your freshman algebra class.

"Several other things should make this new coaching assignment more palatable. There will be fewer wrestling matches scheduled for the upcoming season, and most of them will be right here at the school.

"The first away event happens to be a preseason exhibition match right down the road in Bluefield. And we will not participate in the state championship tournament at the end of the season."

Bob realized that Principal Carter was as dead set in this matter as his look-alike ancestor had been in preventing the secession of the south from the union. "I have a truckload of misgivings, Albert, but if this is your final decision, I'll have a go at it and give it my best shot."

"I knew you'd be a good sport, and I'm confident you'll do an outstanding job, Bob. I'll be talking to the other involved members of the faculty tomorrow, and then on Friday morning, I'll announce the new assignments to the students during our first assembly."

*****

Johnny and OL had been watching the clock for an hour, and upon hearing the 3:00 final bell, wasted no time in exiting the building. The two boys followed Main Street through the heart of town, picking up small rocks to toss at leaves and sticks floating down Laurel Creek as it tumbled beside the roadway over rock ledges and gravel beds.

They stopped at the rusty iron bridge to watch ducks paddling slowly in circles below, then followed Pine Street to the fork where Possum Hill Road turned off toward their neighborhood high in the ridge.

"You want to go over to the town dump and shoot rats?" Johnny asked as they walked along. "I still have a box of .22 hollow points in my dresser drawer, and I'll split it with you."

"I can't go this afternoon," OL replied, running his hand over his red crew-cut. "My old man wants me to finish painting the garage, and I better have it done before he gets home.

"Pa started drinking again when he got laid off at the furniture factory, and he gets mean when he's loaded. It's been a lot worse since Lonnie died. I don't want any trouble with him today."

"Your old man used to do a lot of things with you and Lonnie back when he was working, didn't he? I remember that he took y'all camping on the New River in the summertime, and deer hunting with him in the fall. You told me that he was the one who taught you how to use a fly rod and skin squirrels."

"That all seems like a million years ago. I used to look forward to seeing him coming home from work. Now I try to steer clear of him whenever I can."

Johnny peeled off at his house, and OL continued on to the faded white aluminum-sided house trailer dropped without regard for aesthetics at the end of the pot-holed road.

"I'm home, Ma," he called out as he entered the trailer and headed for the refuge of his bedroom.

His mother was watching a soap opera on an old Crosley TV set while stirring a pot of vegetable soup on the stove. She glanced over at him with a weak smile. OL noticed that her hair had not been combed, and she was still wearing the same house dress she had worn for days.

He knew that her life had gone downhill as dramatically as his father's. She had lost her constant smile and happy ways when the household money started to run out, and her embittered husband began to come home drunk. Then the horrific automobile accident had snatched Lonnie away from her forever, and she had thrown in the towel on life.

OL was dressed in a pair of spattered coveralls a short time later, quickly spreading white paint on the side of the dilapidated garage that his dad had built from scrap lumber right after coming back from the war.

He was finishing the job when his mother called to him from the back door, "OL, you need to get in here to dinner now. Your father just got home, and I'm putting the food on the table."

He quickly put the lid back on the paint can and cleaned the brush before heading into the house to wash up for dinner. His dad was already seated at the head of the table by the time he took his place.

Garner Spellman stared at him, asking sternly, "You finish painting the garage today like I told you to?"

"Yes, Pa. I just finished." OL dipped his spoon into the bowl of hot soup in front of him and started to raise it to his lips.

"Too bad Lonnie's gone. He would have had the job done a month ago without me even having to ask him."

OL glanced over at his tired, expressionless mother, and set his spoon back on his plate, staring down at the table. He knew that both of them were in for another unpleasant evening that would not end until his dad went into his room and passed out on the bed, snoring loudly, still wearing his faded Levis and high-top work shoes.

Chapter 3

"Thank heaven for Fridays," Kaye cheerily called out, walking toward his booth with a steaming mug of coffee mixed with a lot of cream and very little sugar, just the way he liked it.

"Thank heaven, indeed," Bob answered, reaching out to take the cup, deliberately letting his hand brush against hers. "I'll bet Chris is getting along well with his teacher, Miss Stevens."

"You can say that again," Kaye answered, tucking her short blonde hair under her cap. "She makes each one of the children think he's her special pet. Chris can't wait to get up in the morning and off to school. I've been relegated to the number two woman in his life since he started the first grade."

Kaye set his breakfast plate in front of him, continuing, "The only time he gets peeved at her is when she calls the roll and uses his full name, Christopher Robin Davidson. I suppose he'd have been much happier if I'd named him Clark Kent."

"Sounds like he's taking to school like a duck to water. It took me a few weeks to get in the swing of things when I started the first grade."

"The only thing that's bothered him so far is a couple of boys in the second grade calling him four-eyes. He asked me if he could go to school without his glasses, and I told him that since we don't have a white cane and a seeing-eye dog, he's stuck with wearing them.

"Chris has been in glasses since he was knee-high to a grasshopper. The eye doctor said he's very nearsighted, so it looks like he'll be wearing glasses for the rest of his life, but I can think of a lot of things that would be worse."

She was in no hurry to walk away, and Bob seized the opportunity to inquire, "Any chance of me making a date with you after work to drive over to Tazewell and take in *Wanted Dead or Alive* with Steve McQueen?"

"Sorry, Bob, not tonight. I don't get off until 6:00, and I don't have a baby sitter lined up. How about giving me a little more notice the next time?" She brushed a lock of hair from her damp forehead and flashed a pretty smile before turning to walk away, with his eyes following her trim figure all the way back to the kitchen.

Bob finished his breakfast and drove to the high school, observing that, as usual, he was the first faculty member to arrive. It was a standing joke among his friends that on the day he died, he would be standing around killing time in heaven waiting for St. Peter to show up and unlock the Pearly Gates.

Bob had taken his brief case from the back seat and was walking toward the front steps when he saw Becky Thompson walking quickly toward him. He paused to allow her to catch up, expecting to hear her usual friendly greeting. What he got instead took him by surprise.

"Thanks a lot, Slater. I really appreciate your dumping your freshman algebra class on me this fall. I didn't need that free time every morning to look over my lesson plans, since I can always put in another hour at home in the evenings to prepare."

Bob looked at Becky, seeing a trace of her usual smile, but sensing that she was quite upset. He didn't feel it was fair for her to confront him for something out of his control, and he impatiently snapped back, "Don't start blaming me for unloading that class on you.

"Talk to our principal, Honest Abe. He's the one who's handing out the new work assignments. Think you've been dumped on? Well, I've been assigned Buck Callison's coaching duties. If you want to swap, I'll take back the algebra class and let you have the wrestling team."

Bob regretted his words almost before they were out of his mouth. He and Becky were very good friends, and he knew that he had overreacted to her comment.

"I'm sorry, Becky. I didn't mean anything by that. Albert's gotten squeezed by the superintendent on faculty hiring, and he's loaded up several of us with the straw that breaks the camel's back."

"That's OK, Bob. I didn't help to get our Friday off to a good start by flying off the handle here in the parking lot. We'll get into those job reassignments soon enough during the school assembly this morning. I apologize, too."

The bell rang a short time later signaling the stampede to the gym. Students and teachers filed in, filling the bleachers along both sides and the folding chairs arranged in rows across the shiny oak plank floor.

Principal Carter walked to the front of the room, raised his hand to quiet the crowd, and quickly started the meeting.

"I'd like to welcome everyone to Stony Ford High for the start of the new school year, particularly the members of our freshman class. I'm sure that all of you have grown bored with summer vacation, and are excited about starting back to school today."

He smiled as his remark got the expected reaction from the young audience, continuing, "Now will you please stand, direct your attention to the flag overhead, and join me in the Pledge of Allegiance." The room soon echoed with the rhythmic monotone voice of the student body.

"Rev. Jonas Underwood, pastor of the First Baptist Church, has joined us this morning to deliver an invocation," Albert continued. "Then I have a few announcements to make about plans for the school year, including the reassignment of responsibilities for some faculty members.

"We'll keep this first assembly short, since I can see you're all anxious to get started in your new classes." His smile indicated that it was OK for everyone to emit another collective groan, and after the students quieted, he turned the microphone over to the minister.

Rev, Underwood stepped to the podium, bent his head as he spoke, his words heartfelt.

"Lord, last winter Coach Callison and four of our finest young people were taken from us in a terrible accident, but we know they're at home with you now. Be with us today and throughout the coming year, helping us to honor their memory by doing our best in our work, our studies, and our lives.

"Lord, I pray that there will be rebirth in this community. I pray that good times will return to this town. I pray that new jobs will be created, families will be reconciled, lives will be redirected, educations achieved, and the unquenchable spirit of Stony Ford restored.

"And I ask that you start it here this morning in this school, in the hearts and minds of these young people and their teachers. Amen."

The room fell silent as Jonas finished, the usual whispering among students and shuffling of feet not heard. A girl cried softly somewhere in the back of the room, and Albert saw that it was Amanda Smith, younger sister of Tolly, one of the four Eagles killed in the car wreck.

He quickly returned to the lectern, attempting to lighten the somber mood of the audience. "Thank you, Rev. Underwood, for your eloquent invocation. My announcements about teaching reassignments seem to pale into insignificance by comparison, but they must be made, so I'll get started."

Albert reviewed the changes in responsibilities for the school year ahead. He wisely waited until the very last to announce his selection of Bob Slater as the new coach to replace the late Buck Callison, knowing that the boys would be paying no attention to anything else he had to say after hearing that.

*****

"Big Al must have lost his mind," junior class clown Darryl Honaker speculated, taking a big swallow from his Dr. Pepper and then emitting a prodigious belch. "What kind of moron would pick Mr. Slater to coach the wrestling team?"

Darryl and his friends had walked straight from school to Ray's Drive-In, and were now seated in the back booth discussing the events of the day, particularly that announcement.

"Face the other way when you cut loose like that," an annoyed Johnny reacted, throwing a balled up napkin at his friend across the table. "Big Al didn't lose his mind. He didn't have much to choose from. Would you rather that he'd picked old man Akers?"

"It wouldn't matter either way," OL observed, entering the conversation. "The wrestling team is dead as a door knob as far as I'm concerned. I don't see either you or me going out on the mats this year, knowing our brothers won't be there."

He looked down at the table top and began balancing a salt shaker on its edge, hoping to draw his friends' attention from the tears welling up in his eyes.

"I wouldn't want Bull Frog Akers coaching us, but I wouldn't mind if Miss Thompson did," Darryl cracked, trying to lighten the mood. "She could put on a pair of tights and take me out on the mats to work on pins all day long. I wouldn't even try to bridge out from under her."

He looked at Johnny and OL, seeing their grins, knowing that he had successfully raised their spirits.

Terry Blankenship chimed in from his seat beside Darryl, "I think Big Al should recruit Dan Hodge from Oklahoma to coach. If you brought in the outstanding wrestler from the NCAA championship last year, every boy in school would come out for the team. You'd have the entire Bluefield High wrestling team moving to Stony Ford."

"You guys may have a hard time getting Dan Hodge to move to this rundown town," OL said, getting to his feet. "I think you'd better get used to having Mr. Slater as the new coach. Right or wrong, he's a lock for the job."

Chapter 4

Roland and Oliver Hundley walked side by side through the cavernous Southern Styles factory, their footsteps sounding on the dusty concrete floor and faintly echoing back from far corners.

The dim lighting inside the old high bay manufacturing facility came from a string of fluorescent night lights overhead, supplemented by faint sunlight trying to peek through the dirty panes of large windows along the walls.

The entire production area looked as though some cataclysmic wind had blown through the building in the blink of an eye, carrying all of the workers away forever, but leaving the work stations and assembly lines frozen in time.

They paused to peer through a door at the end of the room into a smaller work area, where a skeleton crew was busily engaged in rebuilding furniture which had had been shipped to Virginia for repair after failing quality control inspection at the new plant in Georgia.

"This place is as quiet as a tomb," Roland observed, looking around through gold-framed bifocals as they retraced their steps. "I can remember when we had hundreds of people working here, and the factory noise was so loud you could hardly make yourself heard.

"A damn pity to see it shuttered up like this. I'd like to find some way of using this building again and putting some of our folks back to work."

"I don't see it that way at all," Oliver replied, brushing factory dust from the sleeve of his dark suit. "We're making a lot more money manufacturing our products in Savannah. In my opinion, the best thing we can do with this building is keep the insurance paid up, and hope that someday before long a lightning strike or some fault in the electrical wiring will burn it to the ground."

"Those Stony Ford craftsmen working next door repairing our Savannah manufacturing defects wouldn't agree with you, Ollie. They're the fortunate survivors of our previous work force who still have jobs to keep food on the table and a roof over their families' heads. They take a lot of pride in their work."

"You have a character flaw that will keep you from ever becoming a full-blown business tycoon, Rollo. You're too soft-hearted. You worry so much about your employees that you take your eye off the bottom line.

"I guess that's why you need me to be your controller. Someone has to be a hard-nosed bean counter in order for Southern Styles to succeed."

Roland glanced at his younger brother and smiled, knowing that the two had an entirely different take on life that dated back to childhood. "Sometimes I think that you may be too obsessed with the bottom line.

"Our grandfather and great-uncle founded this company with the goal of building quality furniture while turning a good profit, but they also tried to make a decent life for their employees.

"The company houses they built were much better than those provided by the coal mines. Samuel and Elias arranged for their tenants to have land for vegetable gardens and a place to keep a few chickens."

"I hear what you're saying, Rollo, but I'm sure that even back in the early days those two had an aggressive plant manager working under them, pushing the employees to produce, making the tough decisions and occasionally bending the rules when necessary to keep the business running in the black.

"Nothing has changed today. You still need a man like me who puts the financial success ahead of everything else. Otherwise, a family enterprise will always fail."

The two parted at the door, Roland shaking his head at his brother's flint hard business philosophy. Oliver wasn't paying any attention, walking away deep in thought about more pressing matters, concerns in his life that his brother must never know.

*****

Bob entered the back room of the Ben Franklin Store on Monday evening, joining the leaders of the Stony Ford Boosters Club. Leon Carper, club president, walked over to shake his hand. "Thanks for coming tonight, coach. By the way, are you starting to get comfortable with that new title?"

"Not yet, Leon, and I'm not sure that I ever will. Anyone who coaches, signing up to turn out a winning team every year, should be aware that uneasy lies the head that wears a crown."

Steve Mullins, town mayor, and manager of the local Piggly Wiggly, and Priscilla, Leon's wife, stood to greet him. "You don't have to worry about our putting your head on the chopping block quite yet, Bob," Steve cracked. "We don't usually call for the coach's head until the end of a losing season."

"Y'all are doing wonders for my self confidence. Until I heard that comforting remark, I was worried about being a math teacher trying to take over a decimated wrestling team, with only two years of college experience dating back to the dark ages."

"You know we're just kidding you, Bob," Priscilla interjected. "I can speak for the entire Stony Ford Boosters Club in telling you how excited we are to have you stepping in to bring the wrestling program back. Our group is ready to give you any support you need."

"What would you like for us to do to help you kick things off?" Leon inquired. "Are you ready for us to call a general membership meeting, so that you can tell everyone your plans and ask for help?"

"I appreciate your offer, Leon, but I think that a meeting with the Boosters Club now may be premature. The first order of business for me is to talk to Johnny and OL, and see if I can persuade them to come back out for the team. If I can recruit those two seniors, I'll have the bell cows to help lead the others back."

After the meeting broke up, Leon walked Bob to the door. "I owe it to you to tell you something before you leave tonight. Priscilla may have overstated things when she said that the entire club is behind you.

"You need to watch out for two of our members, Nick and Randy Kowalski. They're very upset that Albert Carter gave you the job.

"They've already contacted the superintendent to protest your appointment. They'll be watching you, hoping you'll make mistakes and fall on your face, so they can pull some strings and get an experienced wrestling coach brought here from the eastern part of the state."

"Thanks for the warning, Leon. The name Kowalski sure rings a bell with me. The first year I started teaching here I had a big kid named Mickey Kowalski in my freshman algebra class.

"He cut school every chance he got, and never turned in any homework. At the end of the school year I gave him an F. He went home afterward, and didn't come back for his sophomore year.

"His father came to see me about the failing grade, mad as a wet hen, acting as though all of Mickey's academic problems were my fault. I think he hoped to provoke me into a fist fight, so he could either whip my butt or get me fired."

Leon raised his eyebrows. "I think you should know that Mickey's father, Buddy, is Nick and Randy's younger brother."

"Thanks for tipping me off. I'm not surprised to hear that all of the Kowalskis are related, since that's a pretty uncommon name in these parts. I'll be watching out for them."

Chapter 5

OL drove his dad's battered '49 Chevy pickup through town until West Main Street gave way to Creekside Road, which continued for another mile to a neighborhood made up of a dozen small frame houses built on a low rise just above Laurel Creek.

The people who lived there called their neighborhood Laurel Glen. Most of the people in town referred to it using a less elegant but more colorful name: Frog Level.

He turned into a gravel driveway leading up to a small white house with blue shutters, climbing the front porch steps two at a time to ring the bell. Betty Ellison, wearing a colorful print house dress, came to the door with a warm greeting. "Come on in the living room and sit down. Julie will be ready in just a few minutes."

OL took a seat on a on a small upholstered chair across the room from Julie's parents. Homer glanced up from his newspaper, taking the old briar pipe from his mouth long enough to say a friendly hello, while Betty continued to chat.

"Tell me, OL, how does it feel to be starting your senior year of high school? Have you started thinking about what you want to do after you graduate?"

"No, ma'am, I never look that far ahead. You never can tell what's going to happen down the road. I pretty much take things one day at a time."

Betty smiled upon hearing OL's philosophy on life. "I definitely think that you should be planning to go to college next year. We've been steering Julie in that direction since she was in grade school."

Homer set down his paper to relight his pipe and entered the conversation, "What's going on with the wrestling team? I heard down at the barber shop today that Bob Slater's been picked as the new coach.

"A few people seemed disappointed. They thought the principal made a big mistake in appointing an inexperienced man like Slater to the job. How do you boys feel about it?"

"Truthfully, Mr. Ellison, it doesn't matter a whole lot to me. I think that Mr. Slater's a good teacher, and everyone likes him, but I doubt that he knows much about wrestling. I don't plan to go back out for the team this year no matter who coaches. I lost interest the night my brother died."

"We're all still saddened by that, son, but it's a shame for you to give up the sport because of it. I went to all of the home matches last year before it happened, and I thought that you, Lonnie, and Johnny Burke were the best athletes on the squad. I hoped that you might do something with it, and earn a scholarship to some college around here with a good program. Someplace like VPI."

At that moment, Julie came through the hallway into the living room, wearing a white sweater and blue skirt, her long brown hair pulled back in a pony tail. OL noted how much she looked like a younger and more athletic replica of her pretty mother.

"Sorry to keep you waiting, OL. The time snuck up on me after dinner. I guess we'd better run if we want to make the start of the first feature at the Zephyr."

"Don't be too late getting home," Homer called out to his daughter, as the two teenagers left the house and the screen door noisily banged behind them. "You know that your mother won't close her eyes 'til she hears you come in."

OL held the door for Julie to slide into the front seat, then walked around the car to climb behind the wheel. She turned to him with an annoyed expression and remarked, "Sometimes Daddy really embarrasses me!

"I hate it when he comes out with a remark like that when I go out on a date. For heaven's sake, I'm seventeen years old and a junior in high school."

"Go easy on him, Julie. Your dad's only looking out for you. A lot of kids at school would be happy to have a father like him. Somebody who cares what happens to them. And that includes me."

Later that evening, they settled into their seats at the theater to watch *No Time for Sergeants*, each with a big box of popcorn, OL reaching out to take Julie's hand. Andy Griffith was perfectly cast as Will Stockdale, a good-hearted country boy but a total military misfit.

During the barracks inspection scene when Will rigged up the row of toilet seats to simultaneously snap to attention, OL laughed so hard you could hear him all over the theater.

Julie snuggled close to him during the ride home, murmuring, "Honey, I enjoyed the movie so much. I haven't heard you laugh like that in a long time."

OL slipped his arm around her and replied quietly, "For a while there I was having a good time. I didn't have my mind on Lonnie."

*****

"Come in and have a seat," Bob invited, as OL and Johnny approached his desk on Monday afternoon. "I appreciate both of you hanging around to talk with me after class. How are things going?"

Johnny glanced at OL, then back at Bob before responding, "OK, Mr. Slater." Both boys slipped into front row desks, waiting patiently to see why they had been summoned, while already having a very good idea as to where the conversation was headed.

"So that we don't waste anyone's time, I'll get straight to the reason you were invited here this afternoon. Plain and simple, it's because I need your help.

"You were both there during the assembly when Principal Carter announced that he had picked me as the new wrestling coach and given me responsibility for reorganizing the program. And you both know that I'm starting from scratch, since the team disbanded after the accident last winter.

"Maybe you're wondering what right I have to bring you in here and ask for your help, so I'll try to make my case. The whole town, particularly the student body, is still devastated. But we can't walk around under a dark cloud with our heads down forever.

" Johnny, I know that isn't what Red would want, and OL, neither would Lonnie. I'm confident that neither of your brothers would expect us to quit. If they were here now, I believe they'd tell us to honor their memory and respect their achievements as champions by getting this team going again.

"I'm positive that Coach Callison would do the same. So now I'll ask you the sixty-four dollar question: Would the two of you be willing to be senior co-captains this year and help me rebuild the team?"

OL stared at the floor and answered softly, "I'm sorry to turn you down, Mr. Slater, but my heart's not in wrestling anymore."

"You have every right to feel that way. But for your own good and that of everyone around, I'm asking you to reconsider.

"Look at this as an opportunity for you to help revitalize your school and the community, then get back to me in the morning with your answer. If neither of you is willing to sign on for the challenge, I promise that I won't pressure you any further."

OL and Johnny glanced at each other, standing to leave. Both had anticipated the new coach's request to come back to the team, but not the forceful way he had presented it as their responsibility to help others.

Bob watched OL and Johnny walk out of his office, trying to read their body language. It seemed that Johnny had an open mind toward stepping up and helping him. And it was obvious that OL had given up, not only on the sport, but also on many other hopes in his life.

At home that evening, Bob spent several hours grading student papers and making lesson plans for classes the next day. It was almost nine o'clock when the phone rang, and he picked up the receiver to hear a teenage boy's deepening voice on the other end.

"Mr. Slater, this is Johnny Burke. I'm calling to tell you that I've been thinking over what you asked me to do this afternoon, and

I've talked it over with my folks. I'll help you get the team going again."

"Johnny, that's what I've been hoping to hear! You won't regret this decision, I promise you. What about OL?"

"I just got off the phone with OL, and he still says no. I tried to convince him that it was up to the two of us to help you rebuild the team, but he doesn't have his heart in wrestling anymore. He thinks that because Lonnie will never go on the mats again, he shouldn't either."

"I'm sorry about that, Johnny, but I'm glad that at least one of you will be stepping up. I appreciate your calling me tonight to give me the good news."

"You're welcome, Coach. I guess I'll see you at school in the morning."

Bob realized as he set the phone down that it was the first time any one of the boys at school had called him coach. Then his thoughts turned again to OL.

He barely realized that he was talking to an empty room when he spoke out, "I take back what I said about not pressuring you, OL. I'll be darned if I'm going to give up on you watch you let life pass you by."

Chapter 6

"Everybody gather 'round over here and take a knee," Bob called out to the boys in the gym, interrupting their game of H-O-R-S-E with a deflated volleyball. "I'm going to hand out sign-up sheets for the wrestling team. You need to get one of your parents to put a John Hancock on the bottom line, and bring it back to me tomorrow. No approved sign-up sheet on file, no participation."

The team knelt in a circle around him, and he continued. "I want to thank all of you for turning out this afternoon. Before we go any further, we're going to bow our heads in a moment of silent prayer to remember Coach Callison, Red, Lonnie, Rick, and Tolly."

After a short interval of silence followed by a soft, collective "Amen," Bob spoke again. "As we kick off a new start to our wrestling program, I want to dedicate this season to your former teammates and coach. We're going to work together to keep their competitive spirit and winning tradition alive. We must not let them down.

"Now let's get down to business. Practice will start this Wednesday and run five days a week from 3:15 'til 5:00. Johnny, our only senior, has accepted my request to serve as captain. Billy Bowman has agreed to take over as equipment manager this year.

"The first thing we'll do is head over to the equipment room, and he'll issue each of you a pair of practice tights and a jersey. You're on your own for towels, jocks, socks, and shoes. Any questions? If not, Billy's waiting for you in the cage next door."

Johnny started to follow his friends when Bob laid a hand on his shoulder to stop him. "Have you talked to OL again?"

"Yeah, Coach, I talked to him on the way to school this morning. He's not coming back out for the team. OL's lost interest in a lot of things that he used to like. About the only thing he seems to care about now is hanging out with Julie."

"Maybe you just came up with something. What if I talk to her? Maybe she could convince him that it's time for him to accept his brother's death and get on with his life."

"You could try, Coach. I don't think it would hurt anything. Lonnie once told me that he'd had a secret crush on Julie since he was in the seventh grade. If OL hadn't started going steady with her, I believe Lonnie would have asked her out himself. He was always watching her out of the corner of his eye when she was cheerleading for the team."

Bob returned to his classroom, noticing that Becky Thompson was still grading homework papers at her desk in the next room. He walked in and took seat at a desk on the front row to inquire, "How's the new freshman algebra teacher doing?"

Beckie glanced up from her work and replied, "Hey there, Bob. I'm doing surprisingly well, thank you, although I must confess that it's taking me a lot more time to work up lesson plans for a subject that I haven't taught before. You're not here now with a guilty conscience, volunteering to take the class back, are you?"

"Nope. I managed to get rid of my conscience a long time ago. I just stopped by to look in on the prettiest teacher in the building."

Beckie rolled her eyes, then gave him a mischievous look. "Slater, you are a man of boundless charm. First you dump a ton of extra work on me, and then while I'm trying to dig my way out from under it, you stop to pay me compliments. Paul Newman could take lessons from you."

"You're determined to hold a grudge, aren't you? Would it help to smooth things over between us if I invited you to go bowling on Friday night?"

"That's not going to happen. You know Principal Carter's rule about fraternization between male and female faculty members. Somebody would report us, and we'd both be in his office on Monday morning getting reprimanded."

"Some things are worth the risk of a reprimand to me, Beck. Anyway, I'll clear out of here now, and let you get your algebra papers graded. Hope it doesn't take too long. See you in the morning."

*****

Bob walked to the podium of the American Legion hall and glanced at the gathering of Boosters Club members seated before him. He recognized a few friends but was surprised to see mostly unfamiliar faces. Realizing that this was not the audience that he had expected, he made a quick decision to jettison his notes and try to wing it with humor.

He took a deep breath and began, "Leon, thanks for that kind introduction. I appreciate you, Steve, and Priscilla getting everyone out tonight to give me this opportunity to talk with the Boosters

Club. I'm new to speaking in front of groups such as yours, so I hope you'll understand if I seem little nervous.

"Some of you may wonder why Principal Carter picked a math teacher like me to pick up the high school wrestling program. I did, too, so I asked him.

"He explained that I was the logical choice, based on his knowledge of ancient history. Since the Greeks developed both math and wrestling, he felt confident that someone who teaches algebra and geometry could coach the sport."

Bob saw the puzzled looks on faces around the room and knew that he was off to a bad start, quickly shifting gears. "That was supposed to be a joke, but obviously I should leave the humor to Bob Hope. Please let me start over.

"Ten years ago, I was a member of the VMI wrestling team for two seasons, which gave me an understanding of the basics. When Principal Carter learned that he would not be able to replace Coach Callison with a new faculty hire, he realized that I was the only teacher on his staff who had any experience, and for that reason he selected me to step in and try to fill Buck's shoes.

"I certainly didn't ask for the coaching assignment, but I promised Mr. Carter that I would respect his decision and do everything in my power to help rebuild the program. Tonight I make the same promise to you. But the only way to succeed in restoring a winning team is for all of us to pull together. I'm going to need the cooperation and support of everyone in the Boosters Club."

Bob could see smiles and nods of assent on many faces in the audience as he quickly surveyed the room. Then he caught sight of two stocky men on the front row, and neither was smiling. He didn't recognize either, but both resembled someone he had met at an earlier place and time, though he could not recall just where or when.

The older one raised his hand to speak. Bob nodded at him and inquired, "Do you have something you'd like to say before I go on to tell you about my plans and progress to date?"

The man stood, speaking in a deep drawl, "My name's Nick Kowalski. If I understand what you just told all of us, Slater, the only reason Carter gave you the coaching job was because you were a walk-on for some college wrestling team ten years ago."

He paused, looking around at others in the audience for effect, then smirked, "That doesn't give me a helluva lot of confidence in Carter's ability to make good hiring decisions."

The room grew silent as Randy sat down, exchanging glances with the man beside him, both breaking into grins while waiting to see how the new coach would react. Bob decided to ignore them, trying to conceal the red flush creeping across his face, and speaking calmly as though he had not heard the ugly comment.

Now he knew who the older two Kowalski brothers were, realizing that they were as headstrong and troublesome as Mickey's father, Buddy. He would be on guard around that family going forward.

"Eighteen boys have signed up. The only senior on the squad, Johnny Burke, has been named captain. We've issued equipment, and started working out five afternoons a week to get into shape.

"Next week, we'll get into the basics: takedowns, control and escape from the referee's position, and most importantly, going for pins. There's a lot of work ahead of us, but things are coming together, and I believe that we can have a competitive team this year, maybe not a championship contender, but one that will go out every match and give one hundred percent."

Bob saw a sarcastic smile pass over the face of the second brother as he raised his hand for permission to speak, but Bob paid no attention and quickly moved forward to wrap up his talk.

"Thanks for coming out this evening. I look forward to a great working relationship with the Boosters Club as we develop a strong wrestling team in the months ahead."

He surveyed the room, making brief eye contact with everyone except the two men, concluding, "I'd enjoy speaking with those of you who are able to stick around after the meeting."

The group gathered around Bob, the Kowalskis drawing closer as if to speak. But when Nick extended a beefy arm, it was only to stub out his cigar in one of the Legion hall's black tarred ashtrays. A moment later the door bounced on its hinges, and both brothers were gone.

Chapter 7

Jonas Underwood entered the Piggly Wiggly, spotting the store manager, Steve Mullins, bending over a counter in the produce department. Quietly walking over to stand behind him, Jonas spoke loudly, "I think all of the oranges are overripe. Are you planning to mark them down and move them out before they go bad?"

Steve recognized the voice and didn't bother to look up before replying, "And I think all of the sermons at the Baptist church on Sunday morning go on too long. I suppose people need to learn to live with the things they can't control."

He turned around to greet his friend, continuing with the dead-pan delivery. "Maybe we both need a complaint department. If you opened one at First Baptist, it would mean a full time job for someone." He watched Jonas stifle a laugh, continuing, "Tell me, Rev, what brings you in here this morning so full of peas and ginger?"

"So full of what? Maybe I better let that slide, and we'll talk about something respectable. Actually, I happened to come here this morning with an exciting idea that I wanted to discuss with one of the young deacons in the church, and you immediately came to mind. Do you have a few minutes?"

"All the time in the world for you, Rev. Fire away."

Last week, I was reading an article in a Baptist periodical about old time tent revivals, and it went on to describe how effective they were in restoring the vitality of churches and the surrounding communities. Revivals were a big thing back during the Depression.

"I started giving this some thought, and I've prayed about it in recent days. Now I'm entertaining the idea of holding a revival here. What do you think of that idea?"

"You mean bring in some charismatic, hellfire and brimstone preacher with a big tent and a choir?"

"I wasn't thinking about putting on a great spectacle. Just an old time, down home revival with an evangelist like the Rev. Barry Greene and his wife Ethel, preaching the gospel on a Saturday night.

"Maybe some of the other churches in town would like to join in with us. I thought that we might be able to hold it in an empty bay of the furniture factory."

"I haven't been to something like that since my mother took me to a tent revival when I was a young kid, Jonas, but if you think it would help this town, I'm all for it. What about the timing?"

"I was thinking about the Saturday before Halloween. Since I seem to have your blessing, I'm going to present this idea to some of the other church leaders after the service on Sunday, and if they go along, we'll form a committee and start making plans. I'd like for you to be the chairman."

"I'll try to help out, Jonas, but I'm already up to my neck in work as mayor, not to mention managing a grocery store which, according to you, has some big problems with over-ripe produce. Maybe someone else at church could take the lead on this one."

Turning back to his work, Steve added, "A week before Halloween? You're planning to hold a Christian revival right before the biggest pagan holiday of the year.

"Imagine converting all those mischievous little heathens in town who go out and soap windows, jam potatoes in exhaust pipes, and steal lawn furniture on Halloween night. Sounds like the opportunity for salvation of their souls. Who knows what good may come of this!"

"Who knows, indeed," Jonas replied, stopping to pick out a half dozen choice oranges. "Should I tell Peggy that you've decided to mark this dead-ripe fruit down to half price for quick sale?"

Steve rolled his eyes and laughed as he watched his friend head off toward the checkout counter.

*****

"Phone call for you," the secretary said quietly to Roland Hundley, who was sitting at his desk in the Bristol headquarters of Southern Styles Furniture. He picked up the phone and found himself speaking to a man with a strong southern accent that boomed across the line.

"Mr. Hundley, this is Jonas Underwood. I'm the pastor of the First Baptist Church in Stony Ford. I wonder if you could find the time to speak with me for a few minutes."

Roland anticipated another solicitation for a cash donation, but he responded pleasantly, "Certainly, Rev. Underwood. What can I do for you this morning?"

Jonas launched into an explanation for his call, a request to use part of the empty furniture factory at Stony Ford to stage a revival. "Our church will clean up the meeting room and rest rooms after the event, and won't make any demands on your company for anything but electricity for an organ and public address system. We'll take up a collection to reimburse your company for all expenses."

"Rev. Underwood, I'll have to look into this matter and discuss it with my staff. There may be some issues with insurance, building codes, and other things I'm unaware of. I won't know until I have a chance to look at this more closely. Let me take your name and phone number, and I'll get back to you within a few days to let you know whether I can help you."

Roland hung up the phone and dialed his brother's extension. A few minutes later, Oliver answered, and Roland repeated the request. He didn't have to wait long for his brother's strong opinion.

"I wouldn't touch that with a stick, not in a hundred years," Oliver said emphatically. "There's not a single thing in it for the company. We get the headaches and expense of making our old manufacturing facility available for some stem-winding tub-thumper to whip a bunch of local yokels into a religious frenzy, and for what purpose? It won't add a penny to the bottom line for our business."

"I wasn't looking at this as a financial venture for the company, Ollie. I was looking at it as an opportunity to provide a service for the townspeople. I feel responsible for leaving so many of them out of work.

"If a revival helps them deal with their problems, I'm willing to provide the venue for a stem-winding tub-thumper, as you call their evangelist, to inspire them not to give up."

"You're going against my advice, Rollo, but if that's your final decision, I'll check to be sure we don't expose ourselves to a huge lawsuit if some old dame goes twirling down the aisle and falls and breaks her fool neck."

Chapter 8

"That's not the way Coach Callison showed me how to do it," Bennie Feldman objected. "He taught me to keep my head up and my back straight when I shoot under an opponent and go for his legs. If I get my chest up against his legs, I can hook his ankle, and take him down to the mat on his back."

It was the second time that day that one of the boys had corrected Bob about the technique he was demonstrating, just as others had since the team had started working on takedowns, escapes, and pins.

Realizing that there were boys on the team who had developed better wrestling skills in high school than he had during his two year stint at VMI, he deferred to their expertise. "OK, Bennie, how about stepping over here and showing us the way Coach Callison wanted it done."

Bob knew that the team respected him as their coach, although they were clearly aware that he was a wrestling greenhorn. The boys recognized and appreciated the fact that he was doing his best.

Johnny, the only senior, had taken over as his right hand in leading the workouts and offering coaching instruction. Bob could not help but think how much better the team would be if OL were to come back to take on the duties of co-captain, but there seemed to be only two chances that he would ever do so: slim and none.

For the next hour, the boys paired off according to weight and went through basic drills. Starting with the lightest team members and working up to the unlimited class, they wrestled three-two minute periods at full speed under match conditions.

The best competition took place when 168-pound, eighteen year-old Johnny Burke took on 157-pound, seventeen-year old Darryl Honaker. Both had wrestled since the eighth grade and knew the sport well. Both were competitors who took no prisoners on the mat.

Darryl's trademark was an old VPI football jersey that he had worn at practice since the eighth grade, but which had seldom seen the inside of a washing machine. "Make him take that thing off before we start, Coach," Johnny pleaded. "I don't want that smelly rag in my face again. Darryl's locker stinks worse than the town dump."

Bob agreed, sending both boys onto the mat without shirts. Johnny was bigger and stronger, and was getting the better of things until he was rolled onto his back with Darryl's chest across his face. Although the jersey was off, the aroma lingered, and Johnny threw in the towel. "I quit, Coach. Pair me up with someone else until you run him through the showers."

Bob put on a sweat suit after practice and joined the boys for the daily two mile run on the cinder track outside. "You want me to call you a cab?" Terry razzed him as they started. "We don't want an old man to have a heart attack and end up in the hospital."

"You kids don't need to worry about my heart. You need to worry about your twenty-eight year-old coach kicking your butts doing eight laps around this track."

That was all the incentive the boys needed, and Bob soon found himself running behind the pack, huffing and puffing across the finish line dead last. The payoff for him was a snatch of conversation he later overheard from one of the boys in the locker room. "I didn't think Coach could go that hard for two miles. In a few weeks, he's going to be running over us."

Bob showered after the last boy had cleared the locker room. He stopped by his classroom long enough to pick up his briefcase before driving to Turner's Café, finding Kaye still on the job, trying to keep up with the evening dinner trade.

She spoke to him as he came through the door. "Hi, Honey. I see that you survived another practice. Grab a seat in that booth by the window, and I'll be right around to check on you." The café felt uncomfortably warm from the hot stove in the kitchen, and Bob could see small beads of perspiration across Kaye's forehead beneath her cap.

"Looks like you're having another busy day."

"That's a good thing for me. I don't make much in the way of tips when I'm just walking around an empty greasy-spoon wiping off table tops. You want the daily dollar special, spaghetti and meat sauce with a dinner roll and a salad?"

"Sounds good to me. I'll hang around until you finish your shift and give you a ride home."

Just then Billy walked over, laughing. "Ask Kaye to tell you how she serves drinks to our customers at lunch time."

He stopped to listen as Kaye turned to Bob with a faint smile and observed, "My boss couldn't wait to spill the beans on me, could he?"

"What's that all about?" Bob inquired curiously, waiting for Kaye to explain.

"A good-looking young truck driver comes through town from time to time, and he dropped in for lunch again today. He thinks he's a lady-killer and he's sure waitresses have an eye for him.

"I brought him a big glass of iced tea and was just setting it on the table when he made a fresh remark, so I picked it up and up and dumped it in his lap. He got up and walked out, and never even bothered to leave a tip. Just between you and me, I'm afraid I cost Billy a customer."

"Oh, don't bother worrying about that," Billy replied. "He'll be back. It's all part of the game to those highway cowboys. His buddies will get an earful about that escapade at every truck stop down the road."

Bob found a newspaper to read while killing time, waiting for Kaye to finish her shift. She picked up her coat afterward and walked with Bob to his car, telling him about her day, including her encounter with a kind old gentleman who had left her a half-dollar tip after ordering the special. She also mentioned the group of ladies who had lingered in a booth for hours, leaving nothing behind but empty coffee cups.

"You're not going to get rich waiting on tables in there. But I still make enough to keep an apartment for Chris and me, and to pay the bills, so who am I to complain?" Kaye was a survivor, always upbeat and cheerful, one of the qualities that he liked most about her.

"I'm sure Chris will be peeking out of the window, watching for you to come home," Bob remarked. "He really loves his mama. You know, there's another male around here who feels the same way about her."

"I wonder who he might be?" Kaye teased. "I have quite a few older men who stop by the café to flirt with me, and none of those gentlemen gets out of line like that young truck driver.

"Maybe you're talking about my favorite, Mr. Ellett. He'll be ninety-two this month, and I'm pretty sure that he's sweet on me. He brought me a bag of peppermint candy from the dime store last week."

"Peppermint candy is sure sign that he's starting to get serious. You'll know he's shopping around for a ring if he brings you a box of chocolates."

Bob had fallen for Kaye the first time he met her at the diner and discovered a sweet girl playing a difficult hand without a trace of bitterness. Everyone in town knew Kaye's story, and the one bad decision she had made early in life.

Kaye became pregnant at seventeen by her twenty year-old steady boyfriend, Lucky Abbott, realizing her predicament just before the end of her junior year. Lucky promised to marry her, but a couple of months before the ceremony was to take place, his luck ran out and he went off the side of a winding mountain road on his Harley, trying to hold forty miles an hour through a tight curve.

His body had not been found for almost a week, leading to a closed-casket funeral attended only by a small group of family members and a couple of his best buddies in the Ridge Runners motorcycle club. No one was aware at that time that Kaye was in a family way, and she was not invited by Lucky's mother Leona to attend the service.

Kaye's pregnancy could no longer be concealed by late summer. She went to work at Turner's Café as a waitress instead of returning for her senior year of high school, staying on the job until a month before Chris arrived.

Kaye and Chris lived with her parents for the following four years, until she finally was able to save enough money to afford a furnished basement apartment in the home of a young widow, Helen Chesley.

Kaye earned a high school equivalency certificate along the way, through correspondence school classes and home study. That was the good part of her life, the Horatio Alger story.

The other part was the hurtful disrespect and ostracism that she had encountered as the single mother of a young child with no wedding band on her finger, living in a small southern town.

There were people she had considered as friends, who treated her with respect and kindness before the pregnancy, but now avoided her and excluded her from their lives.

Kaye dealt with it well, holding her head up and still wearing a smile at the age of twenty-four. But suppressed anger and resentment at her treatment had forged a toughness of character that she lacked earlier.

She now knew how to deal with men who saw her as compromised, who mistakenly thought she was easy. She was eager to prove them wrong, as the cocky young cowboy in the café had learned.

Bob pulled into the driveway leading up to the two-story square brick house, seeing the front door open and Chris come running across the front porch and down the concrete steps to greet her. "Mom! I want to show you what I made in school."

Kaye reached out to wrap him up in her arms. "Aren't you going to say hello to Mr. Slater, too? He drove me home from work."

Chris walked over to Bob and shyly extended his hand. "Would you like to come in the living room with Mom and me to see what I made, Mr. Slater?"

Bob took the boy's hand and held it for a moment as he gently inquired, "Don't you think that Mr. Slater sounds awfully formal between good friends, Chris? Why don't you call me by the same name that the big boys in high school do. How about calling me Coach?"

Kaye took Chris by one arm and Bob by the other as they walked toward the steps leading down to the basement apartment, playfully asking, "Does that mean that I should start calling you Coach, too?"

"I'd prefer that you didn't. I'm hoping that you'll be able to come up with a more appropriate nickname than that for me. Get to work on it and see what you can do."

Kaye turned to him in response and softly mouthed a single word.

Bob read her lips, slipping his arm around her waist to pull her closer, and quietly replied, "Yeah, that's exactly the one I hoped you'd pick. That one's a whole lot better."

Chapter 9

Boys lugging beat-up gym bags stuffed with wrestling gear began showing up at the high school around 7:30 on Saturday morning. No one seemed in any hurry to load up and get on the road, the trip to Bluefield for the pre-season match taking less than an hour, and the weigh-in not until 9:30.

Bob parked his car beside Albert's, behind the two late model automobiles belonging to Tony and Andy Gilbert, members of the Boosters Club. Johnny, Darryl, Ron Sawyer, and Terry Blankenship walked over to join him. "OK if we ride with you today, Coach?" Johnny asked.

"No one wants to go in Mr. Carter's car," Darryl added.

"Fine with me," Bob laughed. "What's the problem in riding with Principal Carter? You think he may want to ask about the incident last week when someone let the air out of his tires?"

He saw Ron and Terry glance at each other in surprise, realizing that he had unwittingly solved that particular mystery. "Pile in. It looks like it's about time to get the show on the road."

The four car caravan was leaving the parking lot when Bob happened to glance into his rear view mirror. A tall boy was standing in the shadows next to the building, almost out of sight, watching them drive away. "I believe that I just saw OL standing back there near the school," Bob remarked.

"I wouldn't be surprised, Coach," Johnny replied. "I thought I spotted his old red Schwinn leaning up against the building.

"OL's still pretty mixed up. He misses the team, but he thinks that coming back would be like walking away and leaving Lonnie behind. I know what he's going through. I had to deal with the same thing."

"You did what was right for yourself and your family in coming back to the team, Johnny. Somehow we need to help OL understand that his brother wouldn't want him to give up everything."

They arrived at Bluefield High around 8:30, where they were greeted by Len Stiller, the legendary coach of the Blue Herons. He limped toward them wearing his trademark grin, extending his hand to Bob. "We've been waiting for you Stony Ford folks to show up. My boys say that they're looking forward to some eagle meat this morning."

"Hello, Len," Bob replied with a smile, feeling his hand crushed in the iron grip of the burly opposing coach. "Good to see you. You might want to give your boys a heads-up that eagle meat can be pretty chewy." That good natured come-back was just what Len was looking for, and he threw his arm around Bob's shoulder, leading him into the building and back to the locker room.

*****

Pauly Durham, Stony Ford's skinny sophomore 106-pounder, stared across the room to size up his Bluefield High opponent, Max Cregger, comparing his own gangly frame with the muscular build of the short, stocky boy checking him out, knowing he was in for a tough one.

He listened to the chatter from the other team as he got on the scales. "Easy pin today, Max. You can put that kid on his back in the first period."

He heard Johnny Burke's reassuring voice. "They're all talk, Pauly. You can take him."

He saw his opponent and the referee waiting, heard a teammate shout, "Go get him, Pauly," felt his coach's encouraging slap on the butt. The whistle blew, and both boys began circling, looking for an opening. In the blink of an eye, Max was on his legs, lifting him, driving him hard to the mat.

It was losing struggle for Pauly for the next six minutes, battling to his feet only to be taken down again, constantly fighting to keep from being trapped on his back.

Pauly bridged out of a tight half nelson and fought his way to his feet for an escape just as the final buzzer sounded, gasping for breath, watching Max angrily throw his head gear across the gym floor and stalk off.

Bluefield fans were making all of the noise as Pauly walked back toward his team. He'd lost by a lopsided score, but given everything he had in a head-to-head battle for three periods. The captain of the Blue Herons had been unable to fulfill the prediction of a quick pin, forced to go the distance and settle for a decision.

Pauly glanced toward his coach, reassured by his smile of approval.

*****

Johnny tightened his hold on the struggling Bluefield 168-pounder and held his back against the maroon mat cover for what seemed an eternity. Finally, he heard the referee slap the mat to signal the pin.

He jumped to his feet, shook hands with his opponent, and stood long enough for the referee to raise his hand in victory, before sprinting off the mat and jumping into the arms of his teammates. The final numbers on the scoreboard were Bluefield - 38, Stony Ford – 5. Johnny's win had just prevented an embarrassing shut-out.

Principal Carter joined Bob and the team in the locker room. Albert was upbeat as he addressed the group. "I want all of you boys to know how proud I am of the way you competed today. I'm looking forward to watching you improve week after week as we go into the regular season.

"On the way home, we're going to stop at the Ridge Top Diner to celebrate, and I'm buying hamburgers and milkshakes for everyone. Coach Slater can worry about how to work that weight off of you at practice next week."

As soon as the adults cleared the room, the boys stripped and stepped into the hot showers. Terry passed a bar of soap to his buddy, and said in a mock reprimand, "I bet you're sorry now that you let the air out of Big Al's tires last week."

Ron flipped a handful of suds in his face, replying, "You know which one of us came up with that bright idea, don't you? Yeah, I wish we hadn't done it. It was a crappy stunt to pull on him."

"We got the living daylights beat out of us today, and still Big Al claims he's proud of the way we tried," Terry reflected. "I think we owe it to him to do a helluva lot better in the matches that are coming up."

Chapter 10

Bob arrived at Kaye's apartment on Sunday morning, running down the basement steps to ring the door bell. She opened the door, strikingly attractive in full makeup, wearing a tailored skirt, matching jacket, and high heels. "Sorry to bother you," Bob remarked starting to turn away. "I didn't realize that the Vogue Modeling Agency had leased this apartment."

"You've got to quit watching so many Rock Hudson and Doris Day movies, Slater," Kaye responded, leaning in to give him a hug. "But thanks for the compliment. Come on in and make yourself comfortable while I finish running a comb through Chris's hair, and then we'll both be ready to go. It takes me forever to get his cowlick to lie down."

A few minutes later, Chris came bounding into the room carrying a small bow and two arrows tipped with rubber suction cups. "Look what Mom bought me yesterday at the store, Coach.

"You can shoot these arrows up against the door and they stick, just like real ones." He shot an arrow across the room and watched it carom off the door and spin across the floor. "They stick better if you lick the rubber tip, but Mom says that leaves marks on the white paint."

Chris led the way out the door, and the three were on their way. They parked beside the First Baptist Church, a classic white Greek revival structure fronted by wide steps.

A group had gathered inside the foyer, making friendly small talk. Several smiled and spoke as the three approached, but a few well dressed, matronly ladies looked at Kaye and then turned their backs to continue a private conversation in low voices.

Kaye glanced at Bob, shrugged her shoulders, and whispered, "Even my new jacket can't conceal the scarlet letter, can it?"

He took her hand and gave it a squeeze as they followed the usher up the aisle. She turned to him and commented quietly, "Don't worry about it. It doesn't bother me anymore. Those women probably have a few skeletons in their closets. The only difference is that theirs are not out in the open. "

Jonas Underwood stood at the front of the church, a rangy black-robed scarecrow, starting the service with a warm welcome followed by the announcement of upcoming church events.

"I'm pleased to report that that the membership of two other churches in the community will be joining us for the big revival in two weeks, our brothers and sisters from Trinity Methodist Church and Grace Brethren Church.

"You're aware that the renowned evangelist, Dr. Barry Green, will deliver powerful, old time preaching, and his wife and the Southern Chorus will bring us their inspirational music. I'm hoping that all of you will participate in this revival, and that it will lead to an epiphany in your lives and a renaissance in our community."

Jonas was waiting at the door to speak to them as they made their way out of the church after the service. "Good to see you three this morning," he said, bending to shake Chris's hand.

"Miss Davidson, I believe this is the first time that you and your son have attended a service here at First Baptist. I hope you'll be coming back regularly from now on. Since I call on you so often at Turner's Café, it seems only fair that you reciprocate by coming here to visit me on Sunday mornings."

"Thanks, Rev. Underwood. You've made Chris and me feel right at home this morning."

When they were out of earshot of others, Kaye turned to Bob and added, "Rev. Underwood is a favorite customer of mine.

"He's never been anything but respectful and friendly around me, ever since I was an unmarried teenager in a family way. After the way I've been treated by some of the upper crust of Stony Ford, that's a lot more important than big tips."

"I think 'upper crust of Stony Ford' is an oxymoron," Bob replied.

Kaye grabbed Bob's arm with both hands and swung him around to playfully kiss him on the cheek. "And I think you've got that Cary Grant gentleman's role down pat. I'm going to let you in on a secret: You're my beau."

Bob wrapped his arms around Kaye and pulled her close. "Thanks for letting me know. I recall that in my favorite childhood book a young boy had to wait until the very end of the story before his favorite girl slipped him a note telling him that."

*****

OL set his napkin on the table, leaning back in his chair to say appreciatively, "Thanks for inviting me for Sunday dinner, Mrs. Ellison. I really enjoyed your fried chicken and mashed potatoes."

"Sure you don't want that last drum stick, OL?" Betty inquired, passing the platter his way without waiting for him to respond. "I think fried chicken's better when it's still warm."

"Go ahead and finish it up, son," Homer added. "After you're through, I'm going to ask you to give me a hand down in the basement for a spell. That is, if Julie can spare you. I've been watching the weather forecasts on TV this morning, and they're expecting heavy rains to move into our area before tomorrow morning. I want to put all of cardboard boxes sitting around on the floor up on the new shelves I made, so they don't get wet if our basement floods again."

OL followed Homer down the steep, narrow steps to the dimly lit basement, leaving Julie and Betty behind to clear the dining room table. Together, they moved dusty boxes containing everything from old family photographs to mason jars filled with canned cherries, tomatoes, and green beans, transferring them from the floor to the sturdy wooden shelves along the walls. After they finished, Homer made one more request.

"Since you've already got dirt all over your clean clothes, I wonder if you'd help me move a few old railroad ties around to the front of the house to block the water if the creek gets up. I don't want to see the front porch steps wash out again like they did the last time Laurel Creek flooded us out."

The thought crossed OL's mind that he should be annoyed at Homer for roping him into some really dirty work when he'd been invited over for Sunday dinner wearing good shoes, his best khaki pants, and his favorite sport shirt. But somehow he couldn't.

Homer was always friendly and appreciative, two qualities OL hadn't seen in his own father since Lonnie's death.

"Sure, Mr. Ellison. Let's go get your hand truck out in the garage, so we don't break our backs carrying those ties."

Watching the storm front move in, the two hauled a number of old railroad ties to flank the front steps, sledging pieces of iron pipe into the ground to anchor the timbers securely.

By the time they were through, the sky had darkened to a slate gray color, with low-hanging clouds scudding overhead, and the wind was starting to pick up and bow the tops of the trees. Julie came out in the yard to join them, taking OL aside.

"I'm sorry Daddy roped you into helping him with these dirty jobs. You came over here to dinner wearing your nice clothes, and now you've ruined them. The creosote from those nasty old railroad ties will never come out."

"Don't worry about it, Julie," OL told her. Your dad needed help, and I'm glad I was here to pitch in. If I've ruined my shirt and pants, it's OK. I'd better head for home now to see if my folks are ready for this storm. It looks like the weatherman may have gotten it right, and that this could be a bad one."

Chapter 11

The rain was drumming on the roof of his white stucco bungalow when Bob awoke on Monday morning and rolled out of bed. He turned on the radio and tuned in to the local station to listen for the list of weather-related school closings.

He didn't have to wait long to learn that all public schools in Tazewell and the adjoining counties were closed. Residents were being encouraged to stay home except in the case of emergencies. Peering out of the window through the rain, he could see water ponding in the yard and flowing across the grass into the street and down the hill.

Bob dialed Kaye's number, relieved to hear her say calmly, "We're doing fine here, Bob, high and dry. There's some water coming down the basement steps, but the floor drain seems to be taking care of it. If water starts coming under the door, I'll let you know."

The second call was to his grandparents, and the response from his grandfather was equally reassuring. "We're safe and sound right now, Bobby. If we start to have a problem with all of this rain, we'll be quick to call on you for help, just like we always do."

The third call to Leon Carper brought bad news. "Leon, I got word late last evening that you wanted to talk to me. I understand it has something to do with the wrestling team."

"Bob, what I wanted to talk over with you yesterday seems pretty trivial. I was calling to tell you that the Kowalski brothers are circulating a petition to have you replaced as coach.

"Right now, I don't care what they're up to, with Laurel Creek completely out of its banks and the lower end of Main Street under water. Three businesses on West Main are all flooded out.

"I don't have any idea what's happening to the people living below town, but I imagine that they're in a heap of trouble from this flash flood. I know one of your boys, OL Spellman, has a girlfriend that lives down that way. I hope the police and fire departments are keeping an eye out for those folks."

"Do you know when the rain is supposed to stop?"

"The Weather Service said that the storm will move out of our area by early afternoon. I sure hope that they got it right."

By noon time, it was apparent that the weather men had called it correctly, the sky becoming noticeably lighter, the rain slowing from a downpour to a drizzle, and finally coming to a stop. An hour later, the storm clouds had begun to break up, and shafts of sunlight were spotlighting the waterlogged countryside below.

On impulse, Bob called the Spellman home, finding himself on the line with OL. 'This is Coach Slater. I was calling to see if you've heard how the Ellisons made out during the storm. Are they OK?"

'They got hit pretty hard, Coach. I talked to Julie, and she told me the creek washed out their driveway and got up high enough to flood their basement with a couple of feet of water.

"A trailer down below them was lifted off its foundation. Julie said it looked like a big barge floating downstream. I told her that I'm going to take the old ridge road over to their place in a little while and see if I can help."

"How about me picking you up at the foot of Pine Street and giving you a ride? I can put on some old work clothes, and carry a shovel and a few other tools in the back of my car. I have an electric pump, and I'll throw that in, too. You think that you could be ready to go in an hour?"

"I'll be ready and waiting for you in thirty minutes, Coach. Thanks for offering to pitch in and help."

Bob picked up OL a short time later, and together they took the winding gravel road along the ridge for a mile until they approached the Laurel Glen neighborhood from the upper end, winding their way downhill through a series of hairpin curves.

Both were startled upon catching their first glimpse of Laurel Creek. The normally clear, placid stream tumbling down in cascades over rock ledges was transformed into an angry, clay-colored torrent which had swallowed Creekside Road and was surging across the front yards of a row of houses including the Ellison home, lapping up against the foundations.

Julie was watching for them from the backyard, and she ran over to the car before they had turned off the engine. "Mother and Daddy are about to have a nervous breakdown," she exclaimed.

"We don't think that the creek's going to get any higher unless something changes, but the weather forecast still calls for a chance of more rain late today. Our basement's already flooded.

"Poor Mr. Fizer who lives down closer to the creek got hit really hard. His trailer was swept away, barely giving him time to get out with his two cats. His home floated away downstream, hit the bridge, and broke apart."

Homer Ellison joined them, and Bob asked, "Do you still have electric power? I brought along a pump that we could use to start getting the water out of your basement."

The pump was installed and running a short time later, shooting a stream of muddy water out of the basement window through a short length of rubber hose. Within hours, there was nothing left on the concrete floor but a deposit of dark silt.

"Good thing we moved all of those boxes up on the shelves, Mr. Ellison," OL commented, using a push-broom to sweep the mud out through an open basement door. "It would have ruined everything you store down here if we had left it on the floor."

Bob followed behind, using a garden hose to wash the walls and floor. "After this room's had time to dry out for a week or so, you'll have to repaint the walls. But it may end up being even cleaner down here than it was before."

Betty looked at Bob with a faint smile. "You could compare our basement to the Augean stables. I recall from high school that Hercules had to clean them, and the only way he could do it was by diverting a couple of rivers to flush them out. Maybe that's what Laurel Creek did for us today. We're pretty fortunate as it's turned out. I only wish all of our neighbors had come through the flood as well."

It was late in the day, and Bob, OL, and Homer were covered in mud from head to foot by the time the three had installed new supports under the front porch steps, leaving the house safe again.

"I can never thank y'all enough for all you've done here today," Homer said appreciatively, extending a hand covered with black silt. "Can you stay around and let Betty and Julie fix supper for everyone?"

"We'd better be getting back to town," Bob answered. "But we'll try to get back here tomorrow and see if we can lend a hand to your neighbors. The creek should drop back within its banks by that time."

He looked around for OL, and caught a glimpse of Julie standing close to him saying goodbye, paying no attention to the mud covering him from ear to ear and now smudging her face and brown pony-tailed hair.

Both Bob and OL were too tired to carry on much of a conversation on the drive back to town, and few words were exchanged until OL got out of the car. "Thanks for everything you did for the Ellisons today. They're not going to forget it, and neither will I."

He hesitated, then changed the subject. "I want you to know that my decision not to come back out for the team has nothing to do with you replacing Coach Callison, Mr. Slater. I just don't feel right about going on without Lonnie."

"I'm not going to press you again today to change your mind, OL, but sometime down the road, I hope you will. Just keep thinking about it, and try to understand what Lonnie might want you to do. I still hear people talking about him, and how much he cared about his teammates and his school."

OL turned his head as he walked away, trying to conceal tears sliding from his hazel eyes down his sunburned, mud-spattered cheeks.

Chapter 12

"Ain't this the biggest damn mess you've ever seen in your life?" Holton Akers queried mayor Steve Mullins, surveying the mud covering the floor of his plumbing supply store.

"I swear it's even worse than the last time this place flooded. Everything I have stored here in cardboard cartons is going to have to be cleaned up and re-boxed or thrown out."

He managed a smile and observed with his trademark humor, "At least I don't have all those copperheads slithering around in here like I did when the creek flooded me out in '48. The last time I could have opened a serpent show and charged admission.

"I even thought about putting up some billboards out on Route 460 showing a beautiful young woman with a python wrapped around her, telling tourists to 'See Snake City'. Bet that would have drawn a few visitors to town."

"Holton, I'm amazed at how well you're dealing with this. The town needs to help you and your neighbors get the hell out from down here and relocated to higher ground.

"This county has a history of floods, and they seem be happening more often in recent years. Y'all shouldn't have to deal with a disaster every time a big tropical storm comes through these parts."

"People have been saying that for twenty years, Steve, but nothing has ever come of it. We both know it would cost a lot of money. The department of highways would have to condemn a bunch of homes further up the ridge to build a new section of highway and move Main Street up there.

"I don't think we have enough votes and political clout in this end of the state to get the governor excited about spending his road funds on something like that."

"I'm not saying it would be easy, Holton, but I think we should at least be fighting for it. There are too many people in Richmond who think all of the money appropriated for roads ought to be spent in the northern and eastern parts of the state that are growing the fastest.

"Hell, we pay taxes around here, too. I'm going to bring this up again in our next town council meeting. But for now, how about me rounding up some volunteers to help y'all clean up the mess and reopen for business?"

"Any help you can bring in will be appreciated, Steve. Just tell anyone planning to come down here and lend a hand that they need to wear old clothes and rubber boots."

Steve turned away, walking back up Main Street to the Piggly Wiggly, situated well above the flood plain. The first call he made was to an old friend. "Albert, Steve Mullins. I heard on the radio that the high school was closed due to the weather, but I had a feeling that you and most of your faculty would find your way into work today."

"All of the staff are here," Albert replied. "I gave the cafeteria workers and the school bus drivers the day off, since classes were cancelled. What can I do for you?"

"I have a big favor to ask. Do you think that you could offer the older boys an excused day off from classes again tomorrow, and get their parent's permission for them to help clean up downtown? There's a lot of work to be done before the business owners will be able to reopen, and it will go a lot faster with a team of volunteers."

High school boys and teachers gathered on West Main Street, ready to pitch in, the next morning at 8:00. Albert and Bob walked to the back of the building facing the creek, seeing that the pools of water had drained, exposing the foundation. They simultaneously spotted the damage done by the flood.

"Look where the water's cut the ground out around the building footers!" Bob exclaimed. "I don't know what's holding up the wall. It doesn't look safe to me."

"I'm going to call the building inspector and tell him to come down," Albert said. "I don't know what he'll do, but I wouldn't be surprised if he hangs a no trespassing sign in front of the building and padlocks the doors until repairs are made.

"A construction crew needs to get started right away stabilizing the building. Maybe the back wall can be lifted with jacks and shored up with timbers until the concrete footers can be repaired. We need to tell everyone the work party for today is called off."

Holton took the news hard. "I thought all I was dealing with was another clean up and figured I'd be open again in a few days. Being shut down until this old building is repaired is a huge problem for me.

"When you're not making any money and are hanging on by a thread trying to keep the lights on, you sure don't need this. Joey Tucker and Leonard Smith are in the same boat with me. Their businesses are both struggling as badly as mine."

He walked away with his head down in discouragement, adding, "You can't buy flood insurance, so none of us have coverage for our losses. Maybe someday the government will offer it, but I'm not going to stand around holding my breath.

"In the meantime, Joey, Leonard, and I are going to be stuck here like ducks in a shooting gallery waiting for Laurel Creek to knock us down again."

Chapter 13

Friday morning, Bob was still shaking off the cobwebs from a restless night when he walked into the café and saw Billy and Kaye standing behind the counter sipping mugs of freshly perked coffee. Kaye set her cup down and walked over to give him an affectionate hug.

"You're up and about early today, Coach," Billy commented, with a wink directed at Kaye. "Getting nervous about the first home match tonight and having trouble sleeping? Starting to worry a little about the Bristol team? I hear that they have most of their starters back from last year."

"We'll have our hands full for sure," Bob agreed. "Yeah, I'm a little nervous about the match. You probably know that there are some people in town who would like to see us take a whipping so they can lay it all on me and hang me out to dry."

"But there are some others in your corner. I hear both sides of that debate in here. The most vocal ones after your head are the Kowalski brothers and a few of their cronies.

"Nick and Randy were in thick with Coach Callison. They're part of the gang that still gets together for weekly poker games at the Moose Lodge. Somewhere along the line, they've gotten the idea that they're on the board of directors for the school athletic program and should have a big say in all of the decisions."

"I'm going to be there tonight cheering for the Eagles," Kaye chimed in. "Billy's closing up early tonight and taking Chris and me over to watch the match."

"I might as well close early," Billy added. "When there's a wrestling match in town, everybody who can still put one leg in front of the other is going to be over at the high school."

"Want your usual this morning?" Kaye inquired.

"No, just get me a cup of coffee and a bowl of Special K with a glass of milk. My stomach's feeling way too nervous to handle bacon and eggs right now."

Bob left the café after breakfast to start his work day. Later that morning, he stood in the locker room watching as each of member of the varsity checked to see that he was down to his required limit before an official weigh-in later in the day. Everything was going fine until Sonny Bowles and Ron Sawyer stepped up and tipped the scales at a couple of pounds over for their 136 and 141-pound weight classes.

"If you two want to wrestle tonight, you're going to have to work it off. Put on your sweats and a rubber suit, and go jump rope in the furnace room by the steam pipes. You won't be able to eat or drink anything until you make weight this afternoon."

The boys slowly meandered back from the furnace room later, dark stains marking their gray fleece warm-ups, sweat dripping from their faces. The scales showed that each had sweated off several pounds, and was now below his weight limit.

"We're going out to get a hamburger and shake, Coach. You want to come with us?" Sonny called back to Bob as he walked out of the locker room laughing.

*****

"I had no idea so many people would be here tonight," Kaye commented to Billy, as they followed Chris into the crowded, noisy gymnasium and carefully climbed up to three vacant seats near the top of the bleachers. "I haven't been back here for a match in a long, long time."

"A lot of reasons for the crowd," Billy explained. "First is the free admission for people without much money in their pocket. Second is the chance for folks to get away from the TV set and enjoy some live action.

"But the biggest draw is the winning tradition of the wrestling team here. There isn't much else in this town to make you hold your head up and feel proud except a squad of tough young kids scrapping it out on the mats against teams from bigger schools."

"Here they come," Chris exclaimed, as the Eagles jogged into the gym and onto the mats to warm up amid the raucous shouts from the home crowd now filling the bleachers. Everyone came to their feet as the cheerleaders, dressed in blue and gold, bounded out in front to lead the traditional school cheers.

"Bob looks nervous," Kaye observed, looking at the young coach standing on the edge of the mats, watching the team go through its drills. "I wonder what's on his mind?"

"I imagine he's concerned about how his boys are going to do against the Bulldogs tonight," Billy replied.

"Opening against one of the best teams in the district is a tough way to start the season. Being a new coach in front of a home crowd with high expectations makes it worse. I wouldn't want to be walking in his moccasins."

Bob turned around to quickly survey the crowd behind him, and spotted the three near the top of the stands. He lifted his hand to wave, seeing Kaye hold her arm high in encouragement.

*****

Sonny Bowles watched the referee raise Gene Lasky's opponent's hand in victory and felt the mounting pressure on the Stony Ford team to start scoring points. The Eagles were down 9 -3, and he needed to turn things around for the team with a win in his 136-pound class, knowing it would be tough. He took off his blue and gold warm-up jacket, tossing it on a chair, and walked out on the mat.

Sonny reacted at the sound of the whistle, dropping to his knees beneath his opponent, hooking an ankle and tripping him cleanly, but quickly finding he could not hold the Bristol boy down. The contest swung back and forth as they battled without let-up, quickness against strength, the score dead-even at the end of the second period.

The match got away from Sonny in the third period. Whether it was because he had not pushed himself hard enough at practice or because he had lost stamina from sweating off the extra weight earlier, he ran out of gas. On the bottom near the end and needing an escape to win, he was unable to fight to his feet. He heard the whistle sound, knowing that he had lost a heartbreaker by a single point.

*****

OL leaned forward, watching his pretty girlfriend and the other cheerleaders as they excitedly urged the home crowd to crank up the noise. It felt strange for him to be sitting in the stands as just another spectator, after his stint as one of the best wrestlers to ever wear the Eagles blue and gold.

He looked over the Stony Ford team seated in a row of folding chairs beside the mat, missing both the excitement of competing and the shared camaraderie. Seeing his team trailing badly on the scoreboard despite Coach Slater's futile encouragement was disturbing and painful. By now, it was a foregone conclusion that the first match of the season would enter the books as an embarrassing loss.

His eyes focused on his best friend, now removing his warm-up jacket, preparing to take the mat in the last match of the evening. Johnny turned to face him, raising his arm. OL returned the salute, feeling a mixed sense of pride and guilt. He could see that Johnny was all business. The whistle blew to start the match, and the boys quickly closed at the center of the mat.

OL watched the two warily move in circles, repeatedly locking up and then breaking away, club-like slaps to the backs of necks sounding each time they came together. The Bristol boy dove hard at Johnny's ankles, and Johnny countered by dropping to a low stance, blocking him head to head.

OL smiled, remembering how many times at practice he and Johnny had banged heads the same way while working on takedowns, how he had accused his friend of being kin to a billy goat.

It seemed neither boy would find an advantage until Johnny stepped in, wrapping his opponent in a tight headlock, taking him to the mat on his back in one sweeping motion. The Bristol 168-pounder struggled to break free, but Johnny tightened his hold, ramming the boy's shoulder blades down against the mat, not letting up until the referee slapped the mat to signal a pin.

The Stony Ford fans were on their feet yelling as the referee raised Johnny's hand, forgetting for a moment that the Eagles had just lost the season opener in a crushing 28 – 8 loss.

OL caught up with Julie, and the two worked their way through the crowd, trying to catch up with the team before they headed back to the locker room. He spotted two burly men approaching the new coach, the short one sounding off in a loud voice.

"Slater, why don't you hand in your resignation and let the school hire a coach who knows what he's doing? These boys deserve someone a lot better than you, someone like Callison. He knew how to build a winning team."

OL started toward them, but Johnny stepped in front of him, cutting him off. "Let Coach handle this. If you really want to help him, quit moping around feeling sorry for yourself. Get off your butt and be part of this team."

Chapter 14

"Standing room only in here every doggone Saturday morning," Jonas commented, walking toward the table at the back of the cafe where Bob, Becky, Virginia, and Virgil were gathered. "Mind if I pull up a chair and join you? There isn't an empty seat in the house."

"As long as you don't mind sitting at the faculty table and abiding by our rule: last man here picks up the tab," Virgil drawled. "Have a seat, Rev. Our friend Slater is trying to drink himself under the table on strong coffee this morning to forget what happened at the school last night. You may have heard that the home team took a fanny whipping."

"Well, Bob, slow down. You'll have to drive yourself home, and we don't want any nervous, over-caffeinated drivers behind the wheel. Maybe things will take a turn for the better.

"Remember that nothing good ever comes easy. The prophets in the Old Testament had to struggle for everything that they accomplished despite the Lord being there beside them all the time."

"I don't think Bob has any reason to hang his head," Becky stated. "The Stony Ford kids gave it everything they had last night. The Bristol team was just a lot better. I don't think that's Bob's fault."

"Thanks for the support, Beck. I'm afraid that not everyone around here has the same opinion. A couple of people talked to me after the match last night, offering to provide me with free transportation out of town. I think what they had in mind was carrying me on a rail wearing a fresh coat of hot asphalt and chicken feathers.

"But let's get on a more pleasant subject this morning. Do you have everything ready for the big revival tonight, Jonas?"

"I think so, Bob. There's enough folding chairs set up in the factory to accommodate up to four hundred worshippers. That might not sound like many to people familiar with George Brunk's tent revivals a few years back, where he'd pull in fifteen thousand people. But for this area, it's a lot of folks gathered together."

"I heard that a truck delivered a big Hammond organ out there yesterday," Virgil chimed in. "I bet people in houses half way back to town will have their windows rattle when the organist hits those bass notes."

"You're probably right, Virgil. The music is certain to bring people up out of their seats. I'm sure the hymns tonight will be just as inspirational as the preaching.

"You've probably seen the posters in store windows around town and know that Dr. Green's message will be about God bringing renewal. It sounds like exactly the message that the people in this town need to hear. You plan to be there, don't you?"

"I plan to come and bring Mildred, but this revival of yours had better be something really spectacular. There's not many things going on around here that will get me out of the house on Saturday night and make me miss Gunsmoke."

*****

"Look at all the cars in the parking lot!" Bob exclaimed to Kaye, as they drove in and parked beside the furniture factory. "There must be over a hundred here already, and they're lined up behind us for a country mile. A bunch of people are going to end up having to park out in the field."

"I'm glad Bob let us ride with him," Becky commented to Virginia, who was sitting across from her in the back seat. "I don't like driving at night, particularly when there's this much traffic."

Chris stared through the windshield in fascination, watching two big spotlights mounted on the back of a flatbed truck play their beams of light across the sky, lighting up low hanging clouds, and projecting between them toward the myriad white pinpoints shining in the black canopy above.

He suddenly spotted a spark of light streaking across the sky and excitedly pointed toward it to catch his mother's attention.

"That's a shooting star, Chris," Kaye explained. "It's good luck for everyone who spots it. You get to make a wish, and it will come true. Just think of all the good things that could happen tonight because of that star. Did the rest of you see it, too?"

"I did," Becky replied. "But don't start asking any questions. I'm not about to give away my secret."

"I bet you wished for a new candy apple red Corvette convertible," Virginia laughed. "You're always talking about wanting to ride around town in a shiny sports car with the top down."

"Oh, I'm not going to waste my wish on a new car," Becky answered. "I'm going for something a lot more important than that. But I refuse to tell you anything more. If I give away the secret, my wish won't come true."

The five climbed out of the car and joined the throng of people pushing through the door into the brightly lit interior of the factory, working their way to seats halfway up the aisle. They could see that a platform had been erected up front, with a podium that resembled a pulpit on the left, and a massive organ and risers for a small choir arranged on the right.

The crowd filed steadily into the building, filling every seat, row-by-row, while a group of men brought in more folding chairs, placing them against the walls to accommodate the last few stragglers.

Animated voices throughout the room subsided from loud chatter to hushed whispers as Dr. Greene entered the room with his wife, making his way up the center aisle, climbing the steps to the platform. A small choir resplendent in red robes proceeded behind them to take its place on the risers.

The two evangelists were imposing figures, standing on the platform and looking out over the congregation, he in a well-cut black suit, and she wearing an elegant white floor-length gown.

Bob had never seen a picture of Dr. Greene, but he had visualized him as resembling charismatic religious leaders like Billy Graham and Oral Roberts. Looking at the man standing before him, he realized he'd been wrong. Dr. Greene was big and barrel-chested with a cleanly-shaved head, reminding Bob of Ray Nitschke, the Green Bay Packers' star linebacker.

His deep, booming voice, amplified by large speaker, was equally impressive. "Good evening and welcome to our old-time revival.

I'm Dr. Barry Greene, and I'll be preaching this evening. To my left at the organ is my wife, Ethel. Standing beside her is our nationally acclaimed Southern Chorus.

"I can see that we've got a fine crowd this evening. I'm sure that each of you sitting in the congregation before me came here tonight for one reason and one reason only: You've been called to this old factory to hear the Word of God."

"You're going to hear the Word tonight, but don't let it be a passive experience. Open your heart, and let the Holy Spirit come in to fill you with joy, bringing you out of your seat, singing, and praising, and praying for forgiveness, and searching for a new purpose for your life.

"To start off our crusade tonight to restore the Lord as the rightful center of each life, we're going to stand and sing *Onward Christian Soldiers*. Ethel will accompany us on the organ, and our choir will lead us.

"I want the sound of your joyful voices to spill out from this room so loudly that they'll have to get up from their celestial seats in heaven and turn down the volume."

A thousand amateur voices, led by a skillful professional organist and a well trained choir, blended to produce a hauntingly beautiful old-time rendition of the hymn.

Becky heard a pleasant baritone voice to her left, and glanced across the aisle to see a clean-cut, athletic young man with a crew-cut who knew the words to all of the verses.

Her gaze lingered, trying to recall whether she had ever seen him before. She had just concluded that he was a stranger to the community when he glanced around and their eyes met. He smiled, and Becky quickly looked away, her cheeks starting to redden.

Dr. Barry's preaching proved to be everything that the congregation had expected to hear, and more. He delivered his message without notes, switching from a soft voice that had older people leaning forward in their seats, then building to a booming crescendo that made some of the ladies cup their hands over their ears.

Beads of sweat formed on his smooth head and rolled down to disappear into his starched white collar. He slipped off his coat and tossed it across the lectern, then loosened his tie, never pausing in his sermon, the now-damp white shirt clinging to his chest, emphasizing his powerful build.

"Do you believe the Holy Spirit is in this building with us tonight?"

"Yes," came back a scattered answer, the audience beginning to respond.

"Do you have an open heart to receive the Holy Spirit? Are you ready for a life-changing experience tonight?" His eyes slowly swept across the audience, giving each person the impression that he was speaking directly to him or her.

"Yes." More people joined in, fervor growing in their voices.

"Are you ready to allow the Holy Spirit to redirect your life, free you from your past sins, and lead you in a glorious new direction, just as Paul in his conversion on the road to Damascus?"

Dr. Greene leaned forward, gesturing with muscular arms. "If you are, let me hear you say it like you mean it. Say it loud enough that it can be heard all the way up there at the gates of heaven. Say it again, and again, and again."

"Yes! Yes! Yes!" The congregation was now fully caught up in the energy and excitement bursting from the pulpit.

Bob glanced at Kaye, seeing her slip a protective arm around Chris, reassuring him that he had nothing to fear from the powerful preacher. He was relieved to hear Chris whisper, "I'm OK, Mom."

Dr. Greene surveyed the congregation again, continuing, "Tonight I'm going to deliver a message taken from the book of Acts. I'm going to tell you how the Holy Spirit converted Paul, leading him to do great works, spreading the Christian faith throughout the known world, from the ascension of Jesus until Paul's arrival in Rome.

"You'll see how the Holy Spirit worked through him to overcome challenges, to accomplish things that no ordinary man could possibly achieve, how through Paul's impassioned evangelical work, men and women, and communities, and nations, were forever transformed.

"The Holy Spirit is here at this very moment. Receive It into your heart and let It take charge of your life, just as Paul did. We'll start now on Paul's miraculous ministry as told by the Apostle, Luke.

"When you understand the truth, and know that it relates to your life, shout out, Amen. Now show me you how you'll answer when I tell you, 'The Holy Spirit will come over you tonight, and you will leave this room a transformed Christian.'"

Dr. Greene thumped the lectern with his fist to cue the congregation, and the room reverberated with a deafening "Amen."

"If you need spiritual help, put your hand up. Bless you, there in the back, and you folks, sitting over to the side. Get those hands up quickly. If you are sinking in sin and need help, reach up, like a drowning man reaches out for a life preserver to keep him afloat.

"That's more like it. I can see hands going up all over this room. Lord, bless these people who are reaching out to You at this very moment for their eternal salvation.

"If you accept the Lord tonight and allow the Holy Spirit to fill your heart with peace and joy, I'm inviting you to come forward, and kneel in prayer at the front of the room, while we sing *Amazing Grace*."

Kaye turned to Bob, whispering, "Are you going up front?" He shook his head, and she instructed Chris, "Stay here with Coach. I'll be right back." She rose from her seat to follow other congregants filing up the aisle.

Becky stood, slipping into line behind Kaye. She had not noticed that the young man sitting across from her had also risen and was entering the aisle at the same time.

The two gently bumped together, the man whispering in a low voice, "Excuse me, ma'am," as they walked toward the front of the room side by side.

Becky cut her eyes to the left, noticing that this time it was the stranger who was wearing a shy look of embarrassment.

Barry closed the service with a benediction which resounded as an emotional command. "Tonight you have been filled with the Holy Spirit. Go forth, and take your light into the world."

Bob saw Jonas as he stepped outside, greeting people just as he did after a Sunday service at the Baptist church. "Great turn out, Rev," Bob commented. "Your man, Dr. Greene, really delivered a compelling message tonight. He had everyone on the edge of their seat the whole time he was preaching."

"He's a powerful speaker, isn't he?" Jonas replied

Becky walked ahead with Virginia, asking softly, "Did you recognize the stranger sitting across from me? I've never seen him around here before."

"Me neither," Virginia replied, laughing. "I don't think that I would have forgotten a man that good looking if I'd run into him earlier.

"It seemed to me that he was right by your side the whole time you were walking up the aisle to answer the altar call."

"Really?" Becky murmured nonchalantly. "I confess that I wasn't paying all that much attention."

Virginia slipped her arm around Becky and remarked affectionately, "People who tell fibs may not go to heaven. I think you should set the record straight when you say your prayers tonight."

Chapter 15

Bob knocked on Kaye's front door, then stepped back out of sight. "Trick or treat," he called out in his deepest voice just as she opened the door to see who was there.

"I know that's you, Bob," she said, in a brave but unconvincing voice. "It is you, isn't it? Come on out now. You're starting to scare me."

Stepping back in sight, he was more surprised than she, as he saw Kaye standing in the doorway wearing a long black wig and a form-fitting witch costume, which emphasized her attractive looks.

"I thought all witches were old hags," he commented. "Your costume isn't in character for gray-haired crones who cook up trouble in boiling cauldrons."

"Not all witches are the kind Shakespeare wrote about, Bob. You'll find a wide variety of witches in literature, some good and some bad, if you take the time to do your homework.

"Remember in the *Wizard of Oz* that the witch of the north who gave Dorothy the silver shoes was good, and the witch of the west who tried to do her in was wicked."

Bob smiled at her reply, no longer surprised at the diverse information Kaye had acquired from many years as an avid reader. Once, while waiting on him at the cafe, she had compared a work experience to an amusing event in *Great Expectations*, and he, the high school teacher, had been the one who had gone to the book shelf in order to confirm the source.

Chris joined his mother at the door dressed in a homemade Snoopy costume. "When did you get the pooch?" Bob inquired. "Does Helen have any idea that you're keeping a beagle in her building? He could bring in fleas."

Chris had been around Bob long enough to know how to take his kidding and dish it back. "Coach, you have a big round head like Charlie Brown."

Kaye was about to reprimand him when Bob replied, "So now you're calling me a blockhead? Is that what you're saying? A blockhead?"

He put his arm around Chris and wrestled him to the floor. "Dog fight! Dog fight!" he called out, as the two rolled around on the rug, stopping only when Kaye began swatting them with her twig broom.

"You children stop that right now, and behave yourselves. I told Miss Stevens that I'd be at the school to help get everything ready for the Halloween party in the cafeteria, and we need to get moving."

"Why are they having a Halloween party tonight?" Bob asked during the drive. "When I was growing up we just went out on Halloween night and did mischief."

"That's exactly why the school is having a party," Kaye explained. "Last year, some kids marked the school windows with wax instead of soap, and it took the janitor a couple of days working with paint thinner and Windex to get it off. I'd really appreciate it if you don't tell Chris any more stories about your childhood as a juvenile delinquent."

"I want to hear about the mischief you did on Halloween night when you were a kid, Coach," Chris managed to blurt, before his mother put her hand over his mouth to stifle further discussion.

Lights were on all over the school when they arrived and entered the cafeteria. Miss Stevens came over to greet them, dressed in a Mother Goose costume. "I'm glad to see Snoopy's here with you tonight. Will Chris be coming later?" she asked, winking at Kaye. Chris responded by giving his teacher a bashful hug.

Two middle-aged ladies glanced over toward them, but turned away without making eye contact or speaking, continuing to work on an apple-bobbing table holding a wash tub filled with water and bright red apples.

"I suppose that I should take you over and introduce you to Mrs. Perkins and Mrs. Garland," Kaye said quietly to Bob, nodding toward the two women now facing away from them. "We're the three who volunteered to be first grade room-mothers. For some reason they never invite me when they get together to plan activities. I wonder why?"

Kaye's smile told Bob she knew the reason she was never included, but also said that any disdain felt by the two ladies was reciprocated.

Children in costume streamed into the cafeteria, many of the younger mothers accompanying them also dressed for Halloween. Bob was surprised to see Becky arrive with one of Chris's classmates in tow, a blonde-haired girl in pigtails, dressed as Cinderella.

Becky was wearing curly red wig, her face painted like a circus clown's.

"I rented a daughter, Patty Perry, so I could come to the party," she laughed, approaching Bob and Kaye. "Actually, her mother asked me if I'd bring her. She wasn't feeling well, and she knew how much Patty wanted to be here tonight to show off her new costume."

The three watched as Patty ran over to Chris, chattering excitedly. Kaye observed both children with quiet amusement. "I thought Chris was the one with the big crush, but looking at them now, I believe it goes both ways."

"Be sure to get her out of here before midnight, Beck," Bob whispered. "It might disillusion Snoopy if he sees Cinderella wearing rags and riding in a pumpkin drawn by a pack of rats."

The party continued for over an hour, the children taking part in games set up around the room and noisily competing for prizes in a best costume contest. Then Bob saw an acquaintance, Stan Carkin, striding toward him. Stan was wearing his deputy sheriff's uniform, his expression grim.

"Bob, there's been an accident over on West Main. The wall of the building that's been shored up with timbers since the flood a while back finally gave way and collapsed. Holton Akers was working in his store at the time, and now he's trapped.

"Our volunteer firefighters and the Tazewell firemen are doing everything that they can, but the part of the building that's still standing is so unstable they're afraid to use a backhoe to clear the rubble, and they're trying to dig their way inside by hand.

"It's turned out to be a helluva job, and it's taking way too much time to get to Akers with the crew on site. That's why I'm here trying to recruit more able bodied men get over there and pitch in."

Bob turned to Kaye, asking, "Can you and Chris get a ride home with Becky? I want to do anything that I can to help. Holton Akers is a good friend."

"Go now," Kaye quickly replied, "but please be careful. It sounds like a dangerous situation. And call me the minute you get home. I'll be on pins and needles until I hear from you."

Bob parked on Main Street a short time later, and walked toward the brightly lit rescue scene. The part of the building still standing reminded him of something he had seen in WWII newsreels showing European buildings damaged by bombs and artillery fire. A gaping hole and piles of debris now showed where the intact back wall of the building had stood earlier in the day.

Bob saw a tall man in firefighter's gear standing in front of the building, and walked over to offer his services.

The man identified himself as Tazewell Fire Chief Roy Bowman, confirming that he was in charge of the rescue operation. He instructed Bob to grab a pair of leather gloves and a hard hat and join other volunteers removing debris at the west end of the building.

"We're working now to create an opening where medical personnel can get in. Holton's been calling to us. He's lying on the floor inside, trapped under a fallen beam, unable to move.

"He tells us that both of his legs are broken, and he's in a lot of pain. We're moving as fast as we can but using extreme caution, since the structure is very unstable. Holton could be crushed if anything should fall."

Bob teamed up with another man wearing a hard hat, and quickly began working with him, using a wheelbarrow to carry away the rubble lying piled up on the ground next to the building. "I'm Bob Slater," he said, introducing himself, neither man pausing from the job at hand.

"Art Lowen, Bob. Glad you're here to help. I happened to be driving down Main Street a couple of hours ago when the building came down. Bystanders heard a man inside yelling for help, and we've been working to get him out ever since.

"You can see that those firemen working next to us have finally opened up a small entry hole, and if we can get a little more of this rubble out of their way, they should be able to crawl inside."

Bob carried load after load of debris away, and was bracing his shoulder against the wall, trying to lift a heavy piece of concrete, when one of the firemen nearby suddenly turned toward him and shouted a terrifying warning.

"Heads up! The cornice has broken off! Bricks coming down!"

He froze, unable to move, not knowing which way to turn. Then he felt a strong hand grab his wrist in a steel grip and give him a hard yank away from the building, slinging him to the ground a dozen feet away.

He remained sprawled on his back, dazed, silently watching dozens of loose bricks cascading down from overhead, pounding the spot where he had been standing, stinging his face with sharp fragments as one collided with another.

Anxious voices called out as he lay prone in the dirt, trying to sort out what had just happened. He realized as the dust cleared that another man was lying on the ground nearby. A closer look told him that it was the volunteer who had been working beside him.

"Is everybody safe?" a fireman called out apprehensively.

"We're OK," Bob yelled back. "But if it hadn't been for my friend here, y'all would be scraping me up off the ground and covering me with a tarp. He saved my hide."

Bob extended his hand to Art and said in a shaky voice, "Thanks for getting me out of there. No way I'll ever be able to repay you for what you did."

Art reached over to clasp his hand, replying, "Glad I was able to help. No need to say anything more. You would have done the same for me."

Firemen were soon able to crawl inside the building on hands and knees to free Holton from the wreckage. A shot of morphine had killed the pain from his two crushed legs by the time he was dragged outside and loaded onto a stretcher.

The emergency crew gathered round to applaud as Holton gave them a feeble wave of thanks from the back of the ambulance, just before the door closed, and the vehicle pulled away with flashing lights and wailing siren.

Bob looked everywhere for his partner after he turned in his hard hat and work gloves but could find him nowhere on site. He called Kaye upon arriving home just as he had promised, telling her about the rescue.

"Yeah, the emergency team got Holton out. He's alive, but I'm not sure whether he's ever going to be able to walk again. It's a sad situation."

"Please let me know when you find out his condition," Kaye requested. "Was anyone else hurt? I've been sitting here by the phone waiting to hear from you."

"No one got a scratch. I'm sorry you were too worried to sleep."

"You're telling me everything that happened tonight, Bob?"

"Everything turned out fine, Honey. Please try to put it out of your mind and go to bed now."

He ended the conversation with an affectionate good night, putting down the phone without sharing one part of the story: the part where he was standing under a lethal shower of falling bricks until a stranger with quick reflexes and a strong arm yanked him to safety.

Across town, Kaye held the phone to her ear until she heard the click on the other end. Bob was home now, so she could check on Chris one last time, then allow herself to relax.

But when she finally turned out the light and put her head on the pillow, her intuition told her that Bob had not been completely truthful.

She had a disturbing feeling that something had happened that had almost taken him away from her, and it was a long time before she was able to shake off the incomprehensible fear and drift off to sleep.

Chapter 16

"Thanks for turning out," Mayor Steve Mullins said, stifling a yawn, opening a meeting of the Stony Ford Town Council late Saturday morning. The four councilmen, Leon Carper, Joey Tucker, Royce Smith, and Tony Gilbert, filled their mugs from the percolator on the counter and pulled up their chairs around the worn oak conference table.

"Before we get down to business, has anyone heard anything from Thelma about how Holton's doing?"

"She called me long-distance this morning," Joey replied. "Holton was in surgery for several hours. An orthopedic surgeon inserted a steel rod and four steel pins in his legs, but the doctor seems encouraged that he'll be able to walk again some day down the road.

Thelma says that they still have him on some pretty strong pain medication right now. She thinks he's going to need a lot of rehabilitation."

"Thank the Lord," Leon chimed in. "I was afraid he was going to lose both of his legs."

"So now we need to make some decisions about that building of ours on West Main," Steve continued. "Y'all have had a chance to look at it in broad daylight, and can tell that it needs to be condemned. The timber footers that were installed to shore up the back wall turned out to be a jury rig.

"Joey, we understand that you, Leonard, and the Akers family need to get your business records out of the building, but other than safes and file cabinets, anything else salvageable will probably have to wait until we bring in a professional demolition team. We don't want anyone else to get hurt."

Joey raised his hand to take the floor. "I can only speak for myself, but I imagine Holton and Leonard will tell you the same thing. I'm ready to move my business away from Laurel Creek and be through with worrying about flooding every time a heavy rain comes along. I'll be looking for new quarters on higher ground if I can get a loan from the bank."

"I don't understand why all of you have been patient with the town this long," Royce interjected. "Y'all have been paying rent on space in that building since the town bought it in '48, and putting up with the creek overflowing its banks over and over.

"Our town council's been talking about getting the Department of Highways to move Main Street out of the flood plain for years. It's time for us to build a fire under our delegate to the General Assembly and get him working on funds for the relocation of that stretch of Route 161 this coming year."

"Amen," Joey added vehemently.

"I'll start making some phone calls and get the ball rolling," Steve replied. "Now, do I hear a motion that we proceed to go out for bids from contractors to demolish the building?"

*****

"That's correct, Mr. Hundley, I wear both sales and project engineering hats for Turnkey Universal Ventures, TUV, out of Pittsburgh. I'm here trying to identify new business opportunities for our company in southwest Virginia. That's why I requested a meeting with you today, hoping that we can put our heads together and discover a new use for this facility.

"I was out here in the vacant part of your factory during a revival a couple of weeks ago, and I had the opportunity to look around a little. It gave me some ideas." Art handed his business card to Roland as the two continued walking through the empty building

"Closing this place was simply a matter of economics," Roland explained. "My brother and I concluded that we could reduce production costs by building our furniture in a new facility in Georgia where labor rates are lower.

"I've scratched my head to find another use for this building, but haven't had any success. There's a very good workforce here that I hated to lay off. Most of our former employees haven't been able to find other work."

"I'm reading that there's a growing market for upscale colonial-style hardwood furniture," Art observed. "Four poster beds, dressers, bureaus, and chests made out of solid walnut, oak, and other native hardwoods, furniture that requires more hand labor but sells for a higher price. Have you given any thought to getting into that business?"

"I'm aware of the growing market for authentic early American furniture, Mr. Lowen. It's a segment that my company doesn't now serve. Let's talk more about it after we finish our tour."

It was late afternoon before Art shook hands with Roland, driving back to the Laurel Lane Motel. He entered his room, breathing the musty, stale cigarette odor of every old motel, pausing to tune in the evening news on a small black and white TV set. Afterwards he showered and shaved before making the short drive across town to Turner's Café.

The small parking lot was full when he arrived, and inside, he quickly discovered that it was a full house, with every booth and table, and most of the counter stools, occupied. He spotted one familiar face toward the back, a man sitting alone in a booth, and started toward him.

"You're Bob Slater, aren't you? We met the other night during the rescue operation. Any chance that I might share your booth?"

Bob looked up to see the man he had searched for after Holton's rescue, the sandy-haired young man with a crew-cut who had pulled him to safety.

"Please sit down and join me. I looked around for you before I left Halloween night, wanting to talk to you again, but I couldn't find you anywhere."

Art slid into the seat across from Bob, replying, "You thanked me then, and that's more than good enough."

Kaye crossed the room to see who had joined Bob, recognizing the stranger. "Aren't you the gentleman who was seated right across the aisle from us during the revival?"

"Yes. I recognized you when I came in. I believe that there was another young lady sitting next to you that I literally bumped into when we were getting up to answer the altar call. I'm Art Lowen."

"And I'm Kaye Davidson. How did you and Bob come to know each other? I didn't realize that you had met."

Bob hesitated before speaking but then realized that this was the time he had to come clean. "Kaye, there's something I didn't tell you when I phoned after helping to get Holton out of that building. I didn't bring it up because I didn't want to upset you."

Kaye eyes narrowed, her smile disappearing. "What went on that you didn't want me to know about?"

"I met Art while he and I were working side by side clearing rubble piled up against the building. A brick cornice near the top of the building broke loose and bricks started falling.

"I heard one of the fireman shout a warning, but I couldn't tell what was happening, and I didn't know which way to run. Art grabbed my wrist and pulled me away from the building. He saved my life."

"My God, Bob. Someone saved your life, and you're only now telling me because you thought that it might upset me? After all the time we've known each other, do you still take me for a child?"

Kaye paused, staring at him angrily. "I had a bad feeling come over me after we talked on the phone. Apparently my intuition was dead right. I cannot believe you kept this from me."

Art stepped in, trying to calm Kaye. "I believe Bob may have overstated what I did, Miss Davidson. I helped him out of a bad situation, but it's unlikely that I saved his life."

"No, Art. I'll take the chewing out from Kaye for keeping her in the dark, but you and I both know that I would have been crushed if you hadn't been there to pull me out of the way. I owe you a huge debt of gratitude."

"If you really feel indebted and want to repay me, just let me have dinner with you here this evening and that will make everything even," Art suggested, with a quick wink at Kaye.

Art's friendly, unassuming ways made Kaye smile, and she looked at him with new respect. "Mr. Lowen, our friend Bob is having the cheapest house special tonight, and he's only getting something that appetizing because the health department won't let me serve him a big plate of road-kill.

"You, however, are getting our best steak dinner and a cold Michelob to go with it. Bob will pick up your check. And I'd like for you to call me Kaye, starting right now."

"Thanks, Kaye. And I'd like it if you'd call me Artie. That's the name I go by with my family ands friends."

Bob and Art enjoyed a leisurely meal, with Kaye joining them whenever she could break away. One common interest surfaced during their conversation.

"So you grew up in Pittsburgh and went on to get your engineering degree at Pitt?" Bob inquired. "The Pitt Panthers have always had a great reputation in sports."

Art perked up at Bob's comment. "I wrestled a little while I was at Pitt."

"As a walk-on or on scholarship?"

"On a four year full ride, Bob, and that was the only way I could afford college. My dad was injured on the job working in a steel mill when I was a youngster, and our family didn't have a lot of money after that."

"I was a two year walk-on at VMI, but didn't do a whole lot with the sport. I look back and regret that today. You must have been pretty good to have gotten an athletic scholarship. How did you do? I assume you lettered."

"Fortunately, I was a starter for four years at 157 pounds, Bob."

"I'm impressed. What kind of record did you have?"

"A teammate and I went undefeated in our conference our junior and senior years. The last year I won gold at the NCAA national championships."

"You're a former NCAA national champion! I can't believe it. What year?"

"It was 1949, Bob, the year I graduated and a year before I shipped out to Korea. But please, I'd rather not get into that."

"Art, I'm a math teacher who's been thrown in as coach of the high school wrestling team. What wouldn't I give to have someone like you helping me with the boys. How long will you be working here?"

"That sort of depends on how things go between my employer, TUV, and the furniture company. My assignment here could go on through the spring, but I never know when I'll be pulled out and transferred somewhere else. Would you like for me to sit in on a practice? I'm available this Saturday.'

"You better believe I'd like that. The team will be really excited to meet a former NCAA champ. I think you'll like the boys. They're good kids from solid blue-collar families. Can we shoot for 9:00 Saturday morning at the high school gym?"

"I'll be there."

"Great. Now, what do you want for desert? Kaye always recommends the banana cream pie."

Kaye was way ahead of them, appearing at the table shortly afterward carrying a tray loaded with two generous slices of pie and three mugs of steaming black coffee. Business had slowed down for the evening, giving her the opportunity to slip into the booth beside Bob and join the conversation.

Bob put his arm around her. "You can see that Kaye never stays mad at me or anyone else for long. She's too good hearted a lady to hold a grudge."

Kaye winked at Art and asked, "Are you listening to that line of malarkey? He's hoping to convince you that I'm some kind of saint, but he knows better.

"Bob, you'll find out at my front door tonight you don't get a pass for keeping me in the dark about what went on Halloween night. You still have some time to spend in the doghouse."

Chapter 17

'Guys, circle up and take a knee," Bob instructed the team, as Art joined them. "I want to introduce Art Lowen, the 1949 NCAA 157-pound national champion out of Pitt."

Art pulled off his tan windbreaker and tossed it on a nearby chair, his black short-sleeve polo shirt emphasizing his wiry, muscular physique. "It's nice to meet all of you boys.

"Coach Slater's invited me to join you this morning to demonstrate some moves I picked up during my years of competition. Why don't a couple of you come out on the mat, and we'll start off working on single-leg takedowns."

Johnny and Darryl moved to the center of the mat, facing each other, eager to learn from an NCAA gold medalist.

"What are your names?" Art asked, and after both teammates replied, he continued. "Let's get started. I want all of you boys to watch closely. After I show you what to do, Johnny and Darryl will demonstrate the technique.

"Then everyone will pair off on my count of three, and start working on what I've showed you. I'll observe and point out anything I see that you're not doing correctly."

Art wasted no time, expertly coaching and critiquing the boys on techniques for takedowns, top control, and escapes from the referee's position. He emphasized the importance of constantly attacking, always working for a pin.

"After you take a shot at your opponent's legs, and he blocks you, he'll often step back and let up for just an instant, and that's when you go again. Bam! Bam! The second time you nail him and take him down. Don't let up when you've got him on the mat, break him down, sink a half nelson, and put him on his back!"

Art led the practice like he was conducting a wrestling clinic, but always deferring to Bob as the team coach, never undermining his authority. Gene caught an elbow in the mouth from Sonny during the workout, reacting with an obscenity. Art whistled the action to a stop, but left it to Bob to reprimand the boy.

The morning quickly slipped by, and near the end of the workout Pauly asked the question on everyone's mind, "Will you be coming back to help coach us again, Mr. Lowen?"

"Only if Coach Slater asks me to," Art answered. "If he does, I'll try to get over here after work on weekdays as often as I can."

Bob was quick to take the offer. "If Mr. Lowen's willing to volunteer his time, we'll take all the help he'll give us."

"Then I'll be back her on Monday to work with you again after I finish up for the day," Art replied.

"The one thing I'm going to ask is for Coach Slater to get me one of those blue and gold jerseys with the Stony Ford Eagle. I've heard that this school turns out winners year after year, and I want to be part of that tradition starting today."

That afternoon, Johnny polished off a couple of hot dogs and a Coke at Ray's before walking across town to knock on the Spellmans' door. OL, who had been watching for him from the window, grabbed his jacket and came outside.

"I need to get out of the house and away from my old man for a while," he said in disgust. "He came home loaded again late last night, and threw up all over the bathroom floor.

"My poor mom had to clean up after him twice during the night. But I don't want to talk about him. Tell me what's going on with the team."

"I was at practice this morning, and you won't believe who was there. What would you say if I told you that a former NCAA national champion is helping Coach Slater with the wrestling team, and that he was at our gym showing us a lot of new moves?"

"The same thing you'd say if I fed you a bunch of crap, like telling you I got a letter in the mail this morning from Lehigh offering me a four year wrestling scholarship."

"I'm not shooting you the bull, OL. A guy named Art Lowen who won an NCAA championship at Pitt is helping to coach us now. I've been busting my tail trying to convince you to come back on the team. There'll never be a better time than right now."

"Is this guy good? Does he know as much as Coach Callison?"

"He's the best wrestler I've ever been around. Coach Lowen's better at teaching wrestling moves than Coach Callie. He showed me the right way to go into the fireman's carry, and put me on my back so quick I didn't know what hit me.

"I'm getting a little tired of begging you to come back to the team, OL. You haven't gone through anything that I haven't. Are you planning to wrestle this season or not?"

"I've been thinking about it a lot. You may be surprised to hear me say it, but yeah, I've decided to come back out for the team. Julie's as bad as you, on my back all the time, treating me like I'm some kind of a quitter.

"I really need something to get me away from the house in the afternoons when my old man's there. I'm going to call Coach Slater tonight to tell him I've changed my mind."

Johnny slapped OL on the shoulder. "There are several matches still left in the season, a couple at home, Wytheville and Radford, and an away match in Roanoke. We'll be the underdog in all of them, but with you coming back out and a NCAA champion helping to coach us, we've got a chance of winning."

OL felt the dark cloud of depression start to lift for the first time since the night his brother had died. Johnny had dealt with the same problems, finding strength to move on with his life, showing him the way.

Ruby gave him a warm, reassuring hug when she heard the news. "I think you're doing the right thing, son, going back to the team. I know that you'll have happy times with all of your friends. The Lord knows you deserve better than being around your father any more than you have to these days."

OL got up enough nerve to make the call to his favorite teacher later that afternoon. "Coach, this is OL. I've rethought things and changed my mind. I'd like to come back out for the team. That is, if you'll let me."

He was relieved to hear Bob's enthusiastic reply. "That's what all of us have been hoping to hear, OL. We never took your name off of your locker. Billy will have your tights and jersey ready when you get there for practice Monday afternoon. Welcome back to the Eagles."

OL hung up the phone, then found his mother in the kitchen, preparing dinner. "Coach Slater's glad I'm back."

Bob was back on the phone at that same moment, relating the conversation to another interested party.

"Art, I've got some great news. We've got the other team leader we talked about. Maybe now we can build a team that will make the school and the whole town proud."

Chapter 18

Becky and Virginia slipped into back row seats at the Zephyr on Saturday night, noting with relief that most of the town's teenagers had left after the first feature, and that the ones remaining were seated toward the front.

"I'm glad there's only a small crowd for the second show," Virginia commented. "I've been waiting for weeks to see *Vertigo*. I really get wrapped up in suspense movies like this, and enjoy them so much more when the audience around me is quiet."

"I've been looking forward to this, too," Becky replied. "Alfred Hitchcock always keeps me on the edge of my seat, and Jimmy Stewart and Kim Novak are two of my favorite movie stars."

As their eyes adjusted to the darkness, Virginia whispered, "I see a couple of our students, OL and Julie, sitting down front, holding hands. It looks like Johnny is right beside them, with his arm around the new girl, Peggy Danner.

"You'd think those kids would see enough of each other at school, the way they spend all of their time hanging out together between classes."

"Come on, Virginia," Becky laughed. "I bet when you and Earl started dating right after the war that you couldn't keep your hands off each other, and you couldn't stand to be apart for a minute."

"A lot of water has gone under the bridge since then," Virginia replied. She would have continued if a young man hadn't entered the theater and quietly slipped into the aisle seat just down the row from Becky.

Virginia tapped Becky's hand to get her attention, saying, "Look who just walked in. It's that same man we saw at the revival. The good looking one."

Becky glanced to the side and found herself once again staring into the eyes of the stranger, but this time neither made an effort to turn away. The man raised his hand in a friendly gesture, and Becky nodded in recognition.

"Did you see that look he gave you?" Virginia whispered. "That's the way Earl looked at me the first time we met. I think that man sees something he likes."

"Virginia, please! He's going to hear you. You always say crazy things like that to embarrass me."

Becky was thoroughly distracted throughout the movie, occasionally sneaking a glance toward the stranger only three seats away, half hoping to find him looking back at her. It wasn't until the violent conclusion when the heroine plunged to her death from the top of the bell tower that Becky's undivided attention was focused on the screen.

Becky and Virginia followed the stranger into the lobby after the movie ended, and the house lights were turned up. The man was walking toward the outer door when Becky stepped up to him impulsively and spoke in a manner uncharacteristic for her reserved personality.

"Excuse me, but didn't I run into you a couple of weeks ago at a church revival?"

The man stopped, his expression welcoming. "I believe it was the other way around, ma'am. I'm afraid it was I who bumped into you. If you'll permit me to introduce myself, my name's Art Lowen."

"I'm Becky Thompson, and this is my friend, Virginia Swecker. She was with me that night, and she recognized you when you came into the theater."

Virginia had never known a bashful moment in her life, and she wasted no time in trying to find out more about him. "Are you new to the area, Mr. Lowen? I don't believe we've seen you around Stony Ford before?"

"Yes, ma'am, I've been working here for only a short time. I take it that both of you live here in Tazewell County?"

'That's right," Becky replied. "We both teach at Stony Ford High."

"Then you also work with Bob Slater. I met him during a rescue operation on Halloween, and I've come to know him well since then."

OL and Johnny walked by with their girl friends, and Johnny called out, "Hey there, Coach Lowen. See you Monday afternoon at practice."

"How in the world did you become acquainted with Johnny Burke?" Virginia inquired. "You've gotten to know a lot of people in our town in a very short time."

"I've been giving Bob a little help with the wrestling team," Art replied. "I drop by the gym in the afternoon after work whenever possible, and I help coach Johnny.

"It looks like the theater manager wants us to clear out so he can close for the night. If it weren't getting so late, and there was a place still open in town where we could get a cup of coffee, I'd enjoy visiting with you longer."

"Maybe we'll bump into each other again at school," Virginia remarked.

"That would be nice. Well, again, it's been nice meeting you, Mrs. Thompson and Mrs. Swecker."

"It's Becky, and Miss, not Mrs. Thompson. I hope we'll see you again, Art, and I'm rather sure that we will, since Stony Ford's such a small town. Good night."

Becky and Virginia shrugged on their sweaters as they stepped into the cool night air, continuing down the street to their car. "Why didn't you give him your phone number and ask him to call you?" Virginia asked curiously. "I bet he would have."

"Good grief, Virginia, I just met the man. I definitely don't want to create the impression that I belong in a lonely hearts club. The next thing I know you'll be telling me to run back down the street and hand him my calling card."

Virginia laughed, "No, I don't want you to do anything that desperate. But if I was an attractive young lady like you without a steady boy friend, and I knew that a good looking man would be in our high school gym in the afternoon to help coach the wrestling team, I'd find some excuse to be on the front row of the bleachers when he got there."

"I guess you're finally letting the cat out of the bag about how you snared Earl," Becky laughed, driving off.

*****

Kaye checked to see that Chris was sleeping soundly, then returned to the living room, where Bob was sprawled across the sofa in front of the TV set watching an exchange between Jack Paar and his guest, the unpredictable Dodie Goodman.

She kicked off her shoes, lying back in his arms. "Are you wrapped up in this program, or can I talk to you about something that's been on my mind for a while now?"

Bob kissed her on the on the cheek, inquiring, "What's bothering you, sweetheart?"

"I guess this all goes back to that Sunday in September when Rev. Underwood preached a sermon about helping to better the lives of people around you. Since then, I've been thinking about my life, and where it's going. Or about where it's not going. Do you realize that I've spent the last six years doing nothing but waiting on tables?"

"Nothing wrong with that, honey. You're good at what you do, and you have more friends than anyone I know. You're a terrific mother to Chris, and an incredible girlfriend to me."

"You wouldn't be satisfied if you had no more than that to show in the way of accomplishments, Bob. You can look back at all the young people who learned algebra and geometry from you, who'll go further in life because of what you've taught them.

"You've told me about some of the brightest ones who've gone on to college to prepare for careers in engineering and science. I don't have the feeling that I'm making the meaningful difference in someone else's life that Rev. Underwood talked about."

"You're selling yourself short, Kaye. There are dozens of people around here whose lives are brightened every single day because of the kindness you show them. Never underestimate how much sunshine you bring them."

"But I want to do more than that with my life, Bob. I've been investigating opportunities to get a two year RN diploma from a hospital somewhere in this area, and maybe someday even finishing a four year BSN degree program. Do you think that's realistic goal, or am I out of my mind?"

"Kaye, there's nothing you can't do if you really want it and set your mind to it. If you decide to go for an RN diploma, I'll help you in any way that I can. It will be a long, hard haul, and I only hope that it won't mean less room in your life for me."

"You don't have anything to worry about," Kaye whispered, putting both arms around Bob's neck to pull him close for a peck on the cheek. "You are my life, Chris and you."

"And you're absolutely sure that this career change you're about to make isn't based on proving to a few unfriendly, judgmental folks in town that they've underestimated your worth as a person? Like that old busybody, Mrs. Tanner, and her daughter Francine?"

"Maybe it is, maybe just a tiny bit, but that's not really the main thing with me. Someday I'd like to have the medical training and experience to help sick folks who need nursing care, people like our friend Mrs. Overstreet.

"She was in the hospital for a month after her stroke before she was able to come home to her family. She told me that she would never have made such a good recovery without the care she got day in and day out from her nurse.

"I think that's the kind of difference in peoples' lives that Rev. Underwood was talking about. What do you think?"

"I think you should invite Jonas to sit with Chris and me during the ceremony when you get your nursing cap. He obviously preached one heck of a sermon."

Chapter 19

"Mr. Hundley's waiting for you in the conference room," the attractive young secretary said with a smile. "It's the first door on the left, Mr. Lowen."

Art entered the room and found Roland Hundley and two other men standing beside a massive dark walnut conference table. Roland introduced them as Cliff Miller, Production Manager, and William Coleman, Marketing Manager for Southern Styles Furniture. He explained that his brother Oliver was in Georgia attending to business.

"We're all looking forward to your presentation, Mr. Lowen. You told me on the phone that you see a promising business opportunity for our company using the empty Stony Ford factory, and we're eager to find out what you have in mind."

Art set his briefcase beside the table and took out a stack of drawings, passing a set to each of the three men. "My proposal is to renovate the Stony Ford facility for the manufacture of premium quality traditional hardwood furniture, an idea that came up during our first meeting, Mr. Hundley.

"We've all read that rapid growth is expected in this segment of the furniture business, and Southern Styles is uniquely positioned to capitalize on the opportunity."

Art explained how a relatively small investment in new equipment and minor rearrangement of the old production line would enable Southern Styles to enter the new market.

"So you think we could start out with a small work force, and expand production without making major facility changes if this market proves to be strong?" Roland asked, glancing at Cliff and William to see if they were onboard with the concept.

"I think that I need to walk through the factory with Art and bring a couple of my industrial engineers along, Roland," Cliff replied. "The plans look reasonable on paper, but I always like to kick the tires pretty hard before I buy something like this. Can we plan to do that after lunch, Art?"

Cliff and his team met with Art that afternoon, spending hours going over the drawings and evaluating down to nuts and bolts the proposed use of the factory for manufacture of a new product line.

"You'll be staying on to see this project through to start-up if we proceed?" Cliff inquired, hearing Art answer that TUV would keep him on site until the line was up and running.

Roland convened his staff in his office late in the day to ask, "Do you two think this is a good business move for us?"

Cliff answered first. "I don't see anything that isn't feasible from a manufacturing standpoint. The existing equipment in the factory has been well maintained, and the new woodworking machinery should fit in the facility as Art proposed."

"I've gone over the numbers from a marketing standpoint, and it looks like a viable business opportunity for the company," William added. "You can never be absolutely certain about a venture like this, but unless the national economy takes a downturn, and the furniture business follows, it looks promising."

"Then I'll call Oliver and tell him what I'm planning to do," Roland decided. "He's always discouraged me from moving any manufacturing operations back into that facility. I'll probably be able to hear him all the way from Georgia without needing the phone when I break the news."

Roland's prediction was dead-on. As soon as he heard the news, Oliver quickly challenged his brother's decision. "I'm totally opposed to this.

"Tell me, Rollo, why are you so dead set on restarting production in that old factory? We can buy all the land we need here in Savannah and add additional floor space to our new manufacturing facility. It will cost more initially, but we'll have everything together in one central location. I can't believe you're serious."

Oliver would have continued ranting, but Roland had heard enough. "Ollie, don't forget that I still run this company. I've made a decision, and it may turn out to be a bad one, but it stands. We're going to produce the new line in Stony Ford and put some people back to work."

Roland called his secretary into his office after hanging up. "Susan, set up another meeting with Art Lowen, and this time include our attorney, Arnold Ronson. Tell him that we'll be contracting with the TUV engineer as a consultant for the renovation."

*****

Oliver slammed the phone down on the cradle, angrily pushing his chair back from his desk. He sat for a few minutes, then picked the phone up again, dialed a local number, and nervously began speaking.

"Ben, we've got a big problem, and I need some help from you. It's about those two large tracts of land we purchased on speculation through our dummy corporation.

"I was betting that my brother would need part of it for a factory expansion, getting the county and the utilities to make upgrades, causing the land value to soar. We stood to make a windfall profit if the chips fell that way.

"Now things have gone to hell in a hand basket. My brother's decided to reopen the old factory in southwest Virginia. Unless something happens to change his mind, Southern Styles won't be expanding the Savannah facility, and we'll be stuck with a couple of very expensive cornfields, unable to pay off our loan."

Olivier listened for a few minutes to the angry buzz at the end of the line. "Calm down, Ben. None of this is my fault. Restarting production in Stony Ford isn't a done deal.

"I recall that the factory took a lot of damage when lightning hit the incoming power line twenty years ago and set the building on fire. I'm sure Roland would think a long time before rebuilding if something like that were to happen again. The insurance he's carrying wouldn't begin to cover the cost of rebuilding."

There was a long pause while Oliver listened, stroking his chin nervously. He replied, "I agree with you. An ex-union miner who knows enough about sabotage to shut down an entire coal operation won't have any trouble with this job. Just be sure your man knows how to cover his tracks and keep his mouth shut."

Oliver put down the phone and leaned back in his chair, realizing that the stakes had just become much higher in his gamble for a big return on a secret venture.

He reached into his desk drawer, pulled out a pint of Jim Beam, and poured two fingers into a paper cup, bitterly speaking aloud. "I don't like being in a situation pitting me against my brother, but when push comes to shove, a man does what he's gotta do to protect his own hide. After all, Rollo brought this on himself."

Chapter 20

At the café on Saturday, Becky found the dining area overflowing with the usual lunchtime crowd. Kaye navigated through the jumble of tables and spoke to her quietly, "I think the Gilberts in the booth next to the window are getting ready to leave now. You can have their place if you'll just wait for a few minutes." She had cleared the dishes away, inviting Becky to be seated, when the door opened and another customer entered.

Becky turned her head, seeing Art glancing around the crowded room. She raised her arm to get his attention, calling out, "There's nothing left but stools at the counter. Would you like to share a booth with me?"

Kaye welcomed him warmly as he slipped in on the bench across from Becky. She placed a menu on the table, commenting, "Nice to have you drop in for lunch today. Bob tells me the wrestling team is improving by leaps and bounds now that you're helping him coach."

"No wonder," Becky interjected. "I've dropped by the gym in the afternoon, watching him demonstrate wrestling moves, and the boys are all paying full attention. I wish they'd listen to me in class the same way."

Forever Eagles

As Kaye left with their orders, Becky tilted her head to study Art with a mischievous smile. "How about telling me something about yourself while we're sitting here waiting?"

"There's not a lot to tell, Becky," he began, leaning forward with folded hands resting on the edge of the table. "I'm a native of Pittsburgh here in your beautiful part of the world on a temporary project engineering assignment for my employer, TUV. I'm staying at the Laurel Lane Motel while I'm in town.

"After work in the afternoon, you've seen me helping Bob coach the wrestling team. That sums it up, short and sweet. Can't think of a lot more to say, and to be perfectly honest, I'd much rather talk about you anyway."

"You didn't even scratch the surface." she replied. "I'll gladly give you a rundown on Becky, but don't think that I'm not coming back to hear more about Art."

"I'm from Logan, West Virginia. Both of my parents died in a car wreck while I was at college, leaving me only one family member, my older sister Ruth. She still lives there with her husband and two daughters."

"I'm sorry to hear about your parents, Becky," Art interrupted. "I know what you've been through. I lost both of my folks not too long after I finished high school. Please go on."

"After high school, I went off to Marshall for my BA, and then on to Radford College for an MA in education. I moved here three years ago hoping that I'd be able to help kids living in the Appalachian region. I've been in these parts long enough to put down roots and feel like this is home."

"What do you like to do for fun in your free time?" Art asked.

115

"Hiking, bicycling, anything outdoors. When I was growing, up my mother couldn't get me to put on a pair of shoes, or come in the house between sunup and sundown, all summer long. My daddy had to hunt me down and walk me home at twilight."

"So you ran around barefoot all summer when you were a kid?" Art interjected. "I can picture a little cutie pie with red pigtails, chasing butterflies and climbing apple trees."

"I also like to sketch portraits when I can find someone willing to pose. And I like to pick out old songs on a piano if I can rope friends into harmonizing with me. I sing in the church choir, too."

Kaye returned to bring their meals. "You two kids need anything else?" she asked, moving back toward the kitchen after both shook their heads.

Becky redirected the conversation as they tucked into their lunches. "The ball's back in your court now. Tell me about your life before you came to the bright lights of Stony Ford."

"OK, if you insist. I grew up an only child on the south side of Pittsburgh. There weren't many kids running around barefoot where I lived, but I liked being outside as much as you.

"My father worked in a steel mill until he lost an arm in an industrial accident, and then my mother went to work clerking in a ladies' clothing store to help pay the bills.

"I had a paper route, delivering The Pittsburgh Press on my bicycle every morning around the neighborhood to help out. Did you have any part-time jobs growing up?

"It might be stretching things to call running a lemonade stand when I was eight years old a part time job," Becky laughed. "When

I was sixteen, I got my first real job at the local drug store. Playing on the girls' basketball team, and working part time kept me hopping, but I loved every minute of it."

"I have happy memories of high school, too," Art commented. "I made good grades in math and science, and I loved wrestling. My senior year, Pitt offered me a four year wrestling scholarship, which meant I was able to get my engineering degree."

"So that brings us up to your assignment with TUV here in Stony Ford?" Becky inquired.

Artie shifted in his seat, and answered, "I volunteered for a hitch in Korea right after I graduated. That's about all there is to say about me until I came here."

It was much later, and most of the noon diners had moved on, when the two realized the time. Kaye had started over toward their booth several times, but seeing how much the two were enjoying each other's company, talking and laughing, she turned back each time with a smile.

Art insisted on picking up the check for both, then followed Becky out of the warm café into the cool, sunny outdoors. He reached out for her hand and held it for a moment. "You told me that you enjoy hiking. Would you be willing to let me tag along with you the next time you go?"

"How would you like for me to show you Burke's Garden? It's a valley completely ringed by mountains that's not far from here. When you drive up the old mountain road through a bunch of hair pin turns and cross the top of the ridge, you feel like you're descending into the crater of a volcano."

"I heard someone at the factory talking about that place. When can we go?"

"How about Thursday when I'm off from school for a four-day holiday weekend? I'll pack a lunch, and come by to get you around 10:00. Better wear comfortable shoes, since we'll be hiking quite a way along country roads."

The two said goodbye in a now empty parking lot, driving away to different sides of town, Becky mulling over the question she had wanted to ask but hadn't dared. The one intended to confirm what Art had told Bob, that there was no other woman in his life.

Chapter 21

"I think we'll do better tonight than we did against Bristol," Wally commented. "We've got Coach Lowen working with us now, and he could write the book on wrestling."

Gene replied skeptically, "Do you really believe that's going to make a big difference? You think Coach Lowen's going out on the mat with you tonight? Dream on, Kemo Sabe. You'll be the Lone Ranger, no Tonto, same as last time."

Gene realized he was not helping Wally's confidence and threw an arm around his teammate. "Look, just follow Coach Lowen's advice and take it to your opponent for six minutes."

The visitor's side of the gym filled with fans in maroon, chattering away, watching their team warm up. Kaye, Chris, and Becky sat halfway up the stands directly across the gym in a sea of blue and gold.

"What do you think of all this excitement?" Becky asked Chris, who was taking everything in, glued to the activity on the floor below them.

"I think the cheerleaders are pretty," he answered seriously.

Becky glanced toward Kaye and winked, "Typical male, and not yet seven years old."

"I think I need to keep him away from Coach Slater," Kaye laughed. "Chris, try watching the boys for a change."

The buzzer sounded to bring the 106-pounders out. Pauly looked back at his coaches for final instructions, and heard Coach Lowen say one word, "Relentless!"

Pauly started fast and fought hard for six minutes against a tough opponent. The lead swapped again and again, both boys still scrapping right up until the final buzzer. Pauly was awarded a point for riding time, winning 11 to 10, walking off the mat to loud cheers from the home crowd.

The team score shifted to favor Wytheville, as Bennie, Wally, and Gene lost close decisions in the next three weight classes before Sonny slowed the bleeding by pulling out a come from behind win in the third period of his match.

The visitors were on their feet, and raucous shouting filled the gym, when a cat-quick 141-pound Wytheville grappler put Ron Sawyer on his back and showed him the lights. They cranked the noise level even higher when their wiry 148-pounder scored a hard-fought decision over Terry Blankenship, making the team score 17 to 6.

Bob glanced at Art, expecting to see frustration, but the former NCAA champion's expression was impassive. "Let's get Darryl, Johnny, and OL over here for a minute."

The referee impatiently signaled for the next Stony Ford wrestler to take the mat as Art delivered a short message. "We can still pull off a team win if you three run the table, two of you scoring pins.

Turn the season around for the Eagles. Attack, wear your man down, put him on his back."

Darryl quickly shot a takedown at the opening whistle and moved into the top position, slipping into a figure-four leg hold and a cross-body ride. The Wytheville 157-pounder was as strong as Darryl but not as experienced, making a classic blunder, reaching backward with his right arm for Darryl's head.

Darryl quickly trapped him, rolling his opponent over onto his back in an unbreakable crucifix, hearing the referee signal a pin two seconds later. Stony Ford fans were still screaming as he shook hands with his opponent, the referee raised his arm in victory, and he walked away, fresh as a daisy. One down.

Johnny tossed his warm-up jacket on the floor and started out onto the mat, feeling Coach Slater give him an encouraging slap on the back. Peggy's high pitched yell could be heard above everyone else in the gym, "Get him, Johnny!"

Johnny went on the attack, shooting underneath the Wytheville boy for a quick takedown, controlling him from the top position. The crowd came to its feet when he broke his opponent down, used a forearm cross-face to drive him into a tight cradle, and rocked him onto his back for a pin with less than a minute off the clock.

Cheers shook the building as the referee raised Johnny's arm, Peggy's shrill voice ringing from the rafters, "Way to go, Johnny!" The scoreboard now flashed, "Wytheville-17, Stony Ford-16." Two down.

"It's up to you now," Bob told OL.

Art added, "He's big. Don't try to muscle him around. Beat him with speed and finesse."

OL nodded his head, glancing back toward his team, spotting Julie watching apprehensively.

Wytheville fans were chanting, "Bear! Bear! Bear!" as their senior heavyweight, Robbie "Bear" Lawson came out on the mat, a red haired farm boy with thick arms and legs, thirty pounds heavier and a couple of inches taller than OL.

Bear instantly went on the attack, bull-rushing OL, trying to overpower him, driving him off of the mat again and again, OL countering with quick shots at Bear's legs, unable to take him down. The first two minutes ended in a scoreless stalemate, the second in a tie at 2-2, leaving everything on the line in the third period, both boys now gasping for breath, unwilling to back off.

Bear got underneath OL as time was running out, locking his arms around OL's waist, lifting him off the floor, driving him into the mat on his back. The instant they hit, OL shifted his weight and bridged on his neck and shoulder, flipping the pair upside down, putting Bear on the bottom. The referee awarded him a two–point takedown just as the final buzzer sounded. Three and done.

Celebrating Stony Ford fans were emptying the bleachers and rushing out onto the floor as Bear jumped to his feet and stormed off the mat, refusing to shake hands. The scoreboard lit up with the final score: Stony Ford 19, Wytheville 17, the first win of the season for the Eagles now in the record book.

Bob pounded Art's back, exclaiming, "OL surprised a lot of Wytheville folks tonight! He surprised a lot of Stony Ford fans, too. That Lawson kid hasn't lost a match this year before tonight."

"OL's got a lot of heart," Art replied. "I could tell that about him from the time he came back, completely out of shape, refusing to quit."

The boys were in no hurry to hit the showers, staying on the floor to receive handshakes and hugs from family members, and congratulatory slaps on backs from classmates. Julie didn't care that OL was soaked with sweat when she ran to him, and he picked her up in his arms.

"That boy was so much bigger than you. Nobody thought you had a chance." She was unable to get another word out as he pressed his wet face against hers.

Nick and Randy Kowalski rose from their front row seats and made their way through the crowd, walking past Bob toward Art with extended hands. "We're glad to have you coaching the team now, Mr. Lowen. This group of kids needed someone like you to come in and take over."

Art looked both men over quizzically without offering to take their hands, replying, "I believe you've been misinformed. This is Coach Slater's team. I've only been here for a short time trying to help out. You need to be congratulating the boys and the man standing next to me for the win."

The Kowalski brothers looked at each other in surprise, offended by Art's refusal to shake hands, sullenly walking away.

Kaye, Chris, and Becky joined the coaches. Kaye stood on tiptoe to kiss Bob, watching as he lifted Chris off the floor and asked, "What did you think of the match?"

"I want to be able to wrestle like those boys," Chris answered. "Will you teach me how, Coach?" Kaye looked on in amusement as Bob picked Chris up on his shoulders like a professional wrestler, twirling him in an airplane spin.

Becky watched for a moment, then impulsively threw her arms around Art in a congratulatory hug. She was happily surprised when he pulled her close and held her as if there were no one else in the building.

*****

"I'm home," OL called out as he came through the front door. "We won the match tonight. I beat Wytheville's undefeated heavyweight."

Glancing across the living room, illuminated only by faint light shining from the kitchen, he could make out his mother, seated in a rocking chair. "How come you're sitting in here by yourself in the dark, Mom? Anything wrong?"

"No, son. Everything's fine. Your dad's is in the bedroom, and I just wanted to be alone for a while."

OL heard a break in his mother's voice and knew that everything was not fine. He turned on a lamp to flood the room with light, looking across at his mother. He saw a livid bruise on her left cheek and streaks from dried tears.

"Did he hit you?" he inquired deliberately, trying to control his anger.

His mother shook her head but broke down, sobbing silently, unable to speak.

"He'll never do it again," OL said quietly, starting for the bedroom where he could hear his father snoring.

"No, OL! No!" She jumped up from her chair and rushed to stop him. "It's not worth you fighting with your dad and getting into trouble. I'm going to handle things. He won't hit me again, I promise you, because we're not going to remain here one more day.

"You and I are going to leave this house and live with your Aunt Francis. She knows what your dad's like since he started drinking, and she's invited us to come live with her for as long as we want to stay."

"I'll start getting our things together so we can be ready to move out tomorrow morning," OL replied.

"He'll be sleeping it off until noon. By the time he wakes up, we'll be out of here, and he'll have the place to himself. But if he ever tries to make you come back and live with him, he'll have to deal with me."

Chapter 22

Albert closed the door to the conference room, soberly surveying the staff seated before him. "I'm about to tell you something in strictest confidence. If what I say should leak out, I'll find out who violated my request for confidentiality, and deal with him or her accordingly."

This remark brought the entire faculty to full attention, including Virgil Akers, who had been staring at the floor in front of him with exhausted disinterest.

Albert paced back and forth collecting his thoughts, then spoke tersely. "The county budget shortfall this year is a lot worse than expected, and the school system is feeling the brunt of it. The board of supervisors has given the school board and the superintendent a mandate to reduce costs, and some radical ideas have been thrown out on the table.

"One of the recently elected and most politically influential board members has proposed that Stony Ford High be closed, and our students bussed over to attend school in Bluefield."

A perceptible gasp was heard as the faculty members looked at each other in consternation. "That's exactly the same reaction that I had when my boss dropped the bomb on me," Albert commented with a wry smile. "Apparently Bluefield High has the capacity to take in our students, with the biggest incremental expense being the purchase and operation of additional school busses."

"You need to realize that this is still only one of several cost-cutting alternatives being investigated, so we shouldn't panic. But when the decision is made, things will happen quickly.

"If our school is to be closed, there'll be no more classes here after graduation this spring. I anticipate that some of you will be invited to interview for teaching jobs in Bluefield, others will be encouraged to retire, and a few will just be let go. I'm sure that at my age and salary, I'll be among the first they'll want to cut from the payroll."

He watched the grim announcement sink in. "I hated to break this news to you, especially right before the Thanksgiving holiday. It's even more regrettable, after seeing signs the town is rallying behind the high school and showing some signs of life."

Albert observed the distressed faces around the table, speaking sympathetically, "I want you to understand that none of this is a reflection on your performance as a faculty. It's all about the county's lack of funds and the financial bottom line. I'll be glad to take any questions you have now and try to answer them to the best of my ability."

Bob glanced at Becky and Virginia, shaking his head in disbelief, then raised his hand to speak. "What can we do to head off this train wreck?"

"Bob, this is a political affair, like almost everything else that goes on around here. With the right kind of support in the House of Delegates, the county could be coerced into taking some other action, such as raising property taxes or delaying renovation of the courthouse in Bluefield. But we're a small town with very little political clout, and finding a champion for Stony Ford will be difficult."

"Difficult, but not impossible," Virgil Akers responded vehemently, showing unprecedented spirit. "Most of us in this room can't afford to retire, and I know damn well that I can't get on at Bluefield High at my age.

"What we need to do is load everybody in town and all of the news reporters we can line up into an automobile caravan and head down to Richmond."

"We can do that, Virgil," Albert replied. "But first we must wait until the school board publicly announces their intentions. Until then, all we can do is make plans for waging a battle to overturn the decision.

"If there are no more questions at this time, we'll adjourn. But remember what I said, everything I've told you is strictly confidential, and nothing can be disclosed to anyone outside of this room."

Bob returned to his classroom, trying to shake off the disturbing thought that he could be out of work and searching for a job within six months. The bell rang to announce the start of first period, and students quickly filled the room, taking their seats for Algebra II.

"Let's open our books to page 84 and get started," he announced calmly, trying to hide his concern. "If y'all are planning to go on after high school and college to become famous rocket scientists, you'll need to understand this stuff. Wernher von Braun will assume you already know the basics when you go to work for him."

Most of the class laughed at his remark and quickly opened their text books, but Bob noticed that OL's mind seemed to be a million miles away. He had nothing to say throughout class, and he did not turn in his paper after a pop quiz just before the bell.

He was walking out the door when Bob called to him, "OL, hold up. I need to see you for a couple of minutes in private."

OL wheeled around and came back into the classroom, kicking the door closed behind him. "What do you want, Coach?"

"I want to know what's bothering you this morning. You're normally one of my sharpest kids, and this morning you're inviting me to give you a goose egg on a simple quiz. Do you have something on your mind?"

"I don't want to talk about it, Coach."

"But I do. When one of my best math students acts like he doesn't care about his grade, I want to know why. Have you got some problem at home with your father again?"

OL hesitated at first but then opened up, raw emotion written on his young face. "He hit my mother while I was at the wrestling match the other night.

"We moved out of the house on Saturday. Mom and I are staying with my aunt in town now. I don't know how we're going to work things out and find money to live on."

"I'm really sorry to hear that, OL. You and your mother have been through way too much already without having to deal with an abusive family member. We're not going to be able solve a problem this serious in a few minutes between classes."

"But I'll be giving your situation a lot of thought over the coming days, trying to see how I may be able to help you and your mother. You got that?"

Bob impulsively reached out to squeeze the boy's shoulder, noticing that OL was shaking with the effort to hold back tears.

"Yeah, Mr. Slater," OL replied, forgetting to call his teacher by the athletic title. "I'd like your help." He turned and opened the door to walk away, calling back appreciatively, "You've always been there for me."

Chapter 23

"The production line should operate efficiently with this new layout," Southern Styles industrial engineer Randle Creech commented to Art, as the two men surveyed the assembly line.

"It's exciting for me to think about building a new line of early American furniture in this old factory, keeping the tradition of wood-working craftsmanship alive here in Stony Ford."

"I've really enjoyed working with a Tazewell County native like you, Randle, trying to restart production here," Art remarked. "Next week, we'll have plenty of time to start checking out the factory electric power system, including the motors and controllers. Neither of us wants any surprises when we start closing breakers to bring the shop back on line."

"I don't anticipate a lot of problems," Randle replied. "This building hasn't been left unattended for years with open doors and broken windows like some obsolete manufacturing facilities.

"I doubt that we'll run into any problems with rats nesting in controllers or blacksnakes coiled up around transformer high voltage bushings. Everything should be just the way it was when our company closed the factory.

"We've employed the Craig brothers to provide plant security, and one of them is here as a watchman around the clock. If you look over by the paint booth, you'll see the youngest one, Marv, on the job now."

Art glanced across the factory and saw a young man with a buzz cut wearing a dark blue shirt monogrammed Craig Security on the front pocket, standing with his hands on his hips, staring back at him.

"It's still hard for me to believe things are going so well, and that we'll start recalling people and have a pilot production crew at work here in just over a month," Randle continued. "News of a recall will be the best Christmas present our former employees could imagine."

"It looks like everything's coming together as planned and on schedule," Art agreed. "So far we've managed to dodge the third part of Murphy's Law: if anything can go wrong, it will. Hope I don't jinx us by saying that."

"I'll keep my fingers crossed," Randle laughed. "Have a good Thanksgiving and don't eat too much turkey. See you back here next week."

*****

Becky drove up in front of the motel at mid-morning on Thanksgiving Day, where she found Art waiting for her on a concrete bench beneath a nearby maple tree.

"All set for our adventure today?" she inquired cheerily, as he slipped into the front seat beside her. "I packed a nice lunch for us in my knapsack: sandwiches, home made cookies, a couple of apples and a thermos of lemonade."

"I've been looking forward to this adventure all week," Art replied. "It looks like the weatherman's giving us a perfect day. By the way, you never told me how Burke's Garden got its name. How about filling me in?"

"I'll give you the *Readers Digest* abridged version. James Burke headed up a survey party in that valley back in the seventeen-hundreds, covering his tracks so the Indians wouldn't find out he was in their neighborhood.

"He and his men buried their garbage, including some potato peelings, and years later, settlers found potatoes growing wild all over the place. That's how it got the name. If you want to know more, you'll have to buy my book."

"It seems like everybody's out to make a buck these days," Art laughed.

There was little traffic on the way, and even less after they turned off at an old wooden *Burke's Garden* sign and began climbing the winding road up the mountain through one hairpin turn after another.

Finally, they crossed the ridge and began their descent into the open valley below, gazing out over a breathtaking vista of open fields and widely spaced farmhouses.

Becky parked the car beside a pond, reaching into the back seat for the knapsack containing their lunch. A red-tailed hawk searching for dinner made lazy circles in the blue sky overhead as Art took the knapsack from her, and they set out together.

"I can see where the creek was dammed to provide water for an old grist mill that once stood here," Art observed. "I bet every young boy and girl who's grown up in the valley has used this old mill pond for a swimming hole. We could have gone in for a dip ourselves if we'd come here in warm weather."

"That might not have worked out so well, Artie," Becky replied with a teasing smile. "I can just see the headlines on the front page of the *Tazewell Enterprise*, 'Schoolmarm and gentleman friend caught skinny dipping in county millpond.'"

"I didn't suggest skinny dipping, Miss Thompson, but since you brought it up, that does sound like fun," Art laughed, dodging a dirt clod that Becky playfully tossed at him. He took her hand, and the two starting off down the narrow country road circling the wide valley, talking as they walked along.

"When I'm outdoors enjoying a beautiful day like this, it takes me back to my childhood in Logan," Becky commented. "I feel like a little girl again. Do you ever get that sort of nostalgic feeling?"

"I think that's pretty common," Art replied thoughtfully. "I don't think we change a great deal in our hearts as we get older. When I was a young boy, I enjoyed hanging out with a few close friends, doing the things most kids like to do, playing ball in the park and riding my bike in the neighborhood.

"I still enjoy quiet times outdoors away from big crowds. I'd far rather be here with you hiking in this beautiful valley than walking along a busy city sidewalk."

Art's reply made Becky smile, and she remarked, "I sometimes fantasize about going back to live in the past for a day, together again with my mom, dad, and sister in our old home on Cedar Street. It was a pretty small house, but I was very happy growing up there. Do you have a place with happy memories that you'd like to go back and visit again?"

"I've never thought about something like that," Art replied. "But if I were to pick a place, it would be my Aunt Ruth's home. She was like a second mother to me. She's my only surviving kin, still living on Forbes Street in the Squirrel Hill section of Pittsburgh.

"It's a beautiful white frame Victorian house with double porches, big bay windows on the ends, and the only widow's walk in the neighborhood. I used to sit up there with a toy telescope and keep watch for pirates."

"It sounds like that house was a wonderful fortress for a child. I'm sorry to hear that you have only one relative left. Do you have any close friends back in Pittsburgh?"

"I'm afraid not. TUV calls the shots in my life, and they keep me on the road. I never know what my next assignment will be. Maybe that's the reason I'm so grateful to be here with you today."

Becky could not help but feel relieved by Art's reply, ruling out a girlfriend back home. She slipped her arm through his, leaning against him as they continued along the quiet country road, passing a cluster of small signs mounted on a post, showing the names and locations of the different property owners.

She voiced concern as they turned onto a road leading toward a farm house off in the distance. "We don't want to go all of the way to the end. The family has two big dogs that run loose, and I've always steered clear of them."

"But we'll miss a beautiful view from the hilltop beyond their house if we stop and turn around," Art countered. "Let's walk a little further and see if those dogs plan to give us any trouble. We can always turn back if you start to feel uncomfortable."

Becky's caution seemed to be well founded as they approached the house and a black German shepherd and red Chow started toward them, barking ominously. "Art, I'm afraid they'll bite. We shouldn't have come this far."

"Stay here," he replied, continuing to walk toward the two agitated dogs.

Becky watched in concern, expecting the dogs to attack. Instead, both quieted and backed away as Art came closer, uncertain how to deal with someone so completely unafraid of them. Finally, they retreated toward the house to sit in the yard and stare in canine puzzlement.

"It's OK, Becky," Art called to her. "Come on up and walk with me. It looks like the two pooches have decided to behave themselves and won't give us any trouble today."

Becky caught up to him, exclaiming, "I've never seen anything like that before. I was sure that you were going to get bitten."

"Maybe they decided that I didn't pass for Grade A meat," Art joked, trying to put her at ease. "Even dogs don't want a case of food poisoning. Let's go on past the house now and check out that view."

The two continued for a half mile further before veering from the roadway through the low stubble of a newly-mown hayfield toward the crest of a round-topped knoll, finding a place to sit on the massive fallen limb of a lightning split hickory.

Quiet enveloped them, and except for the calling of crows in the distance, there was nothing to be heard but the sound of a gentle breeze passing through the leafless treetops overhead.

"Ready for lunch now?" Becky asked. "If you'll hand me the knapsack, I'll get out our four course meal."

Time stood still for a little while as they sat together on the hilltop, alone in their private world, talking and laughing.

Becky surprised Art, reaching into the knapsack just as the meal was finished, and taking out a sketch pad and pencil. "OK, Mr. Lowen, I want you to sit very, very still and give me a nice smile so that I can sketch your portrait."

Art struck a relaxed pose, while she went to work with quick pencil strokes, handing him the finished drawing for inspection a short time later.

Art looked at the picture, observing with a smile, "You certainly have a talent for drawing people, but there's something wrong with this. It looks just like me. Couldn't you have sketched something that would make me look like a movie star?"

Becky took the sketch pad back from him, poker faced as she returned it to the knapsack. "You want me to draw a portrait that shows your resemblance to a movie star? Who did you have in mind? Porky Pig? Personally, I think you're every bit as handsome as he is."

She broke out laughing when Art responded with a perfect imitation of the cartoon character, stuttering out a panicky porcine protest.

Their easy-going teasing might have continued longer if they had not suddenly heard the faint voice of a woman in the distance.

"Help! Can anyone hear me? Please, I need help."

"Someone's in trouble!" Becky exclaimed. "It sounds like a woman calling out from the farm we just passed."

Art was already on his feet, quickly stuffing everything back into the knapsack. "Let's go. We need to get back there on the double. It sounds like there's no time to waste."

Art and Becky were running side by side back down the road when a young boy came rushing to meet them, gasping for breath, tears running down his face. He managed to blurt out, "The tractor turned over on Papa, and he can't move. Mama's with him now and doesn't know what to do. I can take you to them."

The boy quickly led the way along a dirt road running from an old barn across a closely-grazed pasture, and on beyond to an overgrown field on a hillside where the emergency situation became terribly clear.

On the ground lay a semi-conscious man with blood running from his thigh, pinned under a tractor which had tipped over on top of him. His wife was holding his head in her lap, frantically calling his name again and again.

Art's knowledge of emergency medical care picked up from a Navy Corpsman in Korea kicked in, and he quickly checked the man's vital signs, finding him to be in a state of shock from trauma and loss of blood. Pulse and respiration rates were elevated, the skin pale and sweaty.

He turned to the woman and spoke calmly. "We've got to get your husband out from under the tractor so we can try to stop the bleeding. Do you have anything like a steel bar or even a long, stout fence post that I can use for leverage to lift the tractor off of him long enough for you and my friend to pull him free?"

The woman composed herself, turned to her young son, and commanded, "Richie, run to the barn right now and fetch one of those new fence posts. Hurry back here, son. Your Pa's not going to be able to hold out much longer."

The boy ran off in the direction of the barn, while Art continued to probe the man's leg in an unsuccessful attempt to locate the wound and stop the bleeding. "How can I help, Art?" Becky asked, slipping her arm around the distraught woman.

"When the boy gets back with the post, I want each of you to put an arm under one of his shoulders and be ready to slide him out from under the tractor. I'm hoping that I'll be able to lift it a few inches and hold it long enough for you to drag him free."

"I pray that you can," the woman said, staring at him with pleading eyes. "I tried to lift it off of him, but it's too heavy for me to budge."

The boy was soon back, trotting along the path, dragging a long, sturdy fence post behind him, breathing hard from the exertion. Art took the pole and pushed one end under the tractor engine block, while the two woman moved into position, kneeling on either side of the injured man. "We'll go on three," Art said. "One... two..."

Art lifted with his legs, veins popping out on his forehead, the post bending under the load. For a moment nothing moved. Then the front of the tractor began to slowly rise as he strained with every bit of strength he could muster.

He managed to gasp, "Now-" and the two women dragged the unconscious man from underneath the machine. Then he released the post and let the tractor fall back to the ground. Becky caught a glimpse as he dropped to his knees, completely spent, looking upward in silent thanks.

Art used his pocket knife to rip the leg of the man's blood-soaked coveralls, applying direct pressure to a gaping wound in his thigh with a handkerchief in order to slow the bleeding, quietly giving instructions to the others.

"Becky, take over for me and hold this compress tightly against the wound.

"Ma'am, I need for you to go get your car right now and drive out here to get us. While you're at the house, make a call to the sheriff's office and tell the deputy that we'll be coming to the hospital with your husband, and that he's going to need blood transfusions and surgical repair of a deep leg wound. I'll carry your husband down to the road as soon as I see you coming back this way with the car.

"Son, you run along with your mother and help her any way you can. We're going to get your papa to the doctor as quickly as possible."

The woman returned a short time later, driving a battered Ford station wagon, a cloud of dust trailing her as she sped up the gravel road.

Art lifted the injured man into the back seat while Becky slipped in on the other side, maintaining firm pressure against the wound with the makeshift bandage. Then the five were off.

"God, please keep him alive until we get there," the woman repeated softly again and again as they sped along.

A deputy was waiting in a patrol car with lights flashing when they crossed the mountain and descended on the other side. Siren howling, he raced ahead of them all the way to the Jeffersonville Hospital in Tazewell, where a medical team was standing by waiting for them. The man was quickly loaded on a gurney and wheeled away, Art and Becky following the woman and her son inside.

The woman fought to hold back tears as they sat in the empty waiting room. "I'm Norma Bullard, and this is my son, Richie. My husband's name is Vernon.

"I thank you both from the bottom of my heart for everything you did to get him here to the hospital. I only pray he's going to make it." Breaking down in deep sobs that shook her entire body, she buried her face in her hands.

Becky crossd the room to sit next to the woman, consolingly pulling her close. "Don't give up now, Norma. Your husband's in the operating room getting the best possible medical care.

"I'm Becky Thompson, and my friend's Art Lowen. We're going to stay here with you and your son until your husband's out of surgery.

"I have a good feeling that's he's going to be O.K." Becky glanced at Art, her expression less certain than her words.

The only sound in the room as the four waited anxiously was the ticking of a clock on the wall. Finally, a man in a white medical coat appeared in the doorway and walked toward them, introducing himself as Dr. Maxwell Berman.

"Mrs. Bullard, we've treated your husband for shock, transfused four pints of blood, and repaired a deep wound to his leg. He's regained consciousness and is in stable condition, resting under heavy sedation.

"He's asking to see you and your son. I'll take you back to see him for a brief visit if you'll follow me."

The doctor glanced toward Art and Becky, noticing the dark stains covering their clothes. "I don't know what you folks did to control the bleeding and get Mr. Bullard here as quickly as you did, but you're to be commended. If he had arrived thirty minutes later, I don't believe we could have saved him."

Norma followed the doctor, first stopping to thank Art and Becky, relief and gratitude shining from her brown eyes. "I can never repay you for what you did today. I was praying aloud for a miracle, after the tractor rolled over on Vernon.

"I asked Richie to go find help, and he came back with you just in the nick of time. I think the Lord heard me, and sent you to save his life. I'll believe that to my dying day."

Art and Becky sat together in the back seat of the deputy's squad car as he drove them back to Burke's Garden to pick up her car. She looked at him and said quietly, "Norma really thinks the Lord sent you to save her husband today.

"I don't believe anyone else could have lifted that tractor. I was watching with my heart in my throat, expecting the fence post to snap in two."

"You're reading way too much into what went on today, Becky. Sometimes when people are caught up in emergency situations, the adrenaline kicks in, and they find strength they didn't know they had. That's all that happened. Nothing extraordinary or miraculous."

Becky snuggled closer, feeling his arm slip reassuringly around her. Both were emotionally exhausted, neither finding the need to talk, content to ride quietly along in a peaceful cocoon.

The deputy glanced back at them, courteously shifting his rear view mirror to let them rest in privacy.

Chapter 24

Bob saw light beaming from the window of Albert's office as he hurried across the dark school parking lot in the chilly predawn of a mid-December Friday. He stopped by the principal's office on a whim and knocked on the closed door, hearing Albert's deep voice call out, "Hold on for just a minute."

Then he caught the muffled sounds of shuffled papers and a desk drawer closing before the door swung open, his lanky boss standing in the door way to greet him with a friendly "Good morning."

"You're here at work even earlier than usual, Robert. Step in and let me offer you a good cup of freshly brewed coffee that Rachel poured into my thermos less than an hour ago. Then you can tell me why you're up and about at this ungodly hour on a cold winter day."

Bob gratefully accepted the steaming cup and settled into the chair across from Albert. "I just stopped by to see you for a couple of minutes before I head over to my classroom and finish grading some papers.

"Truthfully, I was hoping that you might be able to start my day with some good news about the school staying open next fall. Are there any developments you can share?"

Albert scratched his head, thoughtfully considering the request before replying. "I'm willing to tell you what I've learned recently, Bob, but if you're looking for good news, you may regret having asked me. I'll expect you to keep our discussion under your hat until after I've made an announcement to the rest of the faculty and sent a letter home to the parents.

"To get right down to brass tacks, the news from my boss isn't good. The board of supervisors and the school board have decided to close us down at the end of the school year."

Bob set his cup on the desk top and stared at Albert. "We talked about contesting this decision if it came. Can't we now launch a campaign to save the school?"

"I don't want to give this bad news to everyone until after the Christmas holidays. You and I both know that trying to save the school may be a political lost cause, and I'd like for our folks to have a happy holiday before they learn about this."

Bob shook his head in disbelief, standing to leave, commenting, "I still can't believe they're doing this to us."

Abert watched him sympathetically. "I'm sorry to have to tell you this. I can assure you that Superintendent Williams regrets this decision just as much as you and I. But don't forget, the news that the school will definitely be closing mustn't leave this room until an official announcement is made."

Bob made his way to his classroom, trying to focus on the lessons for the day. He managed to keep a smile and project an upbeat attitude during classes throughout the morning and later at wrestling practice.

But much of the time, his mind was miles away, wondering what would happen to the students and faculty members he had grown to care so much about after commencement in the spring.

*****

The bearded, heavy-set man in work clothes and a loose-fitting jacket parked his pickup truck bearing the Tazewell County logo on the side, and walked toward the uniformed guard at the front gate of the furniture factory.

He produced a grimy plastic wallet, pulling out a surprisingly clean and sharp-cornered identification card showing him to be Thomas Smith, Tazewell County Electrical Inspector.

Security guard Marvin Craig took the proffered card, carefully studied the photo to be sure that it matched the visitor's appearance, and returned it with a smile. "What brings you our here today, Mr. Smith? I wasn't told that I would have any visitors coming by this evening"

"I'm here to look at the utility incoming power feed. I want to check the power capacity of the plant substation and get a feel for any upgrades that may be required before the new production line starts up next month. That way I can offer suggestions to the contractors to assure compliance with codes and regulations before I'm back out here to inspect and sign off on their work."

"Look around all you please. The engineers handling the revamp, Mr. Creech and Mr. Lowen, were both here earlier but have left for the day. I'll be sure to tell them that you came by when I see them on Monday."

Marvin turned back to the guard house, and the bearded stranger headed straight for the plant incoming power substation, a concrete pad enclosed by a gated and padlocked tall chain link fence, containing power transformers and switchgear dating back to an earlier era.

His eyes traced out the utility high voltage power lines dropping down from overhead to connect to a circuit breaker inside the substation. Incoming power cables continued from the circuit breaker to the exposed high voltage bushings projecting upward from one end of a large power transformer. Outgoing factory power cables connected to exposed terminals on the other end of the transformer and disappeared in a cable trough running to the factory.

Sighting across the transformer, he could see that the high voltage and low voltage connections were directly in line, only an arm-span apart. He slipped a pair of fence pliers from his pocket, and using a powerful two-hand grip, quickly clipped the chain link wires to create a narrow vertical slit directly aligned like the sights of a rifle with the incoming and outgoing power terminals.

He slipped the fence pliers back into his pocket and entered the factory, continuing down the center aisle, studying the layout of the production line as he approached the final assembly area in the back.

Something caught his eye as he stopped in front of the paint booth: sitting on a pallet directly below a low hanging industrial light fixture was a steel drum boldly lettered Varnish Solvent. With practiced ease, he pried off the lid and shifted it to the side, exposing the volatile contents of the drum.

The self-identified Thomas Smith disappeared from the factory floor, a malevolent ghost in a blandly unthreatening disguise, but he did not drive back in the direction of the Tazewell Courthouse.

Instead he headed a short distance down the highway and pulled off of the pavement to remove the *Tazewell County* magnetic signs attached to the doors of the pickup, proceeding onward after placing them under the front seat in the cab.

A couple of miles further down the road on the outskirts of town, he pulled into the parking lot of a small diner identified by a neon sign that had last blinked during the Truman administration: Tootie's Short-Order Meals and Cold Beer.

The only other vehicle parked in the lot was an old pickup truck, with a man in the driver's seat leaning back, sound asleep. Thomas approached the truck, rapping on the window, seeing a startled look come across the dozing man's stubble covered face as he suddenly awoke.

The man wiped the sleep from his eyes with a grimy hand and quickly climbed out of the truck to follow him inside the diner, where the two found a booth near the back. A buxom peroxide-blonde took their order, returning with a tired smile and two cold Blue Ribbons in long-neck bottles, then disappearing behind the counter.

Thomas spoke to the man across from him for the first time. "Are you ready to follow-through on the deal we made?"

His disheveled companion held the bottle to his lips, taking a long pull that drained half of the contents, and without looking at Thomas, answered helplessly, "I reckon so."

He had spent several sleepless nights thinking about this deal with the devil, and he couldn't see where he had anything left to lose. He had already lost his job, his life savings, his wife and two sons, and any last trace of self respect.

Garner Spellman hunched over the table, head down, knowing that he had hit rock bottom.

He was still sitting in the booth working on a third round when the bearded man rose and walked to the phone booth across the room, closed the door, and placed a call. "Ben, listen to me. Everything is set for tomorrow.

"I'm here now with the man who's going to do the job. He used to work out there, but now's just a drunk on the skids. He talks about wanting to get even with the furniture company for laying him off, and he doesn't seem to mind what's involved.

"I'll give you a call tomorrow from a pay phone down the road when the job's finished, and tell you where to send the money."

Bud Neese smiled as he hung up the phone, thoughtfully stroking his beard. In another two days he would be clean-shaven again, and back home in Wheeling with a well-earned cash payment deposited in one of his many bank accounts.

He was confident that Ben Turner would also be pleased, knowing what good value he had received on his investment. After all, in the dirty little business of arson, industrial sabotage, and insurance fraud, there was no one in the country who could carry his bag.

Chapter 25

Garner Spellman heard his old wind-up clock shatter the morning quiet at 5:00 AM and struggled to reach across the bed, slapping at the button on top to turn off the head-splitting alarm. He had finished a pint of Four Roses only hours before and was not ready to rise and shine at this unnatural hour.

Then he remembered the reason for setting the clock: the night watchman at the factory frequently left for home shortly before his replacement came in to take over plant security duties at six. If he could be on site, ready and waiting when the plant was briefly unguarded, he would have time to perform his assigned work and slip away with no one the wiser.

Garner rolled out of bed in the same grimy clothes he had worn for almost a week, including his laced-up work shoes. He walked to the window and stood silently peering into the darkness, surprised to see fine white flakes blowing against the glass, remembering there had been no prediction of snow on the radio weather report the day before.

But the unexpected snowfall was not unwelcome. Garner knew that it would be one more distraction for the security guard at the factory.

He wasted no time pulling on his heavy jacket, wool knit stocking cap, and gloves, walking from the warm trailer through the gently falling snow to the garage. He reflected on how much better the rough structure looked since OL had painted it on a day that seemed a lifetime ago, back when he had a family and some semblance of self-respect.

Finding those thoughts painful, he pushed them from his mind as he entered the garage, taking two six-foot sections of round wooden dowel and a similar length of copper pipe from the overhead rafters.

The three pieces had been modified to quickly connect end-to-end into a single long pole intended for a very special purpose. Garner carefully wiped each of the three parts with a rag to remove any fingerprints before placing them in the back of his truck. Then he drove away, wipers on, headlights off.

The darkness and falling snow would have made it impossible for most drivers running without lights to have navigated the route from the Spellman trailer to the factory, but Garner knew the roads like the back of his hand. After all, he had worked at the furniture factory since before the war, right up to the time the business had closed and he had been let go.

He recalled those early, happy years, starting when he had convinced Ruby to run off from home and marry him right out of high school. OL had come along only a year later, followed by little Lonnie two years afterward. He knew that his life would never be that good again.

No living creature was to be seen along the road from the time Garner left home until he approached the old manufacturing facility, turning off to park at a secluded tree-lined spot favored by the local teenagers for beer drinking and backseat romance.

The front guard house could easily be seen from his vantage point even in the dim light and steadily falling snow. He checked his watch and observed that the time was now 5:30 a.m., then settled back in his seat, pulling his collar up to meet his stocking cap against the cold.

He did not have to wait long. A short time later, he watched the security guard leave his post and walk to his car, never stopping to lock the front gate before pulling away. Garner waited until the guard had passed him and was out of sight before starting his truck and driving up to the deserted factory gate.

His heart pounded like a hammer as he lifted the three sections of pole from the back of his truck and carried them quickly toward the electrical substation.

Garner did not need to read the bold red sign posted on the chain link fence- *DANGER – HIGH VOLTAGE – KEEP OUT-* in order to know the risks involved in the job he had contracted to perform. One mistake and he would either be electrocuted or burned to death.

But he desperately needed money in order to keep food in the house and buy the liquor that dulled his grief and remorse. His life had little value to him or anyone else now that everything had fallen apart.

Garner quickly assembled the long pole, two sections of wood attached to a length of copper pipe, and located the previously cut opening in the chain link fence aligned with the high and low voltage bushings of the power transformer inside.

He started to say a prayer before pushing the metal tip through the slit, but then stopped, realizing that he was unlikely to receive help from The Almighty for what he was about to attempt.

Using the chain link wire at the bottom of the slit to support the cumbersome pole, he guided it through the fence at an upward angle until the metal end directly spanned the transformer high and low voltage connections below. He turned away and released his grip, feeling the pole swing downward.

Garner had expected a violent reaction, but he was not prepared for the cannon-like report, blinding flash of light, and blast of superheated plasma created by the intense electric arc which flashed across the transformer, vaporizing the copper pipe, sending 4160 volts surging into the factory 480 volt power system.

He didn't smell the smoke pouring from the transformer or notice the scorch marks on the back of his jacket and cap as he ran toward his truck. He never heard the popping sounds of disintegrating light bulbs and fluorescent tubes throughout the factory building, or the booming explosion of a spark-ignited drum of varnish solvent in the back of the factory.

All he could feel as he drove away was relief that he was still alive and in one piece, uninjured except for the deafening ringing in his ears.

He switched on his headlights a half mile down the road, just as an automobile topped the hill approaching him, turning his face away as the other vehicle sped past. From the corner of his eye, he saw that the driver was wearing a dark blue military-style jacket and knew that the daytime security guard heading for the Southern Styles factory was in for a bad start to his day.

Garner reached under the seat to pull out a half empty pint bottle of cheap blended whiskey and took his first drink of the day.

*****

Marv stared through the cracked windshield of his battered Plymouth coupe, watching snowflakes hurling themselves against the glass like a stream of white tracer bullets. He pressed the accelerator further toward the floor, suspecting that his brother Del would come off the night shift early as he had often been doing lately.

He knew that his sister-in-law had taken a job at a nearby dairy farm, requiring her to leave home well before sunup, and the only way Del could stir up any marital excitement was to get home and catch her before she could go out the door.

Marv didn't want to see the plant unguarded for long. Southern Styles was the biggest account for Craig Security, and if anything went wrong causing them to lose that particular client, the Craig family-owned agency would be out of business.

Marv's contemplation of his brother's home life snapped to an end when he saw the lights shining through windows of nearby farmhouses simultaneously snuffed out.

It must be some sort of utility equipment failure, he surmised, hoping against hope that electrical power hadn't gone off at the factory. He didn't need that kind of problem to start his day.

A pickup truck sped past a half mile further down the road, the driver looking straight ahead, a stocking cap pulled low over his forehead. Marv's curiosity was piqued: who would be driving along a slick, snow-covered road at this early hour, normally the realm of early-shift factory crews, dairy farmers, and newspaper carriers?

Marv's hopes that the factory had been spared an electrical power outage were dashed when he came in sight of the building and saw that all lights were off, as though blacked-out for a wartime air-raid drill.

Then he caught sight of light coming from the back of the factory through the high bay windows, and he knew it was not from the emergency lighting system. The flickering light could only be caused by a fire inside, and it looked like a bad one.

He pulled up beside the gate and braked to a hard stop, sending gravel flying, then sprinted from his car into the guard house. The phone was still working despite the loss of electric power, enabling him to hastily make an emergency call to the dispatcher for the fire department. Then he grabbed a flashlight, ran through the factory door, and raced toward the scorching heat.

The fire protection system had triggered, and water was spraying down from overhead sprinklers across the back of the building, but it was not enough to extinguish the flames leaping toward the ceiling from a steel drum on the floor near the paint booth. Smaller fires were springing into life, feeding on the combustible material spreading across the floor.

Marv grabbed a fire extinguisher from the wall, carried it as close to the burning barrel as the intense heat permitted, and emptied it at the base of the flames. He repeated this with a second, then a third canister, knocking down the fires burning on the surrounding floor, but unable to staunch the column of flame from the barrel which had now ignited the roof overhead.

The fire was not the only thing on his mind as he feverishly searched for more fire extinguishers. He wondered how long it would take for the fire crews to arrive, and more importantly, how he would ever be able to explain Craig Security's delay in calling them out.

*****

Bud Neese stood near the top of the old fire tower on a nearby ridge with his binoculars steadied against the splintered timber railing. The falling snow obstructed his vision, but from time to time, the flurries slowed enough for him to make out what was happening on the dimly lit factory grounds less than a half mile away.

He watched a man approach the electric power substation, and minutes later witnessed an intense flash of light followed by an explosive boom that shook his perch. All illumination disappeared from the property in the blink of an eye, momentarily leaving behind pitch-black darkness until a faint, flickering light appeared through windows at the back of the building.

Bud continued to watch as Garner drove off in his truck, and the day-shift security guard arrived, jumping from his car, dashing into the building. Glowing fingers of flame now pushed through the roof, lighting up the snow covered site with an eerie red glow.

Bud knew that the fire would be out of control if given a little more time, and that it was now a foot race between the spreading conflagration inside and the crews of firemen turning out from their homes and piling into trucks in nearby towns.

He realized that the flames should be spreading more quickly, guessing that the factory sprinkler system had automatically triggered, kicking himself for failing to sabotage the emergency water lines.

He stayed near the top of the fire tower, staring through trained binoculars, watching the Stony Ford and Tazewell fire crews arrive, one team dragging fire hoses into the building while the other played streams of water across the roof.

He lingered until the flames were suppressed, and columns of steam and smoke poured from holes in the roof and out through shattered windows, before descending the snow-covered wooden steps leading down to the ground, starting the quarter mile walk back to his car.

Bud knew that the firemen had won the race, saving the building in the nick of time, but that he had accomplished his goal once again. Left behind would be a smoky, water-sodden shell, its roof a scattered heap of blackened matchsticks.

He planned to meet Garner in the early afternoon at a diner in Wytheville, to give him a cash-filled envelope for services rendered, knowing Garner had requested that location because it was up the street from the ABC store where he could load up with a half dozen bottles of booze. Once Garner was back in Stony Ford, he would pull the shades down in his trailer, and no one would see him for a week.

Bud was pleased with himself. The results reinforced his certainty that the Marine Corps had lost one of its most talented tacticians when they had booted him out of the service with a dishonorable discharge. He summarized the results of the operation with two self-congratulatory words: mission accomplished.

Later that day Appalachian Power restored electrical service to area residents, but not to the factory. The lights would remain out until the company owners could decide whether the damaged building should be repaired or if it should just be torn down to the ground.

Chapter 26

Bob drove into the school parking lot on Monday morning, preoccupied with planning for his last week of classes and final wrestling practices before the Christmas holidays.

He did not notice that Becky had parked beside him until she rolled down her window and lightheartedly called out, "Hey, Slater, are you trying to avoid me this morning, or are you just hung-over from some weekend party?"

"Sorry, Miss Thompson, I wasn't trying to ignore you; I didn't see you in the rear view mirror when you drove up. Guess I'm distracted, thinking about everything that I need to get done before the Christmas break."

"Every teacher in the building is in the same boat. I haven't done a single thing to get ready for Christmas, including mailing cards or buying presents. I'm having a hard time getting in the holiday spirit this year, with all of the uncertainty about the school closing."

"Maybe we should talk about something else," Bob suggested. "Have you heard any more news about the big fire Saturday morning?"

"I may have some information that you haven't heard. Art spent the entire day at the factory yesterday, helping to assess the situation. He called last night, saying that a team of investigators from the sheriff's office and the fire department determined every bit of the damage throughout the building resulted from the sabotage of the main power transformer.

"They're convinced that it took a professional to plan the job and pull it off with such expertise. Art said that Sheriff Holt is determined to find the person who did it and bring him in."

"Does Art have any idea what impact this will have on the factory revamp project?"

"He's not sure yet. It's going to take some time to evaluate the cost of repairing the building and all of the damaged equipment. Then it will be up to the owner of the business to decide whether he wants to keep going and fix things up or throw in the towel."

"You must have been on the phone with Art for quite a while," Bob teased. "I bet you two found something enjoyable to talk about after rehashing all of the problems at the factory.

"Did you get into making plans for celebrating the holidays, or talk about what you would like to find under the Christmas tree this year?

"That's none of your cotton-picking business, Slater," Becky laughed. "How did this conversation suddenly veer off into a discussion of my private life?"

"I can see by the way you're acting that I've stumbled onto something," Bob continued, a dog unwilling to let go of a bone.

"In fact, I'm going to ask the rest of the faculty to help me keep an eye on you and find out why you're acting so defensive. I bet that Virginia can help me get to the bottom of this."

"If you put her up to that and she starts to ask whether something's going on between Art and me, I swear that you'll never see the light of day again," Becky warned. "Your body's going to be harder to find than Jimmy Hoffa's." She could hear him laughing all the way down the hall.

*****

Albert summoned Bob over the school intercom just before noon. He found his boss seated at his worn oak desk, still at work while eating lunch, a sandwich in one hand and several papers in the other.

"Shut the door behind you, Slater, and have a seat," Albert invited. "Something came in the mail this morning that I believe you'll find quite interesting." He reached into a mail tray on a nearby cabinet, took out a document, and passed it across the desk to Bob.

Bob noted the bold letterhead, *Virginia High School Sports Hall of Fame*, and quickly began to read the letter. It opened by offering congratulations to the faculty and students of Stony Ford High School for Buck Callison's upcoming posthumous induction into the VHS Sports Hall of Fame.

It went on to say that Portsmouth High School's legendary wrestling coach, Ben Stanford, had also been selected, along with several others whose names Bob did not recognize, and that the induction ceremony was scheduled for a Saturday in late March at the University of Virginia.

The last paragraph produced the surprise: "We are hereby inviting the Stony Ford Eagles to participate in an exhibition match with the Portsmouth Dolphins as part of the induction celebration."

Albert let Bob finish, then spoke. "It appears that in this commonwealth the right hand doesn't communicate with the left. The Virginia High School Hall of Fame is inviting us to a big honorary dog and pony show.

"At the same time the Virginia Department of Education is busily at work shutting our high school and preparing to lock the doors forever. Tell me what you think we should do."

Bob took a deep breath and let it out slowly. "My first reaction is that we ought to tell the VHS Sports Hall of Fame and the Department of Education folks what they can do with this invitation.

"But trying to be rational and do what we both know is the right thing, I see no alternative but to support this honorary award to Buck. I know that it will mean the world to his widow and two daughters. Betty almost had a nervous breakdown when Buck died, and she's just now getting her life back on track."

"My thoughts exactly, Robert. So you're willing to sign up for a final exhibition match with a perennial state wrestling power after the regular season's over?"

"I'd like the give the boys a voice in this decision, if that's OK. I'm confident they'll gladly do anything they can to honor Buck and his family. I'll talk to them at practice this afternoon."

Albert rose to open the door. "Get back to me before the end of the week and let me know."

That afternoon, Bob gathered the team in the gym before practice started and shared the news. Johnny was the first to speak. "I'm all for it. Everyone knows that Portsmouth's the best team in the state.

"But if we decide to wrestle them in an exhibition match, I say we don't just show up and let them put on a performance using us as sparring partners. I say we train for it like it's the biggest match in school history. Let's show them who the Eagles are."

OL chimed in, "I agree with Johnny. All that anyone east of Roanoke can talk about is the Dolphins. We'll have to work our butts off to get ready, or they'll embarrass us, and we can't let that happen in front of our friends and the Callisons. Let's find out how good they are, and what we're made of."

Out of the blue, Pauly Durham asked a question that changed everything. "Coach, is it true that the school will close at the end of the year? My uncle heard someone down at the barber shop say that's what's going to happen."

Bob knew there would be no way to put the horse back in the barn after that. He decided to give the boys straight answers, while still not confirming the rumor that he realized must be spreading around town like wildfire.

"I've heard that, too, Pauly. I've avoided discussing it with you until some official announcement is made, and I'm authorized to talk with you about it. It serves no purpose for us to get worked up until then, so try to put this out of your minds until after the Christmas break. I should be able to tell you what's going on by that time."

Rumors of changes in the wind that will profoundly impact people's lives do not die easily. Bob listened to the boys talking among themselves in the shower room after practice, then slipped away to call the principal's office from a pay phone in the hallway.

"Albert, this is Bob. The news about the school closing has somehow leaked out, and it's all over town. Pauly got the word from his uncle, who was down at the neighborhood barbershop, and now all of the boys on the team know."

"Did you confirm the rumor?"

"No I didn't, because you told me not to. I acknowledged that I had heard the same thing, and I asked the boys not to discuss the school closing until an official announcement is made after the Christmas holidays. But we both know that's all anyone in town will be talking about."

"The timing of this is regrettable," Albert agreed. "I had hoped to avoid the news getting out so soon, knowing in my heart that it would be impossible to keep the lid on something so big. Do you think the team will stay together now?"

"They're a tough bunch of kids with a lot of pride, and they'll stick it out for now. We need to be standing up for them, and not rolling over for a few small-time politicians who plan to sell us out."

"I like your attitude, Robert, and I agree that it's time to take up arms. I assure you that the old rail splitter has already started sharpening his axe."

"You have the entire faculty backing you up," Bob replied. "If you can win this fight and keep the school open, we'll put up a bronze statue of you swinging an axe out in front of the court house."

Chapter 27

"You're telling me that you still can't find even one partial fingerprint?" Sheriff Holt asked, not bothering to conceal his growing frustration.

"No, sir," Junior Deputy Freddie Lester replied apprehensively, looking back into the dark brown eyes of his tall, wiry boss. "We dusted the remains of the pole he used to short out the transformer, and the chain link fence wires where he cut the hole, but both were clean. Whoever did this was wearing gloves or very careful to wipe off everything he touched."

"And there's no way of tracing those remaining pieces of wood pole or scraps of pipe back to the source," Walter said aloud, more as a rhetorical comment to himself than a question for the two men standing beside him. "What more have we learned about Thomas Smith, the phony electrical inspector who was out here nosing around before the fire?"

"We've had a couple of interviews with the security guard, Marvin Craig, who was on duty at that time, and we've got his description of the man," Senior Deputy Stan Carkin quickly answered.

"We showed him mug shots of all the convicted felons from around this area who roughly matched his description, but he was unable to identify any of them. I'm sure the suspect has shaved his beard by now and will have a very different appearance if we're ever able to bring him in for questioning."

"I don't ever want to hear you say 'if' again, son," Walter reprimanded him. "I want you to say 'when' we bring him in, because the person who committed this crime made one hell of a mistake by doing it on my watch and in my jurisdiction.

"He's not going to get away this time without being apprehended, convicted, and serving some hard time. You can take that to the bank.

"This morning I talked Richard Jenkins, a very sharp investigator for the Atlantic Insurance Company. He's been out here looking around, and he shares my opinion that the man we're hunting is as cunning as a fox, possibly a professional arsonist with a military background.

"The way Jenkins sees it, the fire started near the paint booth after volatile fumes from a drum of varnish solvent exploded. He figures that the man lifted the lid off the drum to expose the contents, knowing that the high voltage surge from the shorted transformer would blow up the floodlight overhead together with other lights all over the building.

"It takes a technically savvy person to come up with a scheme that destroys electrical equipment and triggers an explosion at the same time. Jenkins plans to talk to the factory owner and see what else he can find out. He starts to get suspicious anytime there's an insurance claim for damage to an obsolete manufacturing facility."

"Who owns the factory?" Stan asked.

"Roland Hundley's the principal owner and president of Southern Styles Furniture Company. His brother Oliver is the controller for the business. People I've talked with have a high opinion of Roland, but a much more guarded opinion of his brother. I'll be meeting with both of them."

Freddie looked across the factory, watching a team of men bending over an electric motor drive for a large wood lathe, and inquired, "Who are those people working on the other side?"

"The tall one in the white hard hat is Randle Creech, an engineer with Southern Styles, according to the Craig Security guard. The one in the tan windbreaker is a consulting engineer named Lowen who works for some outfit called TUV.

"The other two are electricians. I was told they would be checking out equipment and accessing the damage throughout the factory. The seven of us are the only people authorized to be in here today."

*****

"This motor has a ground same as the last one," the older electrician commented, handing the tester back to his partner. "I'll tag it as defective, and then we can move on down the aisle to the conveyor and check out the next two."

Randle Creech marked the list on his clipboard with the latest result, replying, "So far only one out of five motors is bad. I thought it might be a lot worse, after taking that 4160 volt spike on the 480 volt bus. Undoubtedly, the surge arrestors we installed last year soaked up a lot of the energy."

"Do you think you can find enough spares in your warehouse in Bristol to let us get the line running while these damaged motors are being rewound?" Art inquired. "We need to start pilot production in February if we hope to get this factory into full operation by spring."

"There's a pretty good chance that I can," Randle replied. "All electrical equipment that's pulled out after factory revamps goes into a warehouse in Bristol, and it looks like Thomas Edison's basement. When we're finished here I'll get on the phone with Barney Cabbler, the old-timer who runs the place, and see what he can do for us."

The four men did not break until the sun had dropped to the horizon in the southwest as if roosting for the night on the tip-top of Stony Ridge. Art said goodbye to his coworkers and drove back toward town, squinting against the flashing pickets of intermittent sunlight and shade created by trees standing beside the road.

He saw several cars parked in front of Tootie's, and he knew that at this time of day, happy hour would be in full swing inside. He slowed and watched curiously as an obviously intoxicated derelict was suddenly shoved through the front door and out into the pavement.

The man was barely able to walk, stumbling toward an old pickup truck, trying to step up on the running board and get behind the wheel. Art hesitated only briefly before turning into the parking lot and driving up beside the man.

"Better let me take you home. You're in no condition to be driving."

"I don't need your help," the man barked, his slurred speech contradicting his words. "That woman had no business throwing me out like that. She was happy enough taking my money all afternoon."

"Give me your keys and get in with me," Art persisted, holding the passenger door open, refusing to debate with the man. "Tell me where you live, and I'll take you home. You can come back tomorrow to get your truck after you've sobered up."

The man grudgingly complied, managing to get into the seat beside Art and close the door. "Much obliged," he said in a more subdued voice. "My name's Garner Spellman, and I live up beyond Pine Street on Possum Hill Road."

"Are you any kin to a Stony Ford High student named OL Spellman?" Art inquired, glancing toward his passenger with growing curiosity.

"Yes, sir, he's my only living son. My younger boy, Lonnie, was killed in a car wreck last year." Garner stared down at the floorboard dejectedly, adding in a slow drawl, "I don't think OL or his mother would claim me anymore. These days I'm nothing but a no-account drunk, and now I've gotten mixed up in some bad business they'd never forgive me for."

Art listened closely, realizing that his mission had escalated into something much more complex than simply transporting an intoxicated derelict from a beer joint back to his house. He turned off the engine after they arrived at the Spellman trailer, patiently listening, encouraging Garner to talk.

Garner told Art about the crises in his life, including the loss of his job at the furniture factory and the financial problems that it had created for the family. He sobbed softly as he related the death of Lonnie, his friends, and his coach, in a terrible automobile wreck. Then he opened up about his turn to alcohol to escape his troubles, and the many problems it had caused.

"I've done some bad things in my life, but the worst one of all was striking my wife. She never did anything to deserve me raising my hand to her like I did. Ruby had every right to pack up and move out, and take OL with her.

"I miss both of them more than I can tell you, but I know I don't deserve to ever be around them again. I never thought I'd end up in such a miserable state."

But Garner didn't say any more about the bad business, the thing he had done that his family could never forgive. He could not bring himself to share the ugliest part of his life, even with a stranger he'd never see again.

Art watched Garner stumble into the trailer, kicking the door shut behind him. He knew the man desperately needed help, but he wasn't sure who might be willing to step in and lend a hand.

*****

Bud Neese developed misgivings about Garner Spellman's ability to keep his mouth shut, beginning to make occasional trips back to Tazewell County to keep an eye on him. His earlier visits to Tootie's and casual conversations with the owner gave him reassurance that even when stumbling drunk, Garner had never hinted about his role in the fire at the factory.

But tonight, Bud was highly unsettled after driving by Garner's favorite watering hole. He saw the man bounced from the building, knee-walking drunk, and watched him accept a ride home with a man Bud knew to be involved in revamping the factory.

He stayed well behind as he followed Art and Garner from the beer joint to the Spellman trailer, parking in the shadows to maintain watch during their long conversation. Finally, he saw Garner get out of the car and walk unsteadily into his home, and Art pull away. Bud ducked his head and waited until Art came past and continued out of sight before starting his engine and driving back to the heart of town.

Bud pulled up beside a pay phone on Main Street, placing a call, waiting until he heard Garner pick up the receiver. His voice carried the ominous message of a timberback's dry rattle, cutting through Garner's alcoholic haze.

"Be careful who you hang out with and what you say. Bad things happen to people with big mouths. If you're not worried about your worthless self, think about your wife and boy. You won't get another warning."

Chapter 28

"Are you positive you made out your Christmas list and mailed it to Santa?" Bob teased, throwing his arm around Chris. "You didn't forget to put a stamp on the envelope, did you? You didn't accidentally send it to the South Pole instead of the North Pole? You didn't address the envelope in pig-Latin? Try to remember! This is very important!"

"Coach, how many times do I have to tell you?" Chris replied in an increasingly aggravated tone. "Patty Perry told me last week that there isn't a Santa Claus.

"She got out of bed on Christmas Eve last year and caught her daddy and mama putting candy in her stocking. She said her mama yelled out to her daddy, and he almost jumped out of his skin when she came down the stairs."

He studied Bob closely, adding, "You're just joking with me, aren't you?" Then, in quiet exasperation, "Coach, you can't be serious for even a minute."

"You may as well give up, Bob," Kaye interjected as she entered the room. "Patty spilled the beans about Santa to the entire class. Some of the mothers weren't very happy after she broke the story."

"Well, I, for one, don't care what Patty says," Bob countered. "I'm hanging up my stocking on the fireplace mantel tonight, and I expect Santa to come down the chimney and load me up.

"Unlike Chris, I still believe in Santa Claus. Chris will get lumps of coal in his stocking, and I'll get lots and lots of candy, because this year I've been very, very good."

"I'll be the judge of that, and I'm going to have to study on it for a while," Kaye replied, giving Bob a knowing wink

"Now get on in to the table. I want both of you to enjoy the special dinner I've fixed and then help me get the dishes done so that we don't miss a single minute of *A Christmas Carol* on TV. Time flies, and before you know it, we'll be scooting out the door to the Christmas Eve service."

"Last one to the table is a rotten egg," Bob called out, jostling with Chris as they both jumped up from the sofa and started toward the dining room. Kaye reached out, grabbing Bob's shirt-tail to hold him back, letting Chris run ahead.

"No fair, Kaye," Bob exclaimed. "That's two on one. Why'd you take his side?"

"Because blood's thicker than water," she laughed as she cut in front of him, feeling his affectionate retaliatory swat across her derrière.

The stars were out in force when Bob drove Kaye and Chris to the church for the candlelight service, and the three made their way to a pew. A modest crowd had gathered inside the dimly lit church for the traditional service with the story of the nativity narrated by a young woman and familiar carols sung by the choir and congregation.

The service ended at midnight, and each of the three took a small candle and joined others standing outside in the early morning chill to sing *"Joy to the World."* The carillon chimes in the tower above pealed accompaniment, echoing across the still countryside, announcing to all in town and beyond that Christmas had arrived.

Chris led the way inside the apartment after their return, stopping by the Christmas tree to survey the brightly wrapped presents. "Will you come over in the morning to unwrap the presents with us, Coach?"

"Wouldn't miss it for the world," Bob replied. "I want to be here so we can check our stockings together. I might even be willing to trade you some of my candy for your coal."

Chris picked up a pillow from the sofa to sling at Bob, cheerily calling, "Good night, Coach," as he headed off to bed.

Kaye followed to tuck him in, returning to the living room carrying two glasses of wine, dimming the lights and settling in beside Bob. "Chris thinks the world of you," she said.

"If you promise not to say anything, I'll tell you something sweet. He just told me, 'I wish Coach was my dad.' And he doesn't know that you bought him a new bicycle for Christmas."

"I'm not sure I deserve a wonderful kid like Chris, Kaye, but hopefully someday I will. I don't deserve someone as good as you. That's why there's a big box waiting behind the tree with your name on it."

Kaye kicked off her shoes to draw closer. "We seem to disagree on whether you measure up, Bob. Lucky didn't, but he was a charismatic older guy, and I was a naïve teenager with very poor judgment.

"I'm not sure that I have any right to claim you. But if things go my way, I'm going to spend the rest of my life trying to prove that I do."

Bob set the wine glasses on the table, wrapping Kaye snugly in both arms.

*****

Garner could hear the sound of the carillon chiming at midnight as he walked down Pine Street, stopping long enough to identify the familiar Christmas carol.

He reminisced that *Joy to the World* had been a favorite of Ruby's during earlier, happy days, and that thought caused a lump to form in his throat, reminding him it was time for his medication. He took the half empty bottle of Catawba Red from his coat pocket, removing the cap to take a deep pull.

One bright glimmer of hope had appeared in Garner's bleak life in recent days. A kind stranger name Lowen had given him a ride home from Tootie's, remaining to listen sympathetically to his troubles. Garner had been surprised when Lowen returned the next day to look in on him and bring him a hot meal.

The downside to Lowen's assistance was the anonymous phone call Garner had received after the ride home, obviously from the man who had hired him to sabotage the factory, now threatening to hurt him if he leaked information about the crime.

Garner was frightened for himself, but even more so for the wife and son he had placed in danger. The bearded man knew their names, and in a small town like Stony Ford, he undoubtedly knew exactly where they lived.

Lowen had suggested that he and Garner meet with OL's high school wrestling coach, a man named Slater, whom Lowen believed might serve as an intermediary between Garner and his son. That seemed to be a good place to start if Garner was to ever get his life back on track.

But how could he when he had broken the law, and a stranger was spying to assure his silence? Garner took the bottle from his pocket, ready to take another drink.

The carillon chimes abruptly stopped, and Garner knew the hymn had ended with the beautiful chorus, "And heaven, and heaven, and nature sing."

Then he became aware of a different kind of sound, the noise made by an automobile rapidly accelerating directly toward him, causing him to drop the bottle in alarm.

He flung himself over the bank and down the steep hillside without looking, tumbling over rocks and briars to the bottom of the ravine, lying quietly on the ground, bruised and bloodied.

He remained motionless until he heard the car on the street above him pull away in a shower of loose gravel, then got to his feet, unsure where to go.

As bad as his situation had been before, it had just gotten much worse.

Chapter 29

"Looks like you're having a really bad day," Art called out sympathetically as he entered the empty gym on Monday afternoon, seeing Bob sitting alone on a folding chair. "Did you call off practice?"

"Yeah, I figured I might as well. None of the boys has wrestling on his mind today, and neither do I. Check out a copy of the newspaper, and you'll see that the decision to close the school at the end of the year is the headline.

"All of the students got a letter with the same message from the superintendent to carry home to their parents this afternoon. You could have made a lot of money earlier today selling Kleenex to the girls and even a few of the boys. I haven't seen the kids this upset since they heard about the car wreck last year."

Art pulled up a chair beside Bob, inquiring, "Would it make any difference if the furniture company were to go back into production this spring and start recalling their employees?"

"That would be great news, Art, and it certainly might fit in as part of a plan to save the school, but I've been led to believe that the situation at the factory is hopeless. I heard that the damage to the building and electrical equipment is bad, and I figure that the company will try to write off the facility and its contents as a total loss and collect on the insurance."

"I thought the same thing myself the first time I walked through the shop after the fire. But I'm more optimistic now because Roland Hundley is committed to resuming production here in Tazewell County. He came out to personally look over the factory situation."

"And he isn't ready to throw in the towel even after seeing all of the damage?"

"He asked Randle Creech and me whether we'd stake our jobs on getting the factory up and running by spring if he gave us his full support, and we said yes.

"The next day, a building contractor showed up to start structural repairs. Meanwhile, Randle and I have made good progress in locating and installing replacements for the damaged electrical equipment.

"But the main reason I've come by to talk with you today has nothing to do with the factory situation. It's about OL's father. He needs your help."

Art quickly related the story of his encounter with Garner, starting with the ride home from the beer joint, and leading up to the Christmas morning knock on his door at the motel.

"Garner was cold-sober and as gray as Marley's Ghost when he showed up, scratches on his hands and face, mud from head to foot, telling me that someone had just tried to run him down with a car.

"I let him wash up and gave him clean clothes to put on, but the whole time I was helping him, he refused to explain why someone had tried to hurt him. He said several times that if he were to tell me what he knew, something bad would happen to his wife and OL.

"I couldn't get him to stick around long, but before he left I gave him enough money to live on for a few days. There's no telling where he went afterward."

Bob observed wryly, "'As you have sown, so shall you reap.' Garner beat up his wife, and now he's terrified because someone's after him. It would be easy to feel that he has it coming.

"But he's OL's father, and that makes me want to pitch in and help. If we can find Garner, maybe OL and his mother can talk him into coming clean, even if it means turning himself in and confessing that he's committed a crime."

"We're thinking along the same lines, Bob. Garner may be on the run, but sooner or later he's going to come home. No one can live outdoors for long in this cold winter weather. I bet he would call Ruby if he found a note from her saying that she's willing to talk with him. Do you think you could make that happen?"

"I'm sure I can, but let me talk to OL, and we can go from there. I'll give you a phone call to let you how it goes."

Art headed to Becky's classroom, finding her working at the blackboard with chalk in hand, busily writing the proof for an algebraic theorem. He quietly walked into the room to stand directly behind her, putting his hands over her eyes, whispering, "Guess who?"

Becky chirped in startled surprise, spinning to face him. "You scared me out of ten years of my life. Why in the world did you sneak up on me like that?" There was no opportunity for him to speak at first as she pulled his face down to hers for a long kiss.

"I think you just answered your own question," Art replied. "If you're about through here for the day, I'd like to drive you to Bluefield for dinner."

Becky put the chalk back in the tray, and walked toward the coat closet, laughing, "I'm through."

Later that night, at a table in the Mayflower Restaurant, talking over a bottle of wine, Becky asked, "Do you have any idea how much I'm enjoying being here right now?"

"I hope half as much as I am," Art replied. "But I doubt that's possible."

*****

Oliver Hundley closed his office door before picking up the phone, knowing that his conversation with Ben Turner would not be one he would want his brother to overhear. "I'm alone in the office, now. Go ahead."

Ben's voice carried over the line so loudly that Oliver held the receiver away from his ear. "The lenders are calling the loan. We've got to come up with the money we owe them plus their commission before the end of the month. They aren't going to give us an extension for repayment, and they're sure as hell not going to take any excuses.

"Somehow, they've been tipped off that Southern Styles won't be picking up any land for a factory expansion in Savannah, and they know we have no buyer for any part of the property. This get-rich-quick scheme of yours has come back to bite us, and now we're in serious trouble."

Oliver had no choice but to listen until Ben finished his tirade, but then he shot back angrily, "Calm down now and get it together!

You're as responsible for the land speculation deal as I am. No one said that we won't be able to repay the loan.

"All it means is that I'll have to do some covert accounting to withdraw the company funds that are in a special accrual account. Eventually, we should be able to sell the land, and then I'll transfer the money back to the company with no one ever being the wiser."

Ben sounded relieved, but still not completely certain that the situation was under control. "How long will it take you to liquidate the account and convert it to cash so that you can deliver your part? I'm going to be sweating bullets until we hand it all over."

"I'll have the money ready within a couple of weeks. I have to be cautious about withdrawing large sums of cash to avoid triggering bank accounting alarms, but it can be done with payoffs to the right people. Let me handle it on my end, and you worry about your part."

Oliver hung up the phone with a sinking feeling in his stomach, his show of bravado over. Then he heard Roland call his name.

"Ollie, come in here for a minute. I've got some good news to share. I just found out that that we're going to start turning out the first pieces of early American furniture in the Stony Ford facility before the end of February. I knew you'd be as excited as I am to hear that."

Oliver opened the door, calling out, "Thanks for letting me in on that great news, Rollo. You just made my day," muttering under his breath, "In a pig's eye."

Chapter 30

"I wonder how many people will turn out for the match with Radford tomorrow night," Bob asked, as Kaye returned to the living room.

"I bet we can set up a few folding chairs in the gym, and won't even need to pull out the bleachers. Are you and Chris planning to be there?"

Kaye kicked off her shoes and settled down on the sofa beside him, picking up her new textbook, *Basic Human Anatomy and Physiology,* from the coffee table. "You know that I'll make every effort to be there, honey.

"I happen to think you're underestimating the turnout. Eagle boosters aren't going to abandon the team just because they've heard what's in store for the school. You may be surprised to see an even bigger turnout than usual."

"I hope you're right," Bob replied. "You've always had a positive attitude, and that's why things you take on turn out well. Judging by that textbook, you're going to need it. By the way, how did your classes go this morning?"

"Quite well, thanks," Kaye replied, apologetically stifling a yawn. "The classes plus the commute to Bluefield are time consuming, but Billy's adjusted my hours to fit the new schedule. My biggest challenge now is figuring out how I can keep going on six hours of sleep."

"You're really sure you want to take on this load for the next couple of years? It's going to be a grind."

"I'm not having any second thoughts yet, but maybe that's because reality and sleep deprivation haven't settled in. I still have a good feeling that I'm doing the right thing, finally getting my life on track."

Kaye opened the textbook, forcing herself to focus on the microscopic text, while Bob thumbed through the latest issue of *National Geographic*. He glanced at her from time to time, watching her battle to hold her eyes open, finally seeing her head droop forward, the book slipping from her hand.

He quietly stood and gently lifted her into a reclining position on the sofa, slipping a pillow under her head and covering her with a throw. He kissed her on the forehead and turned off the lamp, leaving her sleeping, locking the door behind him. She never heard him whisper, "Sleep well, sweetheart. You have no idea how proud I am of you."

*****

Stony Ford fans showed up by the dozen on Friday evening, just as Kaye had predicted, noisily filing into the gym, pouring into the same bleacher seats they filled for every home match. Among the die-hards were the Kowalski brothers, Randy and Nick, taking up their positions in the bleachers at dead center, exactly five rows up.

A caravan of automobiles loaded with Radford fans drove into the school parking lot shortly before the match started, quickly providing a loud and proud Wildcat presence on the visitors' side of the gym.

The perky Eagle cheerleaders, including Julie Ellison, began to pump up the home crowd with the familiar school cheers, performed with flying ponytails and flashing brown and white saddle shoes, to the noisy beat of a bass drum.

The home team locker room was far quieter than the gym, but just as emotionally charged, each boy dealing in his own way with the restless butterflies in his stomach.

Johnny found this a perfect time for a motivational pep talk. "You recall what happened when we wrestled the Wildcats in Radford two years ago? You remember that bunch of kids who were laying for us on the overpass right outside of town after the match?

"They had a trash can full of snowballs they'd stored in a freezer, and when we drove under the overpass, they bombarded us, knocking dents in our friends' cars. One of those snowballs cracked the rear window of Coach Callison's new Ford. Tonight we pay them back for that stunt. Let's win this one for Coach Callie."

Pauly was feeling the pressure when he took the mat for the opener, facing a dark haired Italian boy who looked like a scaled down Steve Reeves stepping off the *Hercules* movie set.

Any psychological advantage for the muscular Wildcat evaporated when a Radford student yelled out in a voice that reverberated throughout the gym, "Come on, Nick, pin that runt."

One minute and thirty seven-seconds later, Pauly rolled the movie star onto his back with his arm trapped beneath him, and it was all over.

Pauly's first period pin was the start of a Stony Ford jail break, the Eagles rolling up win after win. The rout continued without let up through the progression of weight classes until the very end, when it was finally time for the big boys to have it out in the unlimited weight bracket.

Radford fans were screaming for a win to head off a shutout when Tank Atkins lumbered onto the mat to take on Stony Ford's undersized heavyweight. Tank was the size of a college football lineman, standing like Goliath to face David.

As OL heard the referee blow his whistle to start the first period, he quickly closed with the Radford heavyweight at the center of the mat, hearing the home town crowd on its feet, screaming encouragement.

He dove at Atkins' legs in an attempted takedown, but the larger boy sprawled on top of him, forcing him to struggle back to his feet as though crawling out from under a bus, winded and wiser. He knew it would be a battle of his speed and skill against Tank's size and strength, and the scales were tilted against him.

OL glanced at the scoreboard as the final period started, gasping for breath, seeing he was behind on points. He knew that his only chance for a win was to score a pin, and he threw caution to the wind, attacking recklessly, putting a headlock on Atkins in a desperate attempt to turn his opponent and take him to the mat on his back.

The Radford heavyweight got underneath him, locking his arms around OL's chest in a crushing bear hug, lifting him into the air before smashing him down on the mat, his head whipping violently upon impact.

OL rolled onto his back, motionless, the home team cheering section exploding with the sound of boos and cat-calls. The referee blew his whistle to stop the match and signal a penalty against the Radford boy for an illegal slam.

OL was out cold. Bob and Art rushed over and knelt beside him, trying to make him respond. "Are you all right? Can you understand us?" Bob implored him.

They were overcome with relief when his eyes fluttered open to stare up at them, replying weakly, "I'm OK, but I feel woozy. Give me a minute to shake it off, and I'll be ready to go again."

"Not a chance," Bob replied, Art nodding in agreement. "You're through. I want to get Doc Woolwine to take a look at you in the locker room as soon as we can find him."

The referee disqualified Tank for the illegal slam, awarding the match to OL, giving the Eagles their first shutout in years. The gym rocked after the referee's ruling, the home town bleachers emptying as the spectators streamed out on the floor in congratulate the team.

An ecstatic group of fans was still milling around when Nick and Randy passed, and Randy called out to Bob, "You should have let Spellman keep going, Slater. He would have whipped that fat boy's butt."

He would have said more if Nick hadn't cut him off. "Shut up, Randy. Slater did the right thing. The kid's got a concussion."

Embarrassed by his brother's rebuke, Randy walked away without another word, carried along in a tide of delirious Eagles.

Becky, Kaye, Chris, and Julie were anxiously waiting when Art emerged from the locker room.

"How's OL?" Julie asked, on the verge of tears.

"Doc Woolwine says he's going to be all right, but he doesn't want OL to practice for a couple of weeks. He took a hard shot to the head, and it's fortunate that he doesn't have any permanent injury.

"I've been around the sport for a few years, and I've seen some pretty serious injuries during that time. You never get used to seeing a kid get hurt."

"Will OL be coming out soon?"

"Wild horses couldn't keep him from getting out here to see you. Coach Slater and I had to hold him down until the doc arrived."

OL cautiously approached from the locker room, dressed in street clothes, and Julie was off like a shot to greet him. "How bad does it hurt?" she asked.

"Not too bad now, but I still have a headache," OL replied, gingerly running his hand over his rusty crew cut. "That was the hardest shot I've taken since two summers ago when I went off the high dive board and hit the bottom of the pool."

"I'll never forget the day that happened," Julie said, choking up. "I was the first one who got to you when you came up. Promise me you'll never put me through anything like this again."

Chapter 31

"I need to talk with you for a few minutes, Ollie," Roland told his brother as the two met in the hallway on Thursday morning. "I'm not comfortable with the oversight of our accounting department, and I think it's time to bring in an independent accounting team to conduct an audit of our company records."

Oliver halted as if he had walked head-on into a steel post, then recovered his composure and replied, "That sounds like a hell of a waste of company money, Rollo. Why would we want to do something like that? We're not having any problems with the IRS. I'm the company controller, and if we had any financial problems, I'd be the first one to tell you."

"I realize that, but a privately owned company with a small accounting staff can't be too careful. It's not unheard of to find that a long-service employee in a responsible position has abused his authority. I'd like to have some assurance that everything is financially sound, and you only get that from an independent audit."

Oliver realized that his brother's decision was not on the table for debate, and he broke off the discussion. "I think you're making a big mistake, Rollo, but I can see that you've made your mind up and that there's no point in debating this any further. I have a few things to take care of. I'll see you at lunch."

Oliver closed his office door, his stomach tied in knots, muttering nervously, "What can I do? What in the world can I do now? I can't dip into the accrual account, and there's no other source for that kind of money." Finally, he summoned enough nerve to make the dreaded phone call.

"Ben, things have just gone to hell in a hand-basket here, and I didn't see it coming. I'm in a bind, and can't raise my part of the repayment. I'll tell you what's happened if you'll just give me a minute."

Oliver had expected an explosive tirade from his partner, but Turner's flat, emotionless reply was much more unsettling, like the ominous growl of a chained bulldog.

"So you're going renege on repaying your half of the loan, and you're planning to hang me out to dry alongside you? It's not going to work, Ollie, and I'll tell you why. I'm going to pay off my part of the loan and then clear out.

"The people who bankrolled us may try to find me, but you're the one they'll really want to get their hands on. Are you sure you don't want to rethink this and go to your brother for the money? There's a lot worse things that could happen to you than being disgraced and fired."

"I can't go back to my brother this time. He'd throw me out. I got burned investing borrowed money in a business venture a few years back, and Rollo covered my losses. He swore he'd never do it again. I'm willing to sign over my part of the Savannah property to you, and you can throw that in with your payoff. Do you think they'd settle for a deal like that?"

"Hell no, they won't. You're out of your mind, Ollie. You expect me to pay up what I owe, plus my share of the property, while you walk away only giving up half ownership of some real estate which isn't worth damn under the present circumstances.

"Do you really think they're going to take that deal and let us off? You're out of your mind. I suggest that you either get back to me with a plan that makes sense, or start packing your bag for South America."

*****

Albert joined his staff in the faculty lounge after classes were dismissed on Friday afternoon, beginning without fanfare. "I'm here today with a petition protesting the closing of our school, with the intent of circulating it to every citizen in town and the surrounding county.

"I reviewed it today with Superintendent Williams, and I want you to know that he strongly opposes it. I cannot help but believe that his position may be influenced by the fact that his job, unlike ours, is not in jeopardy.

"I don't know what repercussions this may cause, and I can't promise that I'll be able to protect the jobs of those who stand with me, so the door is open for anyone to leave now."

Virgil Akers didn't wait for permission to speak "What can they do to us, Albert? Fire all of us now instead of waiting to fire us in May? Who'd finish teaching our students for the rest of the school year? Tell Superintendent Williams that if he doesn't like our petition, he can lump it."

Scattered applause filled the room after Virgil finished. Virginia chimed in, "Some of us may be jeopardizing our chances of being reassigned to teach in Bluefield next fall, but speaking for myself,

I'm ready to put my John Hancock on the petition right now, and then carry it door to door all over town."

"Any further discussion?" Albert inquired. "If not, I'd like a show of hands from all in favor of taking action." Every hand in the room shot up.

"Fine, then it's a unanimous decision that we move forward. Let's get out there and make a stand for Stony Ford High."

Bob caught up with Becky on their way out, commenting wryly, "Now we know exactly how that Confederate artillery crew felt after firing the first cannon ball at Fort Sumter."

Becky agreed, "This petition is definitely a declaration of war."

*****

Mayor Steve Mullins called the town council to order on Friday evening, causing Joey Tucker, Royce Smith, Leon Carper, and Tony Gilbert to break off their discussion of the Baltimore Colts win over the New York Giants.

"We got a good price from the contractor for demolishing the condemned building on Main Street," he started. "The insurance settlement more than covered the cost, so that matter's closed. By the way, Holton Akers is undergoing rehabilitation treatment now, hoping to go back to work in a few months.

" Joey, we're all anxious to hear where we stand now in getting the Department of Transportation to relocate Main Street further away from the creek."

Joey glanced at his friends around the table. "We've talked before about this being a political matter, and how our lack of influence in Richmond makes it hard for us to fund projects in southwest

Virginia. It's time to change our strategy of council members making phone calls and traveling to Richmond to buttonhole delegates.

"Instead, we should be getting help from area businesses with influential lobbyists in Richmond, companies making big contributions to the politicians.

"One of the most influential ones is headquartered right here in town. That's K&K Construction Company, the Kowalski family business. They've built roads from Roanoke to Bristol."

"You mean we should ask for help from Nick and Randy?" Royce inquired. "I can't think of a civic improvement project in Stony Ford history that they've ever hit a lick on."

"This is different," Joey replied. 'This time their dog is in the fight. If Virginia 161 relocation is funded, K&K Construction stands to get a big highway building contract. I know Nick is ready to jump in and go after it. I've already talked to him."

"Well, I'll be darned," Steve rejoined. "I don't think we need to spend any more time on this tonight. Let's get back together in a couple of weeks, and Joey can fill us in on how things are going. We can throw our weight behind the bill to relocate Route 161 if it makes it through committee and comes up for a vote in the legislature. "

"I guess I'm still a doubting Thomas," Royce concluded. "I never figured to live long enough to see those Kowalski brothers do one damn thing for this town."

*****

Bob was surprised by a round of applause when he entered a crowded Turner's Café on Saturday morning. Billy left the counter to extend a hand and a warm smile.

"Great job, Coach. You and the boys really did a number on those Wildcats last night."

Billy led him to a table, continuing, "I remember challenging you to step up and get the wrestling team going again, and darned if you haven't done it. Nobody was expecting the Eagles to come back this season and pitch a shutout. That's all anyone is talking about. You'd think the high school had won the Super Bowl."

"Thanks for the kind words, Billy, but you know very well that I didn't 'step up' and take the coaching job. Albert hung it on me as a condition of employment. As for turning the boys into winners, give Art all of the credit. He's coached the team to an entirely new level. I could never have taken them there."

"Baloney, Slater. All of us know that none of this would have happened without you."

Kaye joined the conversation, throwing her arms around Bob's neck in a hug. "Billy's right about you deserving credit for bringing the team back. But don't ever change. That's what made me set my sights on you the first time you came through the door."

Chapter 32

"We've collected a lot of signatures in the past two weeks," Becky commented to Virginia, as they rang another doorbell. "We have copies circulating all over town, and so far, not a single household has refused to sign."

"And why should they?" Virginia asked. "If you close the high school, Stony Ford will go the way of Bigler's Mill right after Camp Peary was built during the war. I think the politicians running the county government are fools."

"It's a crying shame to be going through this now," Becky commiserated. "Artie told me that a dozen more workers are being recalled at the furniture factory, and twice that many will be needed by the end of February. He thinks employment will keep growing."

"You talk about Art a lot. Are you and he getting serious?" Virginia inquired, glancing curiously at Becky. "Not that it's any of my business. I never get into other people's business."

"Virginia, you make a living getting into other people's business," Becky laughed, playfully poking her friend. "But that's just part of your personality, and I wouldn't have you change for the world.

"To answer to your question, I'd have to say, yeah, I believe so. I don't know where our friendship is heading, but I know that neither of us wants it to end."

"I've seen you two hanging out together- I already knew what you were going to say. Where's he tonight?"

"Kaye asked him if he would come over and give her some help with emergency first aid techniques for one of her nursing classes. By the way, Kaye has collected more signatures at the cafe than you and I have the entire time we've been walking all over these boondocks."

"The deadline for returning the petitions to Principal Carter is tomorrow afternoon, right?"

"Yep. We'd better step it off now. We have two more streets to canvass before we can call it a day."

*****

Mid-morning, the phone on Albert's desk rang, and answering, he heard the school secretary inform him that his boss was on the other line. She gave him a quick warning before transferring the call. "Superintendent Williams sounds like he's all business."

"Hello, Sanford," Albert said cheerily. Then his boss spoke, and Albert knew that his secretary had read him correctly.

"Hello, Albert. I'm not sure it's starting out to be a very good day, at least not from where I sit. I just got off the phone with Marcus Sloan, the new chairman of the school board.

"He wanted to talk about a petition that's being circulated, apparently by members of your faculty, opposing the school board's decision to close the school. Well, I can tell you right now, Marcus is pretty hot under the collar, and so are the other board members.

"I told you when the decision was made that I would save as many jobs as I could, and try to get most of your youngest faculty members transferred to Bluefield High.

"No one wanted to close your school, but it made business sense to close the oldest and smallest one in the county and bus the displaced students to Bluefield, where there's plenty of space for them.

"Your staff's actions really upset the apple cart. The school board and the supervisors consider it a direct challenge to their authority, an act of insubordination. I don't think I have to remind you that I report to the board, and you in turn report to me.

"So as you can see, there could be a lot of jobs in jeopardy around here, and it's not likely to end well for any of us. I have to ask you, Albert, exactly what part did you play in getting this started?"

Albert bore a faint physical resemblance to Abraham Lincoln, but his philosophy and modus operandi was pure Harry Truman: "The buck stops here." His Silver Star and Purple Heart from WWII proved that he did not lack for courage under fire.

Albert was unafraid to swing the Great Rail-splitter's axe when the situation demanded, and Sanford was taken aback when his normally soft-spoken principal came back at him forcefully.

"I take full responsibility for the petition, Sanford. I initiated it, I directed my faculty to circulate it, and I stand four-square behind it, with apologies to no one. The decision to close Stony Ford High was poorly reasoned and dead wrong.

"This school operates efficiently and does a damn fine job of educating its students. I know that costs have to be cut to balance the county budget, but this is the wrong place to start.

"Closing the high school will destroy our town. A business won't locate where there's no high school. And when the town dies, the tax revenue to the county follows.

"The school board and the board of supervisors think that opposition to their decision is insubordination? Then they should consider me to be the leader of this defiance."

Sanford backed away from a direct confrontation with his principal. "Albert, I've always liked and respected you, but this time you've put yourself and your faculty in a situation where I cannot offer protection. Would you be willing to back off and kill the petition?"

"I'm sorry if my actions jeopardize our friendship, Sanford, but the answer is 'no.' Either the administrators rescind their decision to close Stony Ford High, or you can terminate my employment with the school system. There's no place for me in Bluefield."

"What do you plan to do with your petition?"

"I'm going to drive to Richmond with the town council and personally hand it to the governor. And if he'll give me time, I'll tell him why this would be the worst thing that ever happened to Stony Ford."

Chapter 33

"I knew we'd be late getting home, but wasn't the play worth it?" Becky asked, slipping closer to Art as they drove from Abingdon back toward Stony Ford.

"Getting to watch *Cat On a Hot Tin Roof* with you in the Barter Theater tonight is something I'll never forget."

Becky playfully affected a theatrical voice, reciting one of Maggie's lines. "You know what I feel like? I feel all the time like a cat on a hot tin roof."

Art came in on cue with a low, carrying imitation of Brick, "Then jump off the roof, Maggie. Jump off it."

By the time they reached Becky's apartment, the two had relived their favorite scenes, and playfully improvised absurd new ones never dreamed of by Tennessee Williams. Art walked beside her to the door, and held her in a long kiss before reluctantly returning to his car.

Back at the motel, he glanced at his watch, noting that it was 1:00 a.m. on the first day of February. He was searching in his pocket for the room key when a man in dark clothes stepped out from the shadows and started toward him. Art took a defensive stance, calling out, "Stop right there. Don't come any closer."

"I don't mean to do you any harm, Mr. Lowen. It's me, Garner Spellman. I only want to talk to you somewhere private where nobody can overhear me."

Garner followed Art into his room, pulling the door shut behind him, and spoke dispiritedly. "I can't run and hide any more, Mr. Lowen.

"I'm scared of the man who's after me, and I can't keep looking back over my shoulder wondering if he's there. I'm afraid I'll never be with my family again. I need to clear my conscience and start trying to make things right, and you're the only one who gives a damn about me."

Garner filled an ashtray with nervously stubbed out cigarettes as he told his miserable life story, breaking down as he reached the most recent chapter. He needed a few minutes to regain his composure before he could reveal the worst part, how he had sold any last trace of human decency to a stranger for a pittance, sabotaging the furniture factory to fulfill a criminal contract.

"I'm ready to turn myself in to the law. All I'm asking is that you break the news to my family however you see fit, and tell Ruby and OL I'm sorry for all the hurt I've brought them."

Art listened quietly, without contempt, to the ugly story. He waited until Garner finished, then replied, "I'm ready to help, and if you'd like, I'll go with you to the sheriff's office.

"I have a friend named Bob Slater, who's OL's teacher and coach, and I'll ask him to break the news to your family. I believe that your wife and son will stand by you. Family bonds are strong."

Garner dug out a pack of cigarettes from his shirt pocket, then reconsidered his need for a smoke, tossing them in the trash can. "I'd like to go home now to clean up and get some sleep, Mr. Lowen. I want to turn myself in on Monday morning, if you're willing to take me."

"Are you sure that you'll be safe until then, Garner? Does the man who hired you think you could identify him? You could be in real danger if he does."

"I won't turn on the lights when I get home tonight, so no one will know I'm there.

"The man warned me about talking to anyone, but he probably thinks I can't identify him. I wouldn't be able to pick him out of a line-up if he shaved off his beard.

"But I spotted something that he doesn't know. He's got a tattoo on the back of his right hand, 'Semper Fi'. I think he's an ex-marine."

*****

Garner eased his key into the lock, quietly opened the door, and slipped inside his home without turning on a light, glancing back over his shoulder to be sure no one was watching.

He cautiously entered the kitchen with eyes now accustomed to the faint light, opening the small metal door to a fuse panel to pull out the main power fuse block and kill all electricity. If anyone forced entry into the trailer, they would have to hunt him down in the dark.

Garner cleaned up in the bathroom and returned to the kitchen, making himself a bread and butter sandwich, washing it down with a glass of water. He felt his way along the ink-black hallway to the bedroom, kicking off his shoes before sprawling across the bare mattress on his back, still dressed in his street clothes, snoring as soon as his head hit the pillow.

Garner awoke hours later to the faint creaking sound of the front door slowly opening, followed by the click of a switch but with no resultant light from the living room, feeling the hair on the back of his neck stand on end. An intruder was inside the dark house.

He sat up on the bed, trying to prevent the squeaking of bedsprings, reaching into the drawer of the bedside table for his 9mm Lugar, always loaded and ready for protection.

Garner's emotions swelled from fear to terror as his hand searched the now-empty drawer. The pistol which he kept there was gone. All he could do now was hide.

He picked up his shoes and crept into the closet, closing the door behind him, working his way back into the corner, crouching silently out of sight behind a row of Ruby's dresses. A feeling of hopeless vulnerability overwhelmed him, a quail hiding in poor concealment from a predator.

He did not have to wait long for the hunter. Faint illumination found its way beneath the closet door, dimly playing across the floor as the intruder continued to silently search the bedroom for him in a lethal game of hide and seek.

Garner held his breath when the door creaked open, and a gloved hand thrust a flashlight inside. The focused beam relentlessly searched from wall to wall, Garner's only concealment a few thin layers of fabric. Then the light moved away, and he slowly exhaled, breathing again.

Garner stayed in the closet for what seemed an eternity before fearfully venturing out, finding that he was once more alone in the dark. He finally gathered the courage to lie down again, but with eyes wide open, staring at the ceiling, attuned to any faint sound.

He did not feel safe until the sun came up on Monday morning, when cautiously checking from a front window, he saw a familiar car arrive.

Garner had expected Art Lowen, but as he watched in surprise, four passengers emerged from the car. He would soon be introduced to two men whom he had never met, Bob Slater, and Clint Lorden, the new lawyer in town.

But Garner's eyes could only focus on two faces, his wife and son's. He was crying like a child as he ran toward Ruby and OL, wrapping both of them in his arms.

Sheriff Holt interrogated Garner later that morning at the courthouse, with Clint acting as his defense attorney. Garner made a full confession of his role in the factory arson and was booked for malicious destruction of property and endangerment of lives.

The Spellman family and friends were able to raise his bail, and Garner was released under the protective custody of the sheriff's department in the afternoon.

Sheriff Holt struggled to conceal his disgust. "You've got a hell of a good family to take you back after what you've put them through. I'm surprised they wouldn't let a low-down bum like you sit in jail and think about what you've done until you're tried."

Chapter 34

"Chris, hurry up and get in here to eat your breakfast. You don't want to be late for school this morning of all mornings. Remember to take your cardboard firehouse for show and tell."

Kaye had been up since five o'clock, doing the laundry, packing Chris's lunch, cleaning the apartment, and looking over her notes for the late morning nursing class. She had managed all of that while preparing to dash out the door and work the breakfast shift at the cafe.

Helen would see that Chris got off to school safely, and on time, and to Kaye, with her overwhelming schedule, that was a godsend.

She arrived at work, early as always, getting a warm greeting from her boss. Billy had the coffee ready, handing her a steaming mug while she was still hanging up her coat.

"Kaye, you've got to find a way to slow down," Billy commented sympathetically. "I'd swear that you haven't had a wink of sleep since you left here on the run yesterday afternoon, looking at you right now. Those classes are going to put you in the ground."

"I'm fine, Billy," Kaye reassured him, already busily preparing for hungry customers to arrive. "As long as there's caffeine in this world, I can keep going. But if it ever runs out, or the government starts rationing it, you won't be able to get me out of hibernation until spring."

The breakfast crowd was bigger than usual, but by mid-morning, business had slowed, and Kaye was on her way to class, driving down Main Street toward Bluefield. She had noticed earlier that there were a few slick patches in the road where snow had melted and run across the pavement, refreezing into clear ice during the cold early morning hours. She said to herself, "Watch out, girl. Today's Friday the thirteenth."

There wasn't a lot of traffic, but Kaye noticed that the few drivers sharing the streets with her were in a hurry, pushing the speed limit as if running late. She was approaching the town limits when she looked toward an intersection ahead and saw a light colored sedan skid through a stop sign and into the main thoroughfare, directly into oncoming traffic.

A speeding trucker hit his brakes and steered his flatbed toward the side of the road, but he could not avoid slamming into the automobile broadside just behind the driver's seat, sending it cart wheeling down the road to finally rest upside down on the pavement.

Kaye pulled off the shoulder and ran toward the accident scene. Two men had gotten out of the truck and were standing beside the car, gasoline leaking from a ruptured tank and pooling on the asphalt.

Another car pulled up, and a middle-aged woman called out, "What can I do to help?"

Kaye looked into the twisted wreckage to see an unconscious young woman inside lying on the car roof. "Run to the service station and ask the man to phone for the lifesaving crew and a sheriff's deputy," she called out.

She turned back to the men as the woman drove away, asking "Have you shut off the ignition? There's a lot of gasoline leaking out."

One of them quickly reached inside through a broken widow to turn off the switch and retrieve the key. His friend spoke out, suggesting, "Let's see if you and I can pry the door open and get her out."

"Don't do that!" Kaye exclaimed. "She may have a spinal injury-she could be paralyzed if she's not moved carefully."

"What should we do?" the other man asked, looking to Kaye for direction.

"I'll crawl through the window and see if I can give her first aid until the lifesaving crew gets here. You two flag down traffic and make sure no runs into us."

Kaye managed to squeeze inside the car, ignoring the pain when she gashed her arm on a protruding shard of glass. She first checked for pulse and respiration, finding heart and lungs to be functioning, then looked for signs of life-threatening trauma, relieved to see only superficial bleeding from cuts and abrasions.

Kaye was concerned about the unnatural alignment of the woman's body but afraid to do more than support her in that position. The woman made a low, moaning sound, and Kaye shifted, gently cradling her head.

That was when Kaye recognized who she was holding. Lying in her arms, bruised and battered, was Francine Tanner, daughter of the woman who had scorned her as white trash since her pregnancy was fodder for town gossips.

Kaye realized it no longer mattered; she only wanted to save the young woman's life. She was more surprised when Francine suddenly opened her eyes to stare at her in recognition.

"You must try not to move," Kaye softly cautioned her. "You've been in an accident. The life saving crew is on the way here now to take you to the hospital so that doctors can take care of you."

Francine responded, blinking both eyes to signal that she understood.

Deputy Stan Carkin arrived minutes ahead of the ambulance. Kaye was inside the car, continuing to stabilize Francine's head and neck as she was carefully lifted out through the now-open door, transferred to a stretcher, then driven away in a high speed run to the hospital.

She was working her way back out of the car when Stan alerted her, "Ma'am, you're bleeding worse than that other woman. You need to get to a doctor right away and have that gash stitched up."

Kaye slowed the bleeding from her arm using a scarf as a makeshift bandage before driving to Dr. Woolwine's office. He quickly took her into an examining room, administered Novocain, and sutured her cut, giving her a report that he had just received on Francine.

"The orthopedic surgeon told me that she suffered multiple cervical fractures and a concussion, but the prognosis is good. Francine should make a full recovery without any permanent disability.

"Not bad work on your part for a medical neophyte, Miss Davidson," Dr. Woolwine added.

"The Tanners have been my patients for years. I intend to tell Mrs. Tanner that she owes you a great debt of gratitude for what you did for Francine today."

Chapter 35

"It looks like we're finally getting a break!" Deputy Carkin exclaimed to his boss. "I just got a phone call- Garner Spellman's pistol has turned up in a pawn shop in Grundy.

"The clerk can give us a description of the man who brought it in, but he told me we won't be lifting any finger prints, since the man handed it to him wrapped in an oily piece of flannel. The shop paid him top dollar, and the owner's pretty unhappy that I'm confiscating it."

"I'll send the artist along with you who's helped us out in the past," Sheriff Walter Holt replied, quickly taking charge. "I want you to bring back a good sketch of our man.

"He's playing a game of cat and mouse with us. He doesn't need the fifty bucks he got for that gun. He just wants to tweak our tails a little. I don't think he'd be afraid to come back here again and watch us good old boys bumble around trying to catch him. But underestimating us is going to be the biggest mistake he ever made."

The sheriff pushed open Tootie's dirt streaked door an hour later, finding Tootie Harker busily wiping off the bar and cleaning glasses before the regulars began to drift in for the day. "How you doing, darlin'?" he inquired.

"Just fine, good lookin,'" she replied, glancing up. "What brings the law in here today? I haven't had the first fist-fight break out yet. How about having a cold draft on the house while you're standing around?"

"I'm going to turn down that kind offer, Tootie. I'm in uniform, and it's a little early in the day for me to start bending the elbow. I'd like to ask you if you've seen a stranger hanging out in here in the past few months. He may have been talking to one of your regulars, Garner Spellman."

"Poor ol' Garner," Tootie mused mournfully. "I hear you arrested him for starting all that trouble out at the furniture factory. He sure went downhill fast in the past few years.

"I recall when Garner used to come by long enough to have a cold beer after work and then go on home to his family. I never thought he'd end up becoming the town drunk."

She paused to clear a couple of empty liquor bottle from the shelf behind her. "Yeah, there was a guy with a beard who dropped in here from time to time. I might have seen him sitting with Garner once or twice, but I can't be sure.

"One thing stuck in my mind. The guy had some kind of tattoo on his hand that he kept turned away so you couldn't see it. I was never able to make out what it was."

"Did he ever strike up a conversation with you?"

"Can't say if he did or didn't. All the men want to chat it up with the pretty blond bartender." Tootie giggled at her own joke, and even Walter had to smile.

"I'm going to send my deputy over later today to talk to you. I'll probably send along a sketch artist, too. If that man should ever come back here, I want you to give me a call, and try to keep him around as long as you can, using all your girlish charms."

"For you, hon, I just might take him in the back room and keep him occupied all afternoon. He'd probably want to stay around for the rest of the week after that." Tootie was still laughing as Sheriff Holt went out the door.

*****

Oliver Hundley apprehensively knocked on the door of his brother's office on Saturday afternoon, then gently opened it. "Rollo, may I come in and speak with you for a minute?"

Roland invited him in, and Oliver took a deep breath, stepping inside to take a seat across from his brother, speaking in a voice shaking with emotion. "Rollo, I'm in bad trouble, and you're the only one I can turn to."

He laid out the story of his get-rich-quick land speculation scheme with Ben Turner. His voice broke when he described how the loan had been called, and despite mortgaging his home and cashing in his life savings, he was still short of funds to pay off his half of the note.

"The lender won't give us an extension. A couple of thugs stopped Ben in his driveway yesterday and shoved him around right in front of his family. He fears for his life."

Roland narrowed his eyes and stared at his brother with the hint of a sardonic smile. "How many times before have you gotten yourself into a financial bind because of some hare-brained scheme, Ollie?

"I believe it happened for the first time when our parents were putting you through school, and a second time a few years ago when you speculated on some land in Texas that was supposed to be sitting on an oil deposit."

Oliver dropped his head and hesitated a few seconds before speaking. "I know that I've made mistakes and had to come to you for help before, Rollo. I have a weakness for gambling on big returns on business deals. But I'm in more serious trouble now than I've ever been in before."

"I need to know something, Ollie, before we go any further. Does your involvement in this debacle have anything to do with the damage someone caused at our Stony Ford factory?"

Oliver had told the unvarnished truth until this point, but he could not bear to admit his role as a major conspirator in the sabotage of the family business. "No, Rollo," he lied. "I don't know any more about that fire than you."

"Then I'm going to bail you out again, Ollie, but only because you're my brother. However, if I ever find out you've lied to me, or deceived me in any other way, I'll disown you, and you will never see this place again."

Oliver left Roland's office still feeling the stinging rebuke. He waited until he had composed himself before calling his partner.

"Ben, my brother's advanced me the money, and I'm wiring it to you today. I want you to know our business relationship is over for good. If your man gets caught, I'll deny my involvement and swear on the holy Bible that I never knew anything about what he did at the factory."

He heard a profane outburst from his former partner before he abruptly hung up.

Oliver sat numbly with the phone still in hand, knowing that his relationship with Roland was damaged beyond repair, and that his former best friend, Ben, had just told him to go straight to hell.

Chapter 36

"Where'd the big vase of cut flowers on the mantel come from?" Bob inquired, taking a seat on Kaye's sofa on Saturday afternoon, finding Chris and her playing a cutthroat game of Parcheesi. "Should I be worried that you have a secret admirer?"

"How do you think you'd stack up against Rock Hudson?" she queried, without looking up from the board. "It was delivered by a florist in town, but I'm sure it was ordered by someone in Hollywood."

"Only in your dreams," Bob laughed. "I figure the flowers are from one of the love-struck old timers at the café who found out it's your birthday. Am I right?"

"Not even close, Bob. Read the card, and you'll find out the real story."

Bob picked up the card and began reading a note written in elegant script.

"Dear Miss Davidson,
"Thank you for being the Good Samaritan who stopped to help Francine after her automobile accident.

"Dr. Woolwine told us that you kept her safe until the ambulance arrived, although you were injured while helping her.

"We will be forever indebted to you for your act of Christian kindness, and wish you a speedy recovery.

"Sincerely,

"Josephine Tanner."

Bob returned the card to the mantel. "Holy Moses, Kaye! Did you think this day would ever come? That's a very conciliatory message coming from that old bat, even if it is a week or so late."

"Robert, Robert, Robert, the young boy beside me is listening to every unkind word you say about Mrs. Tanner. I have chosen to forgive her, and I now consider her a reformed old bat. We may even become best friends in the years ahead."

"You have the heart of a saint, Miss Davidson, and more than ever, I know that I don't deserve you.

"Now before your head starts to swell, tell me where you'd like to go for dinner to celebrate your birthday. Pick a really nice restaurant. The sky's the limit this evening. It's a big milestone, joining the quarter century club."

"Are you positive it's just the quarter century club I'm joining, honey? After burning the candle at both ends lately, I feel more like a member of the half-century sorority.

"By the way, I saw you and Chris having a private conversation out under the tree in the back yard yesterday. What are you two up to? Does it have anything to do with my birthday dinner?"

"What we were discussing is none of your beeswax, cornbread, shoe tacks. We don't allow girls to join our club and learn our secrets."

"Oh, stop it, Bob. Sometimes I think Chris is the more mature of you two kids. But as for dinner, I'd really like to go to the Peking Palace in Marion."

"That's where I'd like to go, too, Coach," Chris chimed in. "You can keep going back for more food until you bust your buttons."

"I think your problem with gluttony may be even worse than your mother's chronic nosiness, Chris, but since you and your mom both have your heart set on Oriental food, that where we'll go. Let's plan on leaving around 4:00."

The Peking Palace was crowded when the three arrived at twilight, finding a vacant table near the window. The meal was an enjoyable affair, Chris wearing out the carpet between his seat and the serving table, reloading his plate again and again.

None of the three was able to eat another bite by the time dinner ended, and their fortune cookies were delivered. "What does yours say?" Bob asked, as Kaye snapped her cookie in two and pulled out the tiny note.

"It says the stars are aligned for my great happiness," Kaye replied. "Maybe I'll find a ten-dollar bill on the sidewalk when we go outside."

"You sure think small," Bob laughed. "Wouldn't something else bring you greater happiness?"

"OK, maybe I'll find a fifty-dollar bill on the sidewalk."

"I never realized you had such a mercenary and unromantic nature until now," Bob sighed, as they left the restaurant.

Chris was sound asleep across the backseat by the time they arrived at the apartment. Bob gathered him up and carried him inside, straight to his bed, where Kaye pulled off his shoes, and left him to sleep still wearing his play clothes.

The two moved into the living room, cuddling together on the sofa, neither making a move to turn on the TV.

Bob broke the companionable silence. "You asked me earlier what Chris and I were discussing in the backyard yesterday. Do you really want to know?"

"Yes. Now you're starting to make me really curious."

"I asked if it would be OK with him if I asked his mother to marry me.

"He seemed a little worried at first- he wanted to know what would happen to him if I did. I told him he would be part of a package deal, since I would also hope to adopt him.

"He asked if he could still call me coach, and I told him that he could if he wanted, but I would be mighty happy if he would consider calling me dad. He was OK with that, too.

"Actually, he was pretty excited about everything, but I told him he had to keep it a secret until I proposed to you."

Bob was interrupted as Kaye put both arms around his neck and pulled his face to hers, holding him close for a long kiss. When he was able to speak, he asked, "Don't you even want me to pop the question ?"

"You already know my answer, but go ahead anyway."

Bob reached into his shirt pocket for the engagement ring that he had purchased weeks earlier, slipping it on her finger, asking,

"Kaye Davidson, will you marry me, and allow me to adopt Chris as my son?

Kaye kissed him again, saying softly, "Yes. "I've been waiting and waiting for you ask me.

"Let's not put it off. I'd like to be married in the spring when flowers are blooming and everything is starting out fresh"

Bob stayed on the sofa holding Kaye through the night until the sun came up. He could see from time to time that she was dreaming, and he hoped that she was planning a wonderful future for the three of them.

Chapter 37

"Hard to believe this is our final match," Bob commented to Art, as they, Darryl, Johnny, and OL sped along US 460 East toward Roanoke on Saturday. "We can end the season on a three match winning streak if we pull this one out. That would a big turnaround since the opening losses to Bluefield and Bristol."

"You all have come a long way in the past few months," Art told the three boys in the back seat. "The Eagles look like a different team than the one I saw the day I arrived. It shows how commitment and hard work pay off."

"We're night and day better for having you here with us," Bob agreed. "Hope you'll decide to settle down and stay. I know one young lady who'd be very happy if you did."

"I suppose this will be the best team we face until we go up against Portsmouth in Charlottesville," Darryl commented. "How do you think we'll stack up?"

"They have more athletes in their program, but I think you're better coached, thanks to the man beside me," Bob answered. "It should be a dogfight."

The Eagles and the Generals met in the home team locker room and hit the scales in the early afternoon. Bob took Art to meet the Jackson coach, Davis Smith, the oldest coach in southwest Virginia, a legendary football general whose knowledge of wrestling had been acquired through blood, sweat, and mat burns over many seasons.

"Slater, I'm going to lodge a protest over you bringing in an NCAA national champion to help you coach. I'm not sure any of my youngsters will want hit the mat and be humiliated in front of the home crowd. What do you say that we even things up and start off tonight with your team spotting mine twenty points?"

"And I'm guessing that you'll want points in the unlimited class when that Pennsylvania star of yours, Ernie Callahan, takes on our undersized heavyweight?"

"Certainly seems fair enough," Davis rejoined. "I'm glad you made that suggestion."

"Just how many state championships did the Callahan brothers win in Pennsylvania before the family moved to Roanoke?" Bob inquired.

"The older two had several titles between them. Ernie never got past runner-up a couple of years. I guess your heavyweight spotting my youngster five points ought to make it a fair contest."

Bob looked at Art, commenting, "Let's inventory our equipment before we leave tonight. I suspect Davis might try to take everything we have, including the wheels off our cars."

A noisy riot of Jackson High students and families filled the home town bleachers, electricity arcing between the rowdy crowd and the shouting, strutting red and white clad cheerleaders.

A group of teenage boys in bib overalls began a noisy chant clearly not approved by the principal: "The Generals don't never fail, the Generals gonna whip your tail."

Only a few Stony Ford fans had made the trip to Roanoke, among them the Ellisons and Nick and Randy Kowalski, sitting quietly, incapable of matching the fireworks on the other side of the gym.

OL stared across the mat at the Generals, watching the largest boy perform flips and handstands, effortlessly snapping from his back to his feet, exuding athleticism and confidence.

Ernie had the right bloodlines, with broad shoulders and barrel chest tapering to a small waist, underpinned with long muscular legs and the powerful butt of a competitive weight lifter.

"Want to swap weight classes tonight?" OL cracked.

"Right after pigs learn to fly," Johnny laughed.

The show started when three teenage girls dressed in red and white costumes paraded onto the floor to sing the national anthem. They knew all of the words and delivered a performance strong on patriotism, if weak on harmony, but good enough to get a big hand from the home town crowd.

Pauly led off the Stony Ford lineup, quickly putting the Eagles out front in a freakish opener when his opponent stayed on his back too long, futilely struggling to avoid giving up a two point takedown, ending up pinning himself.

The lead swung back to Jackson when Benny lost a close decision in a wild six minute shootout at 115-pounds, and Wally, always the riverboat gambler, rolled the dice one time too many with a poorly executed Granby Roll, getting trapped on his back in the 123-pound weight class.

Gene put Stony Ford back in front with a decision at 130-pounds, repeatedly taking his man down and releasing him, driving him off the mat into the score keeper's table at the final buzzer. The referee quickly stepped-in and separated the boys, preventing the contest from going into extra innings.

The match was still a seesawing barn burner when Johnny took the mat in the 168-pound bracket. He lined up facing a stocky opponent displaying the cauliflower ears of a veteran grappler, unable to hear Art and Bob over the screaming Waltons Road fans.

The whistle blew, and for six minutes it was a full pitched battle between a couple of street-tough kids, neither of whom knew how to back down. The two traded busted lip for bloody nose, the match stopping several times for team managers to towel blood spots off of the mat cover.

The lead changed hands a half dozen times before Johnny pulled out a hard fought win on riding time at the final buzzer. The two boys shook hands at the center of the match with grudging respect, the scoreboard flashing, Eagles 21, Generals 16.

Jackson High's chance to come away with a win was gone, and a tie for the home team now hinged on Ernie Callahan pinning OL in the unlimited weight class. That seemed a good bet to the Jackson fans, screaming at the top of their lungs, calling for their General to whip his tail.

OL quickly discovered why Ernie had been a star in the tough world of Pennsylvania high school wrestling. He was bigger and stronger than OL, and just as quick and well-coached.

OL tried everything in his arsenal, looking for a way to take Ernie down and hold him on the matt, but nothing worked. The scoreboard showed him dropping further and further behind his opponent. He knew from a team standpoint it didn't matter, just as long as he didn't give up five points to the Generals on a pin.

The Jackson fans were on their feet in the final period, when Ernie executed a slick hip roll and put a half nelson on OL, turning him on his back, using every ounce of strength to hold him down and show him the rafters.

OL struggled with everything he had, sucking for air, shifting from side to side, bridging on his back, repeatedly lifting himself and his opponent off the mat on his straining neck.

The referee curled around the two boys on his hands and knees, carefully watching the constant touch and go between OL's back and the mat, arm raised to call a pin.

OL heard his coaches and teammates yelling for him to fight his way out, Julie's faint voice begging him to hold on. Time stood still for him in a world of exhaustion and pain, and then the buzzer sounded to end the match. He had survived and averted the pin, salvaging the Eagle's third straight victory.

OL was surprised when Ernie rolled off him, extending a hand to pull him to his feet and shake his hand.

"Good match," the Jackson boy told him. "I couldn't hold you down. Only one other guy has gone the distance with me all season."

Randy and Nick Kowalski worked their way over to speak to the team. "Way to gut it out on your back, son," Randy told OL. "You salvaged a win for the Eagles."

Nick caught up with Bob and Art. "Just want y'all to know we think the team wrestled an outstanding match. Coach Callison would have been all smiles if he had been here tonight.

"Randy and I have been down on you since you got the job, Slater, but you've surprised us. You and your friend have turned the Eagles into one helluva fine team."

Chapter 38

Sanford Williams entered the principal's office with a smile and extended his hand. "Albert, there are some developments concerning the school closing decision that I felt we should discuss face-to-face. I hope you don't mind my dropping in."

Albert had not been looking forward to the first encounter with his boss since their confrontational phone conversation, but he managed to conceal it well. "Good morning, Sanford. Always good to have you come by and get a first hand look at how things are going here."

His boss waited until the door was closed and both were seated, then spoke. "Your counterpart at Bluefield High, Preston Brock, has asked that we set up some informal meetings with members of your faculty so he can start getting acquainted with them. He wants to have some sense of their professional and interpersonal skills before he starts conducting formal job interviews in June.

"I realize that this whole business sticks in your craw, but the decision has been made by the powers that be, and all that any of us good foot soldiers can do now is to follow our marching orders.

"I think there may be one detail that will make all of this a little more palatable to you. The school board has agreed with me that you deserve a supervisory position at Bluefield High School.

"Preston will be looking for an area of his operation where he could use some help. You'd be reporting to him as assistant principal."

Sanford looked toward Albert for his reaction, feeling misgivings that the offer might not be kindly received.

Albert thoughtfully measured his words, and the superintendent knew his intuition had been right.

"So Pres is ready to pick the bones of Stony Ford High three months before the school is even dead? I know I shouldn't harbor any ill feeling toward him, since none of this situation is of his making. But it's hard to listen to any proposal that includes an outsider cherry-picking my faculty while the teachers are still busy educating our children.

"Sanford, I understand the enormous pressure being put on you by the school board and board of supervisors, and I know that you are prepared to carry out their directives, but I am not reconciled to the idea that this school must be closed in June, and I'm not prepared to be a good foot soldier.

"Whether there's some job for me in Bluefield or not, I can't throw in the towel. I sincerely regret it if my actions damage the cordial working relationship that you and I have had for years, but I must stand on my principles and fight."

"So you're still planning to take that petition to the governor?"

"Yes. And you need to know that the folks here are organizing a rally and starting a letter-writing campaign to save the school. They want to create as much publicity as possible on television and in the newspapers before the petition is presented to Governor Lindsey."

"Albert, you're a stubborn man, and you're creating an enormous problem for me. But no matter how this comes out, even if it jeopardizes my own job, I'll always greatly respect you. I've never known a man of greater integrity."

Albert rose with his old friend. "Thanks for your kind words, Sanford. I hope you'll permit me to use them in my resume."

*****

"Why are you calling me here today?" Oliver asked anxiously, as he took the phone call from his former partner on Saturday morning. "I got the money from my brother to pay off my half of the loan, and now he's almost disowned me. I don't owe that bunch of loan sharks another dime."

"That part of the business deal is over and done," Ben Turner replied. "Now something else has come up, and it looks like it could turn out to be an even bigger problem.

"Our former agent contacted me last night, and after hearing what he had to say, I'm beginning to think he's crazy."

Ben related the gist of his phone conversation with Bud Neese, while Oliver listened apprehensively. "He wants to go back and put the furniture factory out of business for good, and he isn't asking for any more money to do it.

"He keeps talking about taking pride in his work, and being dissatisfied with the job he did. The weirdest thing is his obsession with making a fool out of the sheriff."

"You've got to find a way to call him off," Oliver interjected. "There's absolutely nothing in it for us any longer if the factory is burned to the ground, and the last thing we can live with is for Neese to get caught and implicate us."

"You're preaching to the choir, Oliver. I know we both want him to clear out of here now and never come back. It's just not going to be that easy to convince him to leave."

"What do you expect me to do?"

"I don't think either of us can do anything, but at least you're aware of the huge risk we're facing. If Neese should get caught and tell what he knows, we're both ruined. They put people away in prison for a long, long time for what we did."

"He's your man, so you find a way to make him stand down and clear out of town," Oliver demanded. "I only want to hear from you one more time, and that's to tell me that Neese is gone, and we'll never hear from him again."

Chapter 39

"The Stony Ford Town Council is hereby called to order," Mayor Steve Mullins pronounced, as councilmen Carper, Tucker, Smith, and Gilbert looked on from around the table on Monday evening. "We have two items of business on the agenda, and if we move right along, we'll finish in time to drop by Tootie's for a cool one after the meeting."

"Joey, start us off with a report on your meeting with the Kowalski brothers. Are they willing to help us lobby the legislature for funding to relocate Main Street? I guarantee that we won't get through spring this year without some sort of Laurel Creek flood."

"Good news," Joey started. "Nick and Randy agreed to support our highway relocation proposal and have started the ball rolling. K&K Construction has even more clout in Richmond than I realized. A number of delegates in the state government have received campaign funds from K&K to help them get elected, and they'd like to keep that pipeline open.

"A high-powered K&K lobbyist has several delegates preparing to submit a bill in this session of the General Assembly calling for VDOT funding to do the necessary roadwork. I believe the bill will pass with little opposition, and the work might start as early as spring of next year."

"If you were a betting man, what odds would you put on the road construction bill getting approved by the legislature?" Leon inquired.

"You're asking Joey the Pigeon for betting odds?" Royce laughed. "I'm putting my oldest boy, Tommy, through college with the money I win off Joey in our Saturday night poker games."

Joey grinned and paused long enough to flash a middle finger toward Royce, then answered, "I'd say about three to one that we get our road."

"I'm good with those odds," Steve commented. "Royce gets to buy the beer tonight for disrespectful conduct toward a fellow council member during an official town meeting. Put that in the minutes."

"He's the one who made the vulgar gesture and I think he ought to pay the bar tab," Royce protested, but the mayor quickly overruled him, and continued with the meeting.

"The next item of business was submitted by Principal Carter and members of the high school faculty. They're organizing a Save Stony Ford High parade down Main Street and a rally at the high school this coming Saturday. We've been asked to support both events and help drum up support. Any discussion?"

"What's there to discuss?" Leon inquired. "The county wants to close our high school, knowing full well that it will kill our town. Hell, yes, we should support both events. I move that we get with the organizers and help contact every newspaper and TV station between Roanoke and Bristol."

"I'll second that motion," Tony chimed in. "Albert Carter and his faculty have gotten everyone in town to sign their petition He's ready to drive to Richmond and personally deliver it to Gov. Lindsey, and I propose that we accompany him and stand beside him when he does."

"I don't think we even need to take a vote on this motion," Steve concluded. "Town Council support of the school closing protests is hereby approved by acclamation.

"Meeting adjourned. All council members are hereby instructed to reconvene at Tootie's in twenty minutes."

*****

"Everybody and his brother has turned out tonight," Kaye commented, as she, Bob, Art, and Becky stood in the center of a throng milling around in front of the high school on Saturday evening. "Just look at the size of this crowd. When Billy closes his café early on Saturday, you know it's a big deal."

"I certainly didn't expect to see so many news people," Becky added. "I suppose that a small town struggling to save its high school makes a good human interest story."

"I've spotted reporters and camera men from both of the regional TV stations and the Tazewell Enterprise. Principal Carter and Mayor Mullins have microphones in their faces every time I look their way."

"I haven't spotted anyone from the board of supervisors or the school board," Bob observed, glancing around. "I don't believe the school superintendent is here either.

"But I'm positive someone or another here will give them a full report on everything that goes on. You can bet there are some very unhappy administrators in this neck of the woods."

"What could they do to Albert?" Becky inquired. "Could the school board and Supt. Williams fire him for insubordination?"

"I'm an outsider looking in on this brouhaha," Art interjected. "But I believe the Constitution is quite clear regarding citizens' rights to assemble and speak freely. I'm sure that Albert has thought out the consequences of his actions and is willing to risk his career for what he believes is right."

"He showed me a copy of the speech that he'll be giving," Bob commented. "He's going to point out that we have the best graduation rate of any high school in this area, even better than Bluefield High's."

"Let's move up a little closer to the front," Becky suggested. "It looks like he's about ready to speak."

*****

Bud Neese moved easily and inconspicuously among the townspeople clustered together in front of the building to hear the principal. He spotted Sheriff Holt talking with two uniformed deputies, and slowly moved their way to eavesdrop on the conversation, turning his collar up and pulling his cap lower over new dark-framed glasses. A crying baby drowned out their low voices until Bud was standing only feet away.

"I think we'll be OK staying here until the rally breaks up, and people disperse, instead of running routine patrols around town," Holt said. "It looks like everyone between the ages of six and sixty is on the premises, so there shouldn't be any speeders or drunk drivers on the road."

The older deputy glanced over the crowd and curiously asked his boss, "Do you think we need to be here tonight? It seems unlikely that anyone among this bunch of law abiding folks would try to start a fight or snatch a purse."

'I've spotted a couple of people milling around the premises who have police records for theft and assault," Walter replied. "I certainly don't expect any trouble tonight, but that doesn't say we don't need to be here on the job. Unless you have a question, let's split up and keep our eyes open to be sure everybody's behaving."

The younger deputy commented, "Wouldn't it be something if one of us bumped into the man responsible for burning the furniture factory?

"We'd never be able to recognize him from the artist's sketch. I thought it looked like one of the guys on a box of Smith Brothers' cough drops."

"The sketch wasn't much help, Freddie," the sheriff agreed. "It was such a poor likeness that I didn't bother to send it out.

"There's a possibility that he could be walking among us right now, mingling with the crowd. Criminals like fire bugs are known to return to the scene of the crime, looking to get in on the excitement.

"This guy might be a thrill seeker, judging by how reckless he was in pawning Spellman's pistol just up the road, like he wasn't afraid of the law."

Bud turned and walked away, smiling. The sheriff was staking both pride and reputation on running him to ground, and a cat and mouse game with a tough lawman only made life more exciting.

He spotted a white patrol car marked Tazewell County Sheriff's Dept. parked in the roadway as he left the school grounds, stopping beside the driver's door. Seeing no one watching, he reached into his pocket for a black marker, quickly drawing a cross centered within a circle, then walked away.

*****

As the crowd dispersed, Sheriff Holt quickly strode back to his patrol car, Freddie and Stan trying to keep up. A heavyset woman who was standing by the car stepped aside as the three approached, giving the sheriff his first look at the bold black symbol emblazoned on his shiny white paint.

"What the hell is that?" he exclaimed, walking up to take a closer look.

"I think someone drew a gun sight lined up on your door," Freddie answered. "He must have done it while the rally was going on."

"Why in the hell would anyone do that?" Stan inquired.

"I'm not sure, but I have a good idea," Sheriff Holt answered. "I think the man we're looking for was here in the crowd with us today, and spit in my eye."

Chapter 40

"I'd like to see Carter fired for insubordination," Parker Weston, Chairman of the Tazewell County Board of Supervisors, declared to Sanford as the two faced one another across the conference table in his office at First National Bank. "The decision to close Stony Ford High for budgetary reasons is perfectly logical.

"But now Carter has sensationalized the school closing, and people are attacking us as if we're a bunch of fools with no common sense. It was bad enough when he stirred up the Tazewell newspaper editor and the TV station owners with his rally, but then he personally delivered that damn petition to Governor Lindsey last week with the entire Stony Ford Town Council standing right beside him."

"He's within his rights to do so, Park. Everyone has the right to free speech. Albert's a man of enormous integrity, and I can't help but admire the way he's handled this situation. He's made a strong argument for raising property taxes in the county to cover the budget shortfall,"

"We've made our decision and moved on now, Sanford. The county supervisors and school board expect you to implement the plan."

"I don't have my heart in any part of this, Park, but I'll follow orders. If I were younger and didn't have two children in college, I might show a little of Albert's backbone myself."

Sanford returned to his car reflecting on Parker's words, convinced that the bank president was overconfident in the county administrators' ability to rule by fiat. He mused, if Parker thinks that the town of Stony Ford is going to roll over and allow the high school to be closed, he's misjudging a lot of strong-willed folks.

*****

"Turner's Café's becoming a political hot house," Jonas observed as he sat nursing a mug of Maxwell House with Bob and Art on Saturday morning. "This place has been buzzing ever since the rally."

"I think that Carter hit a home run with his speech" Art commented. "The local newspaper is squarely behind him."

"The biggest card is yet to be played," Bob interjected. "We received word last week that Gov. Lindsey will be attending the Virginia High School Sports Hall of Fame induction ceremony. It turns out that he lettered in wrestling at Princeton back before the war, and he later came to know Buck Callison well."

"Albert and our town councilmen didn't get much time to talk with the governor when they delivered the petition, but they heard that he read it afterward, and was impressed with the number of signatures. A career politician like Gov. Lindsey knows that petition represents a lot of votes in the next election."

"But how does the induction ceremony have any bearing on this matter?" Jonas inquired curiously.

"It gives Stony Ford High a platform to put faces on the school closing issue," Bob replied. "Gov. Lindsey will get a firsthand look at some of the outstanding young people who've become pawns in Tazewell County politics.

"I'm confident that the boys on the wrestling team will make a good impression on a man who knows the sport, hopefully earning his respect. That could be important if the governor reevaluates the school closing decision."

Kaye, who had been at work since the café opened, swung by their table to join them, speaking excitedly to Art, "Has Bob or Rev. Underwood told you the good news? We've set the date for our wedding- the last Saturday in May. Rev. Underwood has kindly consented to officiate."

Bob added, "And now I'm going to put you on the spot by asking you to be my best man."

"It's an honor for me to accept, Bob" Art replied, without a moment's hesitation. "I'm sure you two have your hands full making plans."

"The wedding's a work in progress, but Rev. Underwood is helping us make the arrangements at the church," Kaye said. "I've just talked to Becky, and she's going to be my maid of honor. Everything is coming together nicely."

A look of concern flickered across Art's face, disappearing as quickly as it came. "I hope that the wrap-up of my work here won't interfere with my being in your wedding."

"How could that be a problem?" Bob inquired.

"My contract with TUV has a clause regarding reassignment at the end of a job. Right now I'm working to get it straightened out."

Sensing Bob and Kaye's concern, he added reassuringly, "But your wedding's very important to me. Rest assured, one way or another, I'll be standing at your side on the big day."

Chapter 41

"I've been looking over the latest report of thefts and burglaries in our area, and it shows a pretty wide mix of stolen goods this time," Stan commented to his boss. "Let me grab a copy off of the bulletin board and I'll fill you in on the whole laundry list."

He returned with a sheet of paper and began to read aloud: "One Holstein heifer missing from a pasture in Bland County; one '47 Chevy pickup with farm use tags taken from a barn in Tazewell County; twenty-five sacks of nitrate fertilizer stolen from a Southern States store in Wythe County; seven pairs of ladies underwear missing from a clothes line in Tazewell County; two fifty-five gallon drums of heating oil taken from a distributor in Wythe County. Sounds like everything you'd need to stock a general store."

Sheriff Holt looked up from his desk, giving his deputy his full attention. "Go back over that list again, but skip over the livestock, the lingerie, and the clunker. What was that about nitrate fertilizer and fuel oil?"

"A thousand pounds of nitrate fertilizer and a hundred and ten gallons of heating oil are reported missing in Wythe County.

Someone's going to stay warm this winter and have a big crop of vegetables in the spring."

"Yeah, you just might be right. And then again, someone might be planning to blow a hole in the ground big enough to bury the First Baptist Church right up to the steeple.

"Do you know anything about blasting in a strip mine? They drill big holes, load them with a mix of nitrate fertilizer and fuel oil, and set them off with blasting caps. If you've ever watched the miners shoot and all at once seen several acres of rocky land rise up about five feet, you'd know how explosive that mixture is."

"You think there might be a connection between those thefts and the guy who sabotaged the furniture factory?" Stan asked.

"I don't know for certain, but it sure as hell looks curious," Sheriff Holt replied. "We need to take a trip over to Wythe County and talk to Sheriff Foley. That is, unless you'd rather stay here and check up on that lady's missing undergarments."

"I'll get my cap and ride with you," Stan replied. "Freddie can go out and try to lift some fingerprints off of Mrs. Fanning's clothes line. That's part of the duties around here for a junior deputy."

"I bet you would have pulled rank on Freddie and taken that assignment if the lingerie robbery victim had been an attractive young lady and not an elderly widow, isn't that right?"

"Probably so," Stan laughed. "My mama didn't raise no fools."

An hour later, Walter and Stan were talking with Wythe County Sheriff Carson Foley inside the small warehouse of the local Southern States store. "I figured the same thing as you when that fertilizer and fuel oil both went missing," Sheriff Foley commented.

"Someone's planning to create a helluva big fireworks show. The thought crossed my mind that there could be some nut running loose who's unhappy about his day in court and plans to come back and blow up the courthouse here in town."

"Got any suspects?" Walter asked.

"We don't have much to go on so far. The lock on the outside door was broken with bolt cutters, and they're a few faint tire tracks in the dust where he carried the bags of fertilizer off in his truck, but that's about it. Why are you Tazewell County folks so anxious about this?"

"Because we've got our own lunatic, and he seems to be as anxious to get after at us as we are to bring him in. We have a feeling that he may be the person behind these thefts, and that the big fireworks show he's planning is for somewhere around Stony Ford."

"We're still looking around, Walt. I promise to let you know right away if we find anything, and I'll ask you to do the same."

"Fair enough, Carson. By the way, the nut we're hunting used a black marker to draw rifle scope crosshairs on the door of my patrol car. If you catch him decorating one of your vehicles, just hand him over to me, and I'll trade you my secret formula for getting the black out of your auto paint."

Walter and Stan were halfway home when Stan asked a question that had been troubling him. "How far are we prepared to go in arresting this man? He hasn't killed or injured anybody so far, although he threatened Garner Spellman's life. If I were to spot him and he was about to get away, should I use lethal force to stop him?"

"Regulations say we're to use the minimum amount of force necessary to subdue and control the person we're arresting,"

Walter replied, shifting his wad of Red Man chewing tobacco further back in his cheek.

"But I'll tell you, if I thought this man was armed, and he didn't obey me when I called out to him, I'd be ready to use my sidearm. Does that answer your question?"

"Yeah, but I'm still not sure how I'd react if I had him in my rifle sights and knew that I had to shoot him to keep him from escaping," Stan replied. "Maybe I'd try to nail him in the leg."

"You could do that, son, but if he was armed and you shot at him, he'd probably be aiming for your vital organs when he returned fire. It might be better in the long run if you held that rifle a little higher and put a bullet in him where it would put him down."

"Jesus Christ!" Stan stammered. "You hear about people having to make life or death decisions, but somehow you never picture it happening to you."

"From time to time, we come up against some vicious people, son, and things quickly get out of hand," Walter said, reaching over to turn on the radio and dial in a country music station. "That's why law enforcement officers like us make so much money," he added sardonically.

*****

Becky entered the gym on Monday afternoon just as the team was wrapping up practice and following Bob out the door for the daily two-mile run. She found Art looking over his practice notes, and after glancing around the gym to be sure they were alone, threw her arms around his neck to give him a long, affectionate kiss. "How was your day, sweetheart?" she asked.

Art held her close, looking at her affectionately "I'm having trouble remembering right now. We just wrapped up a good practice. The exhibition match with Portsmouth High's only a month away, and the boys are working hard to get ready."

"Would you like to take your pretty girlfriend to dinner this evening?" Becky asked. "And don't start asking 'which one'."

"I've never had but one, and never will," Art answered. "Would you settle for burgers at Ray's? I've only got five dollars on me, and I don't want for us to end up washing dishes to work off the cost of our meal."

A short time later, the two were leaning toward each other across a table at Ray's, sharing a second plate of French fries, talking about everything under the sun. "How did work go today?" Becky inquired. "Things moving along as well as you hoped on the factory renovation project?"

"Even better than I had expected," Art replied. "Things are going so well it seems like Murphy's Law has been repealed. Southern Styles is starting up a second production line next week and recalling twenty five more of their former employees. That's got to be a big boost for the entire town."

"This doesn't mean your assignment here is nearing the end and you'll be leaving, does it?" Beckie asked anxiously. "TUV wouldn't reassign you to another location where we couldn't see each other?"

"Do you think that anybody or anything could keep us apart?" Art asked. "You've got to trust me when I tell you that nothing will ever come between us, Becky. I promise you that. Absolutely nothing."

Chapter 42

"I know y'all may think we've pushed you beyond the limit, but we're down to the final two weeks before the exhibition match," Bob told the team. "The Dolphins wrapped up a great season with another first place in the state tournament. Art thinks that might work to our advantage."

Art explained, "Undoubtedly, the Portsmouth team planned their season to peak just in time for the state championships, and it paid off. The tournament's over, and they won big again this year. But it's almost impossible for athletes not to let up when it's done. All-star games after the regular season are boring.

"That's why we think you may be able to pull off a big upset against a stronger team. We've preached the word 'relentless' all season, but for this match it will be crucial. Near the end of your matches, you'll still be attacking, and they'll be running on fumes.

"Make them work hard in the first two periods, then dial it up and go for a pin in the third. Now give us the one-two-three- Eagles, and hit the showers."

The boys walked away, leaving Bob alone with Art to discuss a private matter. "OL seems to be handling his father's conviction well. The judge was lenient, sentencing Garner to only five years, and suspending all but one based on good behavior."

"The judge let him off easy," Art agreed. "Having no prior record helped Garner get that light sentence. His family's testimony and the death of his other son made him more sympathetic. I also believe the judge was influenced by Roland Hundley's offer to give him a job after he gets out.

*****

The guests attending the Virginia Sports Hall of Fame Convention on the UVA campus wrapped up dinner and settled back for the induction ceremony for Buck Callison and four peer living legend athletes and coaches. Families and friends sat together near the front of the room, Gov. Lindsey presiding at the head table.

While the Hall of Fame inductees were honored, the Stony Ford and Portsmouth coaches and teams quietly exited the banquet hall, moving next door into Memorial Gym to prepare for the exhibition match to follow.

Bob and Art gathered the team in the visitors' locker room while guests were still making their way into the gymnasium, taking their seats. "It's going to feel mighty quiet when you enter the gym in a few minutes," Bob pointed out. "There'll be no cheerleaders and no rowdy fans.

"But don't be deceived into thinking that this match isn't important. It's going to be the biggest one of the season, the most important ever for our school.

"Your audience will judge the character of Stony Ford High School by the way you compete. Keep it clean and show good sportsmanship. Give it everything you've got.

"Show everyone including Gov. Lindsey that small schools in one-horse towns produce winners. Help Principal Carter prove that Stony Ford High's too good to close."

Art added, "Coach Slater has said it all. There's no dishonor in losing, only in doing less than your best. Push yourself to the limit, and give it everything you have for the full six minutes. When the match is over, win or lose, act like a champion.

"This is the last time I'll be assisting Coach Slater, but I'm an Eagle forever. It's been a privilege to work with you, and I count each one of you as a friend. You've made Coach Slater and me proud throughout the season. Now do it one last time for your family, your school, and your home town."

*****

Gov. Lindsey watched closely as the Portsmouth Dolphins, dressed in bright new red and white tights and trunks, and the Stony Ford Eagles, wearing faded blue and gold wrestling gear that had seen better days, filed into the gym. The Portsmouth boys trotted onto the blue and orange UVA Cavaliers mat to warm up, while the Stony Ford team jogged to a nearby canvas practice mat and paired off.

The governor was aware that the big eastern Virginia school was the perennial state wrestling powerhouse under the expert coaching of former NCAA collegiate champion Ben Stanford.

He also knew that the southwestern Virginia school had been invited in a gesture of sympathy following the death of iconic coach Buck Callison and four members of his team, with the school now on the brink of closure, and the small squad of wrestlers coached by a math teacher. He was unaware that there was one wild card in the Stony Ford deck, another former NCAA national champion.

The governor noticed the confident way the Dolphin wrestlers carried themselves, proficiently running through moves on the mat with a flair developed over years of excellent coaching and intense competition. They exuded the nonchalant confidence of young lions, accustomed to dominating their twenty eight-foot circular den.

The Stony Ford team stood in contrast, workmanlike and all business as the boys precisely executed their drills with little chatter. Gov. Lindsey liked that. He grew up a farm boy in a rural community, and he had paid his dues in the summer sun out in the fields before good fortune sent him off to an Ivy League school on a scholarship.

The scoreboard clock counted down to zero, signaling high noon for the young gunslingers, both teams filing past each other in a series of quick handshakes without eye contact, Bob and Art trailing their boys to greet Coach Stanford and his two assistants.

The two squads took their seats in folding chairs on opposite sides of the gym, and a muscular young referee in a white shirt called out the 106-pounders to the center of the mat, Pauly joining two-time state champ, Brad Stillson.

Pauley heard the referee's whistle blow, and quickly moved forward to engage his opponent. For the next two minutes, Brad took Pauley to school, shooting lightning quick takedowns and then releasing him, toying with him for the entertainment of the crowd while running up the score. Pauley never let up, constantly moving forward to attack with a bulldog's focused determination.

The second period also belonged to Brad, as he executed slick reversals and controlled his opponent from the top, still holding a commanding lead on points, but now breathing deeply, trying to wrap up the contest with a pin before he ran out of gas. He soon realized that a pin was not in the cards, pacing himself to go the distance in a full six minute battle.

The tide turned in the third period under Pauley's relentless attack, as finesse and experience yielded to guts and conditioning. Pauley succeeded in turning an exhausted Brad on his back again and again, and though unable to pin his shoulders to the mat, racked up points on repeated near-falls.

Pauley was ahead by a single point when the horn sounded to end the match, and the referee raised his arm in victory. Gov. Lindsey stood to let out a spontaneous whoop of excitement.

The team score seesawed back and forth through the 115, 123, and 130- pound brackets, before Portsmouth pulled out wins in the next three weight classes to take a commanding lead. Bob and Art huddled with Darryl, Johnny, and OL, hammering home one message: You veterans can still win this match for Stony Ford.

Darryl stepped onto the mat to face Robbie Brandon, 157-pound state champion in his first year as a Portsmouth starter, seeing that his opponent was a half-foot taller than he and lean as a greyhound. The referee blew his whistle to start the match, and Darryl quickly discovered Robbie to be lightning fast on takedowns, far stronger on the mat than he had expected, the best leg wrestler he had ever taken on.

The two boys fought evenly through two periods, Robbie moving ahead on points in the third, using his strong legs to tie up Darryl, wearing him down. With only a minute remaining, Darryl executed a flawless switch to score a reversal, relying on guts to push beyond exhaustion, breaking the Dolphin wrestler down and driving him into a tight cradle for a pin. Eagle teammates mobbed him in congratulation as he came off the mat, too tired to stand, too winded to speak.

Johnny was the next to head into battle, trotting out to the center of the mat to shake hands with Ernie Bardell, replacing two time Dolphin state champion Tom Bowers, sidelined with cracked ribs. Johnny knew that Ernie was a mat veteran, spotting the cauliflower ears before his opponent pulled on his headgear.

He was encouraged by drawing a second stringer until the whistle blew and Ernie quickly dumped him on the mat, driving home a half nelson to turn him on his back. Johnny was gasping for breath and sporting another mat burn on his cheek by the time he struggled loose and worked his way back to his feet, feeling new respect for his opponent and much less confident of winning.

Johnny continued to fall further behind on points throughout the first two periods, and was trapped underneath his opponent and under attack in the third. Ernie tasted blood, leaning dangerously off balance in an all out effort to leverage the Eagle co-captain's shoulder blades the final inch downward against the mat, the referee hovering nearby watching for a pin.

At that instant, Johnny suddenly shifted his weight and rolled, the two boys trading positions, Ernie now on the bottom. The referee shifted his focus to Ernie, watching the wrestler in blue and gold struggle to force his opponent's back against the mat, slapping the mat cover two seconds later to signal an Eagle pin.

With Johnny's last minute miracle, a comeback victory for Stony Ford now rode on the results of the unlimited weight class.

OL charged out to the center of the mat at the opening whistle, locking up with burly, well-coached Brandon Carson, state heavyweight champion and recipient of a Crimson Tide football scholarship for the coming fall. He discovered that Brandon was quick, agile, and strong as an ox, quickly aware that a pin to win was not in the cards and that a decision on points would be a six minute brawl.

The two banged heads, pushing and turning, constantly looking for an opening to shoot their opponent's legs. Brandon found one, diving under OL to lift and dump him hard on the mat. OL fought his way to his feet and broke free in an escape, but the Portsmouth boy was now ahead on points, and would stay that way into the third period

OL saw the clock counting down to the final thirty seconds, behind by a single point and completely winded, needing a takedown to win. Brandon made a move to put him away, dropping his head and driving at OL's legs like a linebacker taking on a fullback at the goal line. OL dropped his head to block, and the two collided, both momentarily stunned, the Portsmouth boy stepping back.

Subconsciously OL could hear Art coaching him: shoot again-Bam! Bam! Without hesitating, he instinctively dove at Brandon's legs, pulling them into his chest, hooking an ankle, driving him to the mat.

The referee raised two fingers only seconds before the buzzer sounded, awarding OL a takedown, and with it, a hard fought win. The scoreboard flashed Portsmouth 19, Stony Ford 19 as OL shook hands with Brandon, his arm raised in victory before he stumbled off the mat toward his excited teammates and coaches.

Gov. Lindsey joined the two teams afterwards to offer his congratulations, taking time to shake hands with each boy and coach. He made an impromptu speech, telling the group, "It's appropriate that the match ended in a tie, because there's no loser in this gymnasium today.

"The Dolphins and Eagles both put on great performance, and I'm proud of each one of you. You represent two outstanding schools, and exemplify the finest tradition in Virginia high school athletic competition. Watching you today makes me proud that I went out on the mats myself a few years ago. Well done, boys! Well done!"

The governor sought out Albert Carter, standing face to face with him as the teams filed into the locker room. "I forwarded your petition to Roland Burnette, State Superintendent for the Virginia Board of Education, asking him to review Tazewell County's plan to close Stony Ford High. Today more than ever, I believe that action would be a big mistake."

Chapter 43

Bud Neese used a hand truck to carefully wheel the steel drums from the back of the abandoned shed up a makeshift wooden ramp into the back of a nearby panel truck, knowing that accidental detonation of the loaded containers would leave nothing behind except a crater. Concealed beneath the cover of each drum was an electric detonator with a pair of wires routed out through a small hole near the top.

As soon as the drums were secured, he loaded the truck with a battery powered short wave receiver, a suitcase containing a battery powered controller, and a cardboard box brimming with micro-switches, wire, and electricians' tools.

Then he went to work mounting switches to sense the opening of a door or the release of the hand brake. Installing wiring to connect the controller with the switches, radio receiver, and detonators completed the transformation of the panel truck into a mobile blockbuster.

Bud covered everything in the back of the truck with a tarp, concealing the lethal contents while leaving a few cartons of wood screws visible through the truck windows to deceive the curious.

He climbed into the driver's seat, wearing faded blue work pants, matching denim shirt, and a cap emblazoned National Wood Fasteners. Battered steel-frame eyeglasses, a stubble beard, and shock of hair sticking out from beneath his cap gave him the appearance of an older man.

Bud stopped by Tootie's on the way to the factory. "Good afternoon, ma'am," he called out to the blonde proprietor as he took a vacant stool at the bar. "Could I have a cold Dr. Pepper?"

"Sure, hon, but wouldn't you prefer something that'll wet your whistle better than that?" Tootie inquired with a broad smile, chatting it up with the old-timer in her friendly way while setting his open drink on the counter.

"No, ma'am. I switched over to soda pop after I went through the twelve-step program a few years back." He took a deep swallow from the bottle, continuing, "I suppose you're the owner of this fine establishment. Does an old friend of mine, Walter Holt, ever drop in?"

"Walter's the county sheriff," Tootie answered, looking quizzically at the stranger, with an intuitive feeling that she had seen him before. "How did you come to know him?"

"I'm a man who's had a lot of different work experiences. I did a custom paint job on one of his cars sometime back. He appreciates good work and friendly service. A fine, fine man." Bud finished his drink, wiped the condensation from the bottle with a handkerchief, and set the clean bottle and a carefully folded dollar bill on the counter. "Time for me get back on the road now. Thanks for the soft drink."

"Wait a minute before you leave, hon," Tootie called out as Bud slipped on his driving gloves and walked toward the door. "Who should I tell Sheriff Holt stopped in and asked about him?"

"Tell him Vincent Vango inquired. He'll recognize the painter who came up with the fancy emblem for his car door." Then Bud was out of the building and on his way to make a delivery, humming a song.

*****

Art and Randle finished marking a set of blueprints to show the locations of machine tools and fixtures for a new production line, then took a break outside, noticing the delivery van parked against the side of the building.

"That truck wasn't parked there when we came in," Randle observed. "It's curious that a delivery's being made on Saturday when no one's working in receiving. I think we ought to check and see if the driver's dropping his shipment at the wrong location."

Security guard Marv Craig was thinking the same as he walked through the factory to join Randle and Art. "My brother Del called me to come over. He let a deliveryman through the gate a while back, and the man's still here. Del thinks something might be wrong."

The three men approached the vehicle, but no driver was to be seen. Marv peered through the back window of the van, commenting, "I can see a few cartons of wood screws and some other stuff under a tarp, but I can't tell what it is. I'm going to find out whether we have a lost deliveryman wandering around inside the building."

Art and Randle examined the truck, inside and out. "All the doors are locked," Randle observed.

"I can make out the shape of some objects under the tarp," Art interjected. "They look like steel drums, but that doesn't make any sense. No company's going to ship wood fasteners in that kind of container."

It wasn't long before Marv was back with news. "There's no one inside the building. Del called the sheriff's office to report what's going on, and Sheriff Holt told him he's on the way over.

"The sheriff thinks something may be up. It seems that Tootie Harker called him and said a stranger had stopped in claiming to have painted the sheriff's car. He thinks it could be a man he's been looking for, the one who drew the cross-hairs of a gun sight on his car door."

"Where do you suppose he went?" Randle mused.

"Look at that top strand of barbed wire across the chain link fence," Art called out. "There's a torn piece of blue cloth snagged up there. I'm betting that the driver rolled the fence to get out and left a piece of his britches behind. Now the sixty-four dollar question is why?"

"I'm wondering if it could be the same man who tricked me into thinking that he was an electrical inspector before the power transformer was sabotaged and the building caught on fire!" Marv exclaimed. "If it is, that truck could spell big trouble for us."

Sheriff Holt and his deputies arrived in two patrol cars a short time later, Stan Carkin eager to help. "I have an auto entry tool in the trunk to pop the locks on that van," he said. "Do you want me to get it?"

Sheriff Holt exclaimed "No! Don't do anything until we find out what we're up against." "What do you make of this?" he asked the others.

"I'm thinking the truck could have been left by the stranger who caused all of the factory damage earlier," Marv said. "Art thinks there are steel drums in the back under the tarp."

"Jesus Christ! That could be the missing nitrate fertilizer and fuel oil Sheriff Foley's been trying to track down. I'll going to call in the state police bomb squad. We need to clear everyone out."

"I'd like to stay," Art requested. "I had training and experience in disarming explosives during my Marine Corps hitch, and I have a plan that might work."

"What have you got in mind?" Sheriff Holt quickly inquired.

"If there's a bomb in the van, it's likely that there are trigger mechanisms designed to electrically detonate the explosives if the doors are opened, the engine is started, or the truck is moved.

"There could even be a timer that is counting down to zero while we're standing here. And the bomber might be somewhere in range with a radio transmitter ready to trigger the explosives.

"But if we can get several canisters of liquid nitrogen, we should be able to cut a hole in the back window of the truck and pump in the nitrogen to freeze the detonators and disable any battery powered controls."

"Do you really think the state police could get hold of liquid nitrogen and bring it here in time?"

'They probably keep emergency canisters of oxygen, acetylene, and nitrogen on hand, but if they don't, there are commercial gas suppliers who can provide it, and some businesses, like hospitals, keep it in stock."

Holt relayed a message to the state police through his dispatcher. "The bomb squad's been notified and they'll be here as soon as they can. I've requested help from other law enforcement people in this area to help me set up roadblocks and search the grounds.

"I suspect that our delivery man may be hanging around right this minute, enjoying the show, ready to set the explosives off if he thinks we're about to disarm them."

Randle quickly interrupted, "There's an old fire tower in sight of this place. Maybe one of your deputies could get up on top with binoculars and look around."

"That's a good idea," Sheriff Holt replied. "Stan, get my binoculars and the 30.06 with the scope, and you and Freddie get over there and see if you can make out anyone who looks suspicious. Leave the glass cutter here for me, and I'll get to work on that back window."

He turned to Art and Randle as soon as the two had left, commenting, "Both of those boys have young families. If things should go to hell out here today, I don't want them leaving behind a couple of widows and three young children with no daddy."

Two patrol cars followed by an armored truck arrived within the hour, just as the sheriff was removing the round glass disk he had cut from the back window of the panel truck.

The state police performed their own quick examination of the vehicle, then carried several heavy canisters of liquid nitrogen toward the opening in the back glass, inserting the attached hoses. Minutes later, the van was shrouded by a heavy coating of frost.

*****

"It's dark as hell out here under these trees," Freddie whispered, holding his .38 caliber service revolver in front of him with both hands. "I can't see crap. What if we walk right up on him?"

"You yell, 'Freeze!'" Stan answered quietly. "If he turns around and points a weapon at you, holler 'Drop it' and be ready to blow the crap out of him with that six-gun."

"I've never shot at anybody in my life."

"Neither have I, but there's bound to be a first time. It could happen sooner rather than later. We better quit talking now. We're almost there."

They cautiously approached the old fire tower, scanning it from the ground up to the enclosed room on top. Stan was the first to spot the dark figure on the uppermost landing, quickly freezing in his tracks, calling for silence with a finger across his lips before pointing toward the man standing high above.

Stan raised the rifle to study the stranger through the four-power scope, whispering, "He's looking toward the factory through a pair of binoculars, and he's got a revolver sticking out of his pocket."

"Can you see anything else?" Freddie asked softly, voice quivering and hands shaking uncontrollably.

"Yeah, I can make out some kind of box sitting on the railing beside him. It looks a lot like one of our portable short wave radios."

"What do we do now?"

"Let's sit here and watch for a few minutes. If he makes a move to pick up the radio transmitter, we'll have to stop him. He's plenty close to communicate with a receiver in the truck, and he might be planning to set off explosives."

A grouse that had been huddled motionless in the mountain laurel beside them picked that moment to flush, its wings booming as it took flight.

"Oh shit!" Freddie apprehensively muttered under his breath.

The man at the top of the tower turned to look in their direction through his binoculars, staring eye to eye at the deputy peering back at him through the telescope sight of a rifle.

"Freeze!" Stan shouted, his tense voicing breaking like an adolescent's.

The stranger stopped cold, letting the binoculars drop to hang by a strap around his neck, dead still except for his right hand which was moving quickly toward a short-barreled Smith & Wesson .357 Magnum in his pocket.

"Get your hands up in the air now! I said right now, dammit!" Stan commanded, his voice crackling with authority.

The stranger's response caught Stan and Freddie by surprise. A bright muzzle flash, loud report, and the sound of a slug whistling directly between them caused both men to flinch.

Freddie instinctively reacted in self-defense, raising his service revolver in a two-handed grip, quickly unloading six rounds upward in the direction of the man on the tower, each shot flying wide.

Two more muzzle flashed hollow-points flew at them from the top of the tower before Stan moved the cross hairs on his scope down toward the bottom half of the dark figure above, squeezing off a round.

The 30.06 slug hit Bud Neese in the thigh, knocking him backward, shattering the bone. He reached for the nearby radio transmitter and threw the switch, expecting to hear a bomb go off at the factory, but nothing happened.

He tried to throw the switch a second time, but his leg collapsed, sending him tumbling head first down the steep steps, his neck striking a timber on the landing below, whipping his body around to a stop.

Stan and Freddie worked their way slowly up the tower steps, shaking with apprehension, holding their weapons ready to deal with a wounded and deadly quarry waiting in ambush.

When they stumbled onto Neese, he was lying immobile in a pool of blood, head twisted to the side, eyes wide open as if staring at the sky. They knew without going a step closer that he was dead.

"I don't think my slug killed him," Stan stammered. "I was aiming at his leg. He must have died after falling down the steps."

"We're lucky it happened this way," Freddie said in relief. "If we'd walked up on him and he was only injured, he might have picked us off."

Stan and Freddie were running back toward the factory when Sheriff Holt and two state police officers met them. "We heard a lot of shooting," Holt exclaimed. "What happened?"

Stan started to explain, but choked up. Freddie tried to piece together the story. "The man we've been looking for is dead at the top of the fire tower.

"Stan shot him, but didn't kill him. He fell down the steps and broke his neck." Freddie stopped, unable to continue.

No one would ever see tough lawman Walter Holt lose control of his emotions, but he had to pause a moment himself, draping an arm around each of his young deputies. "You boys did exactly what you were trained to do. I'm just glad neither of you was hurt."

*****

After the bomb squad had completed its work, Art finally walked back toward the factory, breathing a sigh of relief as the truck itself was towed away. He noticed a figure standing almost out of sight beside the corner of the building, curiously turning to see who it was.

When recognition dawned, he called out in surprise, "Becky!" She ran toward him and threw her arms around him wordlessly.

"How long have you been there? How in the world did you get past the guard?"

The words came tumbling out. "I learned that there was a bomb threat at the factory early today after someone picked it up on a police scanner and phoned in to the radio station.

"I knew you were working here, so I made a phone call, and the security guard told me what was going on. I drove over, found no one was in the guard house, and sneaked in. I didn't want to create a distraction, so I stayed out of sight and watched."

"Why in the world did you do something like that?" Art gently reprimanded. "You'd have been killed along with me and everyone else out here if those explosives had gone off."

"I know that," Becky answered softly. "But if you had died in the explosion, it wouldn't have mattered."

Art pulled her close and held her without saying a word, pressing his cheek against her auburn hair.

Chapter 44

"Tomorrow's the big day," Bob said to Kaye, pulling her close as they approached her apartment door. "That is, if you don't run away. You're not going to get cold feet and back out on me at the last minute, are you?"

Kaye laughed and gave him a quick kiss. "I think you've got it backwards. I've always heard that it's the groom who waits until the organist plays 'Here comes the bride,' and then bolts for the door, leaving the girl standing alone at the altar."

Inside, they headed for the kitchen, where Kaye made peanut butter and jelly sandwiches for lunch. "Is this what you're planning to feed me after we're married?" Bob asked. "I'm afraid I'll end up fat and toothless."

"Oh, hush!" Kaye reprimanded him with a friendly swat. "We've haven't even tied the knot, and you've already started griping about my meals. You always seem to enjoy the food I serve you at the café."

"Yeah, but Billy does all the cooking there." Bob tried to say more, but found it hard to do anything but laugh under the wet dish towel Kaye draped over his head. All he could manage was, "Emily

Post says it's bad etiquette for a hostess to dry towels on her dinner guests."

"I wish that I'd dropped you off at school to have lunch with Chris," Kaye rejoined. "You'd fit right in with the other kids."

That afternoon, Bob and Kaye went to the office of attorney Jeff Snead, who joined them carrying a manila folder full of legal documents. "This will be a very straightforward adoption process, since Chris's birth father is deceased," he commented encouragingly.

"I've completed the petition for adoption document to be filed with the court. You'll need to provide Chris's birth certificate and your marriage certificate after you two tie the knot tomorrow. Then you'll get a court date, Chris will get a new birth certificate, and you, Bob, will be the proud father of a six year-old son."

"You make it sound easy," Bob commented.

"It is. I've already gotten the court date set two weeks from today, to give you time to enjoy your honeymoon. May I ask where you're going?"

"We're going to spend a couple of days at Mountain Lake, and then we'll drive back to Stony Ford to get Chris and spend the following week at Nags Head," Kaye answered.

"I suppose Chris is pretty excited to be getting a new father," Jeff commented.

"You have no idea," Kaye replied. "He thinks it's the best thing that's ever happened to him."

"One of the two best things that's ever happened to me," Bob added. "Right up there with marrying his beautiful mom."

Later, Bob dropped Kaye off at her front door. "I'll see you at the rehearsal dinner tonight. It was kind of Becky and Art to host the party since your folks are coming in from out of town. I hope there's a bright future ahead for them."

Kaye hesitated before entering the apartment. "I'm going to let you in on a little secret. Do you recall that cold, blustery night this past winter when Chris was away, visiting his best friend?

"It was getting really late, and you just kept hanging around until I finally told you that we needed to call it an evening. I was actually hoping that you wouldn't go. I wanted you to stay."

"Now you tell me!" Bob laughed, watching the door close behind her.

*****

"Chris, you need to get in here and put on your Sunday best," Kaye called out just after lunch on Saturday morning. "We're leaving for the church in an hour, and Grandmother and Granddaddy are dressed and ready to go."

Kaye's mother, Doris, sat across the room, beaming at her daughter. "Your daddy and I are so proud of you, honey. You've raised Chris to be a young gentleman, and you're well on the way to becoming a registered nurse.

"Today you're going to marry a man who makes Lucky Abbott pale in comparison. Everything seems to be turning out so well for you."

"It hasn't been an easy life for you up until now, has it, Katherine?" her father George observed. "I know you've worked your fingers to the bone and put up with a lot of guff to get where you are."

"Now don't go making me feel sorry for myself, Dad," Kaye laughed. "My life hasn't always been a bed of roses, but you have to learn to live with the good and the bad.

"Mom never thought much of Lucky, but he gave me Chris and made you and Mom grandparents. The nursing career ahead is frosting on the cake, frosting made from a very difficult and time-consuming recipe. Marrying Bob and having my own family, that's like the ending to my own special fairy tale."

Chris gave up a losing battle with his cowlick, and the family piled into Kaye's car, speeding off to the church. They spotted Bob's sparkling clean '55 Chevy parked out front.

"Remember, it's bad luck for him to see you before the ceremony," Doris reminded Kaye. "Can we wait out of sight somewhere in the church until it's time for things to start?"

Everyone seemed to have that same idea, and the Davidsons were soon joined by Becky and the three bridesmaids, Helen, nursing advisor Sue Wilson, and best friend, Bonnie Jones.

"Anyone got a deck of cards?" Becky asked. "We can get up a poker game to help Kaye relax. She's a nervous wreck."

"That might help my nerves," Kaye agreed. "But it wouldn't be good if Jonas came in and caught us. There's no one else to perform the ceremony if he backs out."

Kaye's caution was well founded, Jonas striding into the room almost as the words were out of her mouth. "You are a delight to the eye," Kaye," Jonas remarked. "Possibly the prettiest bride to ever grace the halls of this church.

"It's almost time to get things started. Folks are arriving, and I'd like for Chris to join Albert and Billy, helping to show guests to their seats."

*****

"Coach Slater looks more nervous than he does before a match," OL commented to Julie. "Coach Lowen is cool as a cucumber, but he's not the one getting married."

The two were seated with Johnny and Peggy Danner near the front of the church, surrounded by other teammates, waiting for late arriving guests to be seated.

"We better quit talking," Peggy whispered. "I think the ceremony is about to start."

The organist struck up the wedding march, and Kaye, wearing a striking ivory dress and beaming a pretty smile, entered the sanctuary on the arm of her father, walking slowly to the front of the church.

Bob and Kaye were married in a traditional ceremony. Despite the gathering of family and friends surrounding them, for a brief moment in time they were alone and setting out to sea, embarking on a new life together, launched by Jonas's soft words, "I now pronounce you man and wife. You may kiss the bride."

The wedding party moved from the sanctuary into the church parlor for the reception. Bob and Kaye cut the first slices from the wedding cake, Kaye feeding Bob a large bite. Those standing nearby heard her tease, "Don't forget my tip."

The bridal bouquet pitch and catch was a setup, Kaye aiming directly at Becky, who fielded it on the fly. Becky turned to Art, flowers in hand, with a quizzical tilt of an eyebrow, seeing him nod in reply.

As the pianist struck the first chords of *I Only Have Eyes For You*, Bob led Kaye out on the dance floor, the two quickly finding an easy rhythm, soon joined by other young couples.

Johnny signaled to his teammates that there was work to be done, and they disappeared from the room, gathering around Bob's car. "Don't get any white shoe polish on his black paint." Darryl cautioned, while marking *Just Married* and *Wrestling Clinic Tonight*, on the rear window.

Bob and Kaye ran through a shower of rice to the car, waving goodbye to family and friends as they drove off, tin cans creating a clatter that echoed throughout the neighborhood as the car sped away.

Kaye slipped closer to Bob as they turned the corner and headed toward Mountain Lake. "Tonight's the night I finally stay with you," Bob whispered.

"Tonight's the night!" Kaye laughed, feeling the car accelerate as they flew away into the warm twilight.

Chapter 45

Becky joined Bob and the other teachers filing into the faculty lounge on Monday morning.

"I wonder what bad news we'll get from Albert this morning?" Virgil Akers asked apprehensively. "Classes ended for the year on Friday, and now he's getting us back together again. I'm betting that he's going to hand us our walking papers."

"Don't borrow trouble," Virginia replied cheerily. "Let's wait to hear what he has to say."

They were all seated when Albert joined them, unexpectedly followed by Superintendent Williams, who quietly closed the door. Virgil turned to Virginia and whispered, "I told you so."

"I appreciate everyone getting here so promptly," Albert started. "I've gathered you to hear an important message from Superintendent Williams this morning. I'm going to turn the floor over to him without further ado."

"Thank you, Principal Carter and good morning to all of you," Sanford started. "I imagine you're concerned that I may be here to deliver bad news."

"Damn straight," Virgil whispered under his breath.

"Well, you can relax and take a deep breath, because that's not why I'm here this morning." A collective exhaled sigh of relief rolled through the room.

"Quite the opposite. I've come here to deliver some very good news. The board of supervisors and the school board have rescinded their decision to close Stony Ford High School. Principal Carter deserves much of the credit for this turn-around.

"Governor Lindsey has responded to your town-wide petition by designating part of an Appalachia Relief federal grant to help fund the continued operation of your school next fall.

"Tazewell administrators have agreed to make up the balance through an increase in property taxes beginning next year.

"So if you'd like to give Principal Carter a round of applause for his role in saving your school, please do so. You might also want to thank your teaching associate, Bob Slater, and his boys on the wrestling team, all of whom made a very favorable impression on Gov. Lindsey during their meeting in Charlottesville."

Following Virginia's lead, the other teachers stood to thank Albert for saving their jobs, Virgil the most enthusiastic of all.

Sanford waited until the teachers were seated, then continued, "I want each of you to know that by taking on this fight, Principal Carter put his own career on the line. His conviction and courage convinced me to change my position and take a stand with him.

"I commend you for the excellent results you're achieving in educating your students, and I encourage you to continue graduating more of your pupils than any school in this part of the state."

*****

OL wiped his greasy hands on a rag, calling out to the elderly owner of Carver Engine Repairs as he left for the day. "I was finally able to get the head off that '49 Ford engine block after I steam cleaned it, Mr. Carver. I'll install a new head gasket and put everything back together tomorrow."

Daniel Carver nodded at him. "See you in the morning, son. You're going to make a good auto mechanic if you stick with me." Daniel liked the big, friendly redhead, knowing he was a wrestling star for the Eagles, learning that he was a good summer employee, willing to take on any dirty job.

At home, OL quickly started dinner, knowing his mother was working overtime at the furniture factory and would be along later

He had seen a big change in his mother since she had gone back to work: new self confidence and a much happier outlook on life. When his dad finished serving his time and came back home to live, OL knew he was going to find a more independent, happier wife.

He left a note on the kitchen table before taking his shower. "Mom, I cooked you a piece of cube steak and some fried potatoes, and left them in the skillet. All you need to do is warm them when you get home. Love, OL." Then he was off to clean up and dress for his date.

Julie was waiting on the front porch with her folks when he arrived. The three called out to him as he climbed the front steps two at a time and bounced onto the porch swing beside Julie.

"Mom has a big surprise for you," Julie informed him, as her mother scooted into the house, returning with a cake topped with chocolate icing.

"What's the occasion?" OL inquired curiously. "I didn't know anyone had a birthday coming up."

"This isn't a birthday cake," Betty answered.

"We wanted to do something to celebrate the good news," Homer interjected. "Julie told us that you've applied for admission to VPI this coming fall, and we couldn't let something like that just slip by. Have a piece of cake, and tell us all about it."

OL smiled gratefully as Betty offered him a slice of cake and glass of lemonade. "Mr. Slater and Mr. Carter get all of the credit.

"They've been encouraging me to go to college since my junior year, telling me that I can earn enough money working summer jobs to cover half the cost. Mr. Carter's going to help me make up the difference from the school's scholarship fund."

"You deserve a lot of credit yourself, OL," Betty chided. "You kept your grades up through some difficult times at home. Homer and I are very proud of you."

"He'll be in the cadet corps, and he's going to take engineering," Julie added excitedly. "I'll be right up the road at Radford College next year, so he can hitch a ride and come to see me on weekends."

Homer and Betty quietly ceded the front porch to the younger couple, moving into the living room.

OL and Julie held hands in the slow drifting swing, listening to the creaking of rusty chains, watching lightning bugs flash mysterious messages in the warm summer night, making plans for their life adventure ahead.

Chapter 46

Becky and Art pedaled their bicycles side by side along the quiet country road following Little Walker Creek as it ran past rock ledges, through stands of rhododendron now in full bloom. They found a shady spot under a spreading sycamore tree to stop for lunch.

"I think this is one of the most beautiful places I've ever seen," Art commented, gazing around the rural countryside. "I like this even better than Burke's Garden. How many more natural wonders do you have to show me?"

"Enough to last a lifetime," Becky replied, moving closer. "If you hang around, I'll be your personal tour director 'til the cows come home."

"I think that's a wonderful way to measure time," Art said, slipping his arm around her. "I can just picture us sitting on this rock for hours on end, watching for a herd of cows to plod their way back to the barn."

Becky looped her arms around Art's neck for a long kiss. "Everything seems so perfect now, and I don't want it to end. You're never going away, are you?"

"Nothing will ever separate us, Becky. You can trust me on that.

"There isn't much need for my services here any longer, since the factory's running at full production, and most of the laid-off work force has been recalled. Randle Creech is handling all of the manufacturing problems that come up.

"I haven't had the chance to tell you up 'til now, but I heard from TUV yesterday. I need to get back for an important meeting. "

"When are you leaving?"

"I have to be there by the end of the week, so I need to get on the road day after tomorrow."

"And then you'll be back?"

"You have my word."

"Don't make me wait 'til the cows come home."

Art pulled her close and held her. "Just hang a light in the window for me. I'll be back soon."

*****

Art left, and the days passed slowly for Becky. Getting her home room cleaned up after the close of the school year took only so long, and there was little preparation she could make for the next school year.

She found time in the evenings to visit with Bob, Kaye, and Chris, who had set up housekeeping in Bob's small bungalow while looking for a more suitable home with a third bedroom and a bigger yard, but Becky felt guilty in taking up Kaye's limited free time.

She asked Kaye for copies of the wedding pictures, having only the pencil sketch of Art she had made at Burke's Garden. Unfortunately, some of the film could not be developed, and Becky was disappointed to learn that none of the album photos included Art.

She continued to wait patiently for Art throughout the week, but still there was no sign of him. Calls to the Laurel Lane Motel always drew the same response, "There's no Arthur Lowen registered here."

On Saturday, Becky tried to find the phone number and address of Turnkey Universal Ventures in Pittsburgh. But there was no such company listed. Nor was there any listing for a company called TUV.

Becky broke down on Sunday, calling Bob and Kaye. "Would you be willing to drive me to Pittsburgh to see if we can find Art? He has an elderly aunt living there, and I have a description of her home and its location.

"Maybe his aunt will be able to tell us where he is and what's going on. I'm heartsick thinking that he may be in trouble. He promised that he would be coming right back to Stony Ford, and I know he would never break his word unless something bad happened."

Bob gently replied that he and Kaye would arrange for Helen to take care of Chris, and they'd ready to go with her, starting out the first thing on Monday morning.

Becky was able to control her emotions long enough to hang up, sitting on the sofa in tears. She kept her vigil there throughout the night, dozing fitfully, listening hopefully for the sound of a telephone that stubbornly refused to ring.

Chapter 47

Bob and Kaye found Becky waiting by the street when they arrived at sunup, suitcase at hand. Both tried to make small talk as they started out on their drive north through southwest Virginia into West Virginia, and onward into Pennsylvania, but neither could succeed in drawing Becky into conversation.

Finally, they turned on the car radio, mostly a buzz of crackling static with stations that faded in and out, and sat back in silence to watch the mountainous countryside slip by their windows.

Bob had studied his worn Esso road map carefully before starting out, knowing that Pittsburgh was tough to navigate. He knew that the town had grown up where the Allegheny and Monongahela Rivers joined in hilly terrain to form the Ohio River, resulting in many roadway bridges and tunnels.

He had to stop several times to ask for directions before finding his way onto Forbes Avenue and up into the Squirrel Hill neighborhood. "Go over the description of the house we're looking for one more time," he requested.

"Artie told me his aunt lives in a white frame Victorian," Becky replied. "It has wrap-around porches upstairs and down, and bay windows on either end. There's a widow's walk on the roof."

"You got that, Kaye?" Bob asked. "One of you watch the right side, and the other keep a look-out on the left. I'll work on avoiding all of these axle-busting potholes along the trolley tracks."

They didn't spot the house until the second trip up Forbes Street. "That's it," Kaye called out suddenly. "I'm sure that's the one. Pull over and park. We missed it the first time because the paint looks gray instead of white. It's run-down today, but it must have been spectacular when it was first built."

Becky climbed the steps and walked across the sagging porch to the front door, a manila envelope in her hand, ringing the door bell while Bob and Kaye waited on the sidewalk below.

There was no response at first, but Becky persisted, and finally she saw a curtain move and a gray head appear at the nearby window. The door opened as far as a safety chain allowed, and an elderly voice nervously called out, "Who's there, and what do you want?"

"I'm Becky Slater, ma'am, and I'm looking for Mrs. Lowen."

"There's no one named Lowen at this address."

"Do you have a nephew named Arthur?"

"I believe you're at the wrong address, Miss," came the reply from behind the door, now sounding a little less apprehensive. "This is the Lowenstein residence."

"But you do have a nephew named Arthur?"

"Yes. Why do you want to know?"

"I'm looking for a man named Art Lowen, and he told me he had an aunt living on Forbes Street in Squirrel Hill. The home he described is exactly like this one. I have a hand-drawn sketch of him in this envelope. Would you be willing to look at it?"

Becky passed her portrait through the narrow opening above the safety chain, watching an age-spotted hand take it. Nothing happened for several minutes, leaving Becky to guess that the woman was now studying it in front of the window. She heard the safety chain slide back, and the door swung wide.

Standing in front of her was a tall, slender gray-haired woman in a dark blue dress, tears in her eyes. "Please come inside and tell me where you got this portrait of Artie." Becky signaled to Bob and Kaye to join her, following the fragile figure into the house.

"Come in the parlor and I'll pour you a cup of tea," the shaken woman invited. After the three introduced themselves and were seated, the woman poured tea for them from a tarnished silver service, then spoke.

"My name is Ruth Lowenstein, and I'm pleased to meet you. You've inquired about my nephew, Arthur Lowen, and I'll try to provide the information you're seeking as far as I'm able. Then I'd like for you to tell me how you came to have his portrait.

"My only brother, David, Arthur's father, left the Jewish faith and converted to Protestantism after falling in love with a pretty young girl who was half his age. He married her, and soon afterward, he legally changed his name to Lowen, at her request.

"The two had only one child, a boy they named Arthur. David was injured while working in a steel mill, and though he and his family endured financial hard times afterwards, he was too proud to take money from our parents or from me.

"Artie was his parents' pride and joy, and he meant as much to me. He was a bright, kind, well-mannered boy who never missed an opportunity to help others.

"I never cared for the sports that mean so much to other people in this town, but when Artie became a wrestler on his high school team, I didn't miss a single one of his matches.

"Later, when he became the star at Pitt and went on to win a national championship, I was his biggest cheerleader. Rather hard for you to picture that, I'm sure.

"Everything was so promising for him then. He made excellent grades in his engineering studies at Pitt, and after graduation, he was hired by Westinghouse at their plant east of town.

"But then the Korean War started, and Artie felt it was his duty to enlist. If only he had picked a branch of the service other than the Marines, but that was what he felt compelled to do.

"He went through basic training at Camp Lejeune, and then shipped out to Korea as a 2nd Lieutenant. For months following his deployment, I received several letters each week. He never complained about his situation, but he wrote about the hardship and casualties he saw all around him.

"And then the People's Republic of China entered the war in October of 1950, and the flow of letters slowed to a trickle. The last one arrived in early November."

"Two men in uniform came here in December. I saw them through the window coming up on the porch, and I knew what they were about, even before they told me that Artie had been killed in combat.

"They said that Artie died a hero, and that a commendation would follow. Doesn't a medal seem like a trivial token to receive for the loss of the one who gives you everything to live for?

"Artie was like a son to me, and I'd give every medal that has ever been made, and everything I own, just to have him back here for one day."

The woman realized the impact her words were having on her three visitors. "I'm sorry if I'm upsetting you. Here, let me go get the medal. You can read the commendation for yourselves."

Ruth returned with a glass-fronted case that protected an ornate star-shaped medallion suspended on a wide blue ribbon beneath an eagle and a bar marked VALOR.

Beckie, Bob, and Kaye instantly knew that they were looking at the highest military award given by any branch of the United States Armed Forces, the legendary Congressional Medal of Honor.

"I'd be glad to recite the citation aloud for you," Ruth offered. "My poor eyesight makes it difficult for me to read the words, but I memorized it long, long ago.

"LOWEN, ARTHUR S.
"Rank and organization: 2nd Lieutenant, US Marine Corps, Company C, 1st. Battalion, 1st. Marines, 1st Marine Division. Place and date: Chosin Reservoir, Korea, 05 Dec. 1950. Entered service at Pittsburgh, Pa. Born Sept. 23, 1927 Pittsburgh, Pa.

"Citation: For conspicuous gallantry and intrepidity at the risk of his life above and beyond the call of duty while serving as platoon leader in Company C as part of a 30,000 man UN force engaged in battle with 60,000 enemy aggressor troops in bitter cold weather south of the Yalu River in North Korea.

"Following orders from his commanding officer to withdraw, Lt. Lowen led his platoon of thirty-eight men across a valley exposed to enemy machine guns and mortars positioned on nearby hills. Thirty-six Marines made it to the shelter of a low ridge on the south side of the valley despite sustaining causalities.

"Two Marines in the fourth squad, Sgt. Howard Corbin and Cpl. William Broman, were hit by enemy fire, and remained on the ground, wounded and unable to withdraw to safety from their exposed positions.

"After moving his troops into position on the south side of the valley to provide covering fire, Lt. Lowen went back to retrieve his two injured men, crossing the valley, dodging heavy fire from enemy combatants.

"Lt. Lowen was shot in both legs and knocked to the ground, but he struggled onward to the first downed man, placing his own helmet on Sgt. Corbin before lifting him onto his shoulder, and carrying him on the run two-hundred yards back to safety.

"Bleeding profusely from his wounds, Lt. Lowen set out across the open field a second time under intense fire to rescue Cpl. Broman. He was shot a third time while lifting the wounded Marine and carrying him back toward safety.

"Lt. Lowen was within fifty yards of his troops when an enemy mortar round exploded directly overhead, instantly killing him and Cpl. Broman.

"Lt. Lowen's courageous leadership on the battlefield played a major role in the safe withdrawal of his platoon and the remainder of Company C. His selfless courage and heroism upheld the highest traditions of the U.S. Marine Corps. He gallantly gave his life for his brothers in arms and his country."

Ruth's voice faded away, and she sat silently, tears running down her cheeks. Bob swallowing a lump in his throat before he could speak. Then he told Ruth about the Art Lowen they had known.

"Becky, Kaye, and I first met Art back in October at a religious revival in our home town of Stony Ford in southwest Virginia. Six days after I met him, he saved my life."

Bob spoke of how Art had stepped in to rebuild the high school wrestling team and along with it, the town's pride. He described Art's role in restarting the furniture factory, putting unemployed townspeople back to work again.

Becky brushed aside tears as she told of falling in love with Art the first moment she saw him, describing the many wonderful experiences they had shared since that time, the life he had saved at Burke's Garden.

"We were together a week ago, and he promised when he left that he'd come right back to me. Now it seems he's gone forever.

"How can I cope with knowing that I'll never see Artie again? How can I make sense of everything that happened after we met? If only I could find the employer that sent him to Stony Ford."

Ruth asked Becky, "What company was that?"

"Turnkey Universal Ventures. He always called it TUV. I thought it was a project engineering firm."

Ruth smiled for the first time. "I doubt you know that "tuv" is actually an ancient word."

The three visitors stared at Ruth as she continued to explain. "In the Hebrew language of the Old Testament, 'tuv' means 'goodness.'"

*****

No one spoke for miles as they drove along in the darkness toward home. Finally Becky broke the silence, asking, "How is it possible for us to understand and accept what's happened?

"Could anyone explain how Art could become the center of my world, and then vanish, leaving me alone in the blink of eye?"

"I'm afraid there are mysteries in life that none of us will ever understand," Kaye said sympathetically. "All Bob and I can do is to tell you how sorry we are, and how much we care about you.

"Art was everything to you, Becky, but don't forget that you were also everything to him. He told you he'd come back, but something beyond his control made it impossible for him to keep that promise, or he would be here now."

Kaye's words comforted Becky, and she replied, "When I made my wish on a shooting star, I didn't say for just a little while, I said forever. That's how long I'll keep waiting."

Chapter 47

Summer came and went in a blur of green and gold. It troubled Bob and Kaye to think that their life, which had taken such a happy turn following their marriage and Bob's adoption of Chris, now contrasted so starkly with Becky's. Try as they might, it was impossible to help her break out of the doldrums.

Becky went home to Logan in August, staying with her sister for a week, but even family couldn't to fill the void in her life.

She submitted her resignation to Principal Carter when she came home, taking a teaching position at a small high school in Beaufort, North Carolina. She rationalized that the only way she could start a new life and be happy again was to get away from everything that reminded her of Art.

The entire school faculty and many of Becky's close friends gathered for a farewell party in Bob's and Kaye's back yard on Saturday afternoon. "I don't know how we're ever going to get along without you," Virginia told Becky, her voice breaking.

"You were always the Pollyanna in our group of malcontents. The faculty lounge will be like a morgue without you around to liven up the place."

Becky smiled and hugged Virginia. "I'll miss you ever bit as much as you'll miss me. Your dry sense of humor always made me laugh. Promise that you and Earl will plan a vacation in Beaufort, and I'll be your guide."

"Get a room ready for us," Virginia replied. "We'll be coming."

Finally, it was time to present the farewell gifts. Albert gave Becky the first one. "Miss Thompson, I'd like for you to have this framed picture of Stony Ford High School. It's been signed by every teacher and student. If you should ever get homesick, just look at it and remember all of the friends you have here.

"And if you should ever decide that you want to come back to live in Stony Ford, you'll always have a teaching job waiting for you at the high school."

Bob hugged Becky as he handed her the final gift. "We know that you enjoy sketching portraits and are a very talented artist, so we decided to give you an easel and oil paints. We hope that you'll enjoy many happy hours painting.

"We've tried our best to keep this party from becoming a long, sad good-bye, but if you look around, you'll find that everyone here is having a very difficult time letting you go.

"Our wish for you is that you'll find the happiness you're searching for and richly deserve, the same joy you've brought to our lives since the first day you came to Stony Ford High. Don't ever forget that you're one of the Eagles."

Becky gazed about at the loving faces of her friends, warmed by their kindness, replying softly, "Thank you for everything. I'll never forget any of you. No matter where life takes me, I'm an Eagle forever."

Epilogue

"You could have fried eggs on the sidewalk today," Becky commented, sitting down at the kitchen table where Kathleen McClelland was working.

"I heard that the temperature got up to a hundred this afternoon. When I came to Beaufort to teach school last year, I had no idea the summers would be like this. But with the sun going down, it's already starting to feel a bit cooler."

"This has been unusually hot for the first day of June, particularly here on the coast," Kathleen commiserated. "Glad you were working in an air-conditioned restaurant. Did you have a nice day?"

Becky had been living at McClelland's boarding house for less than a year, but already a special bond of friendship had linked the two. Kathleen's question was not a casual remark, but rather the sincere inquiry of a surrogate mother hoping that everything was going well for her daughter.

Becky hugged Kathleen, her youthful white shorts, sleeveless candy-stripe blouse, and white Keds contrasting with the older woman's pale blue cotton shift and comfortable brown sandals.

"Yeah, thanks for asking, Kathy. We were rather busy at lunch and dinner. I'm not getting rich from tips at Blue Crab Heaven, but what I took in today does help supplement my teaching salary and help me through the off season."

Kathleen was glad to see Becky in such a cheerful frame of mind. There had been months following Becky's arrival the preceding fall when she had little to say, spending her time after teaching either in her room or taking long, solitary walks on the beach.

Kathleen was surprised when Becky suddenly asked, "Kathy, you were married to John for twenty-five years before he died. Did you ever think after he was gone that you might be able to find someone like him and have a happy second marriage? I notice that Carl Barnhart can't take his eyes off you at the dinner table."

"I doubt it, Becky, for quite a few reasons. I'm no spring chicken, for one thing. I lived too many years and had too many wonderful experiences with John for anyone to ever step in and replace him in my life, for another. But Carl is a true gentleman, and I do enjoy his attention.

"Your situation is entirely different. You are still young, and I know that your happiest days are yet to come."

"Thanks for your understanding, Kathy. I couldn't have gotten through this past year without your taking me into your home, and more importantly, into your heart."

"I got a letter from Kaye Slater today, with all of the latest news from Stony Ford. Chris did well in the second grade and is playing Little League baseball this summer. Bob's been promoted to assistant principal, and he's decided to go on coaching the wrestling team.

"Kaye will get her nursing cap in January. She said that she's going to lie down and sleep for twenty years like Rip Van Winkle when her nursing classes are over.

"They're coming to Beaufort in July for a week's vacation, and you'll finally get to meet them. I warned them that it will be hot as an oven then, and they'll need lots of suntan lotion."

"I'm looking forward to meeting your friends," Kathy replied. "If they're anything like you, I may not let them go back home."

Becky gave Kathy a peck on the cheek, and turned toward the outside door. The resident boarding house black cat, Inky, streaked across in front of her, and without thinking, Becky exorcised possible misfortune, quickly chanting, "Buttermilk, buttermilk, buttermilk!"

"Another of your mountain superstitions?" Kathleen inquired with a laugh.

"Yeah, mom, you can take the girl out of the hills, but I'm afraid you can't take the hillbilly out of the girl. I'm off to take my walk now. See you later. "

The sun had dropped from sight as Becky rambled along the waterfront. She saw that several charter fishing boats had returned to dock beside the inland waterway, handling freshly caught fish, and cleaning decks and fishing gear at the end of a long day.

She paused at the pier to walk out on the boardwalk, dimly lit by small lamps along the edge, stopping to stand quietly at the end, staring out over the dark water.

Becky was startled when she unexpectedly heard someone pleasantly say, "Beautiful evening, isn't it?" Glancing to her left, she saw a lone man fishing.

He continued in a voice that she seemed to have heard before, yet couldn't place, "Please don't let me frighten you, ma'am. I'm just out here after work drowning worms, or giving swimming lessons to a couple of bait shrimp, to be more accurate."

Becky could see a clean-cut, handsome young man with short, sandy hair, wearing tan Bermuda shorts and a blue polo shirt.

"Having any luck?" she asked, throwing her better judgment to the wind by speaking to the stranger.

"Nothing's biting right now, but this is a mighty pleasant place to spend a summer evening whether you're catching anything or not.

"My name's Andrew Lofton, by the way. I prefer to go by Andy. I live a couple of miles east of here. Might I inquire if you're from these parts? I haven't seen you here before."

"I live in Beaufort now, and I teach math at the high school, but I came here from southwest Virginia. Do you and your family enjoy living in such a beautiful place? I've heard the town used to be called Paradise."

"I've never been married, and I live alone. But I can see how Beaufort could be considered paradise. Blackbeard must have thought so a few years back when he was hiding out here."

Becky started to walk away, when Andy inquired, "Can't you hang around for a little while? You just got here, and I was hoping to enjoy some friendly company this evening."

She answered over her shoulder, "That would be nice, but I really do have to go, much as I hate to leave this beautiful waterfront. I've enjoyed sharing the cool air with you after the heat today. The midday sun..."

She heard him finish her sentence in that same soft, strangely familiar voice, as if speaking a rehearsed line, "...makes me feel all the time like a cat on a hot tin roof."

Becky wheeled around in startled surprise to see his warm smile, as familiar to her as her own face in the mirror.

She walked back to him in a daze, with the feeling that a hand as soft as a sea breeze was gently touching her, lifting away the cloud of loneliness that had engulfed her for so many months.

She didn't realize that behind her, a spark of light was briefly tracing an arc across the star-studded heavens to disappear out of sight over the blue-black ocean. She needed no such omen.

Becky knew he'd kept his promise. He'd come back.